Annie pressed her fingers in

in through her nose. 'I'm sorry, love. We've . . . we've reconsidered and we don't want you riding.'

'Is this because I fell off?' Lydia cried. 'I didn't even hurt a hair on my head! Not even my little finger! Christine said I did a great job staying on. She said I was a natural!'

'My darling, I'm sorry. I'm so, so sorry. But we've decided. No more lessons.'

Lydia jumped up, dropping her spoon on the counter and scattering sugar all over the place. 'You know what you are?' she screamed. 'You're a big, fat *meanie*!' And she ran for the stairs, heaving with sobs.

Annie stood in the middle of the kitchen, arms folded to stop her hands from shaking visibly. 'So,' she said out loud to Patches, who was licking sugar off the tiles, 'that went surprisingly well, don't you think?'

Elise Chidley is South African by birth but now lives in Connecticut with her husband and three children. Her short stories have been shortlisted for the Nadine Gordimer award and the Ian St James award. This is her second novel.

Visit her website at www.elisechildey.com.

By Elise Chidley

The Wrong Sort of Wife
Married with Baggage

Married with Baggage

Elise Chidley

An Orion paperback

First published in Great Britain in 2009
by Orion
This paperback edition published in 2010
by Orion Books Ltd,
Orion House, 5 Upper Saint Martin's Lane
London WC2H 9EA

An Hachette UK company

1 3 5 7 9 10 8 6 4 2

A CIP catalogue record for this book is
available from the British Library.

ISBN 978-1-4091-0341-7

Typeset by Deltatype Ltd, Birkenhead, Merseyside

Printed and bound in Great Britain by Clays Ltd, St Ives plc

www.orionbooks.co.uk

For my mother

Huge thanks to Peter Robinson, and to everybody at Orion, especially Kate Mills and Jade Chandler. Gratitude also to Debbie Lynn, Odette Watson, Nicola Featonby-Smith and Julie Camarillo. And thanks, of course, to Patrick and the crew.

Chapter One

'Let's see, lunch box, water bottle, backpack, pencil box,' Annie muttered as she sailed regally along Shady Oak Road in her brand new silver minivan. 'Bread for sandwiches. What else? Cheese. Peanut butter? Hang on, isn't there some ban on peanut products? Marmite, then. And jam.' Preoccupied with her mental shopping list, she made it all the way to the four-way stop before she glanced in the rear-view mirror and realised with a jolt that something was wrong. Horribly wrong.

The booster seat was empty.

'Oh *God*!'

The minivan leapt forward as she gunned it around the corner, feverishly searching for a place to turn. She shot into a driveway, executed a seven-point manoeuvre in front of some stranger's garage, and then nosed out into the street again. It was only when the driver of an oncoming vehicle hooted and made rude signs at her that she realised she'd forgotten to pull over to the right-hand side of the road. 'Sorry!' she mouthed at the indignant face behind the windscreen as she veered out of the way.

OK, calm down, she told herself. Getting killed at this point would *really* screw things up.

She pictured seven-year-old Lydia trailing around the empty house, calling, 'Annie! Annie?' while, just a block or two away, ambulances used the Jaws of Life to extricate her charred body from the wreckage. Simon would be on the news afterwards, walking around in a blanket, saying, 'I never dreamed she was the type to go off shopping and leave a kiddy alone at home. You think you know a person ...'

He'd never say 'kiddy', of course. But words to that effect.

By the time she pulled up in her own driveway at number five Maple Tree Ridge, she was sweating and shaky.

The place was still standing, at least.

And what an impressive place it was, too. Set in a small, highly exclusive Connecticut town called Norbury, her new home was a two-storey, five-bedroom, five-thousand-square-foot example of New England colonial architecture, complete with glossy black shutters and freshly painted cedar shingles that gleamed brilliant white in the sunshine.

At the tail end of summer, the front borders were still bright with massive late-blooming hydrangeas and mounds of impatiens tucked under neat box hedges trimmed in alternating ball and cone shapes. The relocation agent had pointed out a clump of tall rhododendrons near the triple garage. 'Those will be fabulous in July,' she'd said. 'And look at those lilacs and dogwoods – you'll have a mass of blossom in the spring.' Annie, whose only experience of plants revolved around care of a temperamental African violet on the kitchen window sill of her tiny flat in Islington, had filed away the horticultural names with relish so that she could recount them to her mother.

The enormous front door of her new house was flanked

by two impressive round pillars that oozed substance and prosperity. Even the knocker – a large copper lion's head – was a statement of power and wealth. If someone had told her, just a few short months before when she was still ensconced in her one-bedroom flat in London, that she'd soon be living in America, in a house that was bigger than her whole block of flats back home, she would have dismissed the whole idea with a laugh.

Yet here she was.

She'd been in the house exactly a week now, and the novelty had far from worn off – but as she pulled up in the minivan she didn't pause for even a moment to admire the architecture.

Instead, she ducked under the garage door while it was still rolling up, and burst into the quiet kitchen. Casting a quick eye around, she shot past the gleaming granite countertops, on through the family room with its cathedral ceiling and massive plasma TV screen, across the gleaming floorboards of the centre hall (skidding a bit on the Persian rug) and up the main staircase. In the carpeted corridor she hurried past several closed doors, then stopped, breathless, in front of a door with a handmade sign taped to it.

The sign read, 'No groan-ups ecsep Daddy'.

Annie threw the door open without knocking.

Thank God! There she was. Safe and sound.

Lydia Keeler, Annie's stepdaughter, was kneeling on the rug, her fair hair falling over her face, the picture of concentration. She seemed to be wrapping a doll in strips of tissue paper. She didn't so much as glance up as Annie burst in. She obviously hadn't even noticed that she'd been gone for a good twenty minutes or more. Excellent, Annie thought. No need to erode whatever modicum of trust the child was beginning to have in her by blurting out the story of her slip-up.

'Lydia? Um – are you ready to go? Remember, I said we have to buy stuff for your first day of school tomorrow?'

Lydia turned the doll over and began tucking away loose ends of paper with the businesslike air of a nurse.

'Lyddie? You can bring the doll, but we have to go.'

The child looked up with a frown. 'I don't want to go.'

'I know. It's a pain. But we have to do it or you won't have any lunch tomorrow, or any backpack to put it in. Do you think you want a pink backpack?'

Lydia gave her a withering look, but began to stand up.

'Here, let me brush your hair.' Annie went over to the dressing table, picked up the hairbrush and brandished it briskly. ('Look as if you mean business,' her friend Henny had told her when she'd asked for advice about getting Lydia to do as she was told.)

Lydia heaved a deep sigh and shuffled towards the dressing table. Folding her arms over her narrow chest, she allowed her stepmother to run the brush through her tangles. Every time it caught in a knot, she winced dramatically and shrank a little further away from Annie.

'How's that?' Annie asked after a moment, meeting Lydia's eye in the mirror. 'Your hair is so pretty.'

Lydia stared at herself with an unreadable expression. Then she looked at Annie's face in the mirror. 'You have weird-coloured eyes,' she noted.

Annie glanced at her own reflection. It was true; her eye

colour was unusual. Most people called it hazel, but it was lighter than true hazel. She'd once seen a goat with eyes exactly that colour; a sort of greenish gold.

Her hair, at least, was an ordinary colour. Brown.

Annie shrugged. 'I know. There's no exact name for the colour of my eyes. But yours are definitely blue, like your dad's.'

'And my mum's.'

Annie paused a moment. 'That's right. Come on, are you ready?'

'I suppose. Why do I have to go to stupid school, anyway? I hate school.'

'You never know. You might like this one.'

'I won't.'

Dragging her feet and complaining steadily, Lydia followed Annie down the stairs, through the kitchen, through the garage, and into the car. 'Right,' Annie murmured to herself, glancing back at the booster seat full of peevish little girl, 'let's try this one more time.'

They returned two hours later loaded down with, among other things, a Hannah Montana backpack and a Barbie lunch box. Lydia sat at the kitchen counter examining her new possessions one by one, while Annie poured tea for the two of them. Lydia's was mainly milk.

'I can't wait to meet your teacher,' Annie said, stirring Lydia's mug and setting it down in front of her.

'Why?' asked Lydia. 'What's so great about her?'

'Well, I don't know. But I bet she's really nice. I wonder how many kids you'll have in your class.'

Lydia shrugged. 'Who cares?'

'Lyddie, I know you're a little nervous about tomorrow ...'

'I'm not nervous.'

'Really? Great. I'm happy to hear it. It's hard to be the new girl, but you'll soon settle in.'

Lyddie didn't even grace this comment with a reply. Instead, she finished her tea, banged the cup on the counter, slid off the bar stool, and left the room.

'Nice chatting to you, too,' Annie said to the empty air.

As Simon opened the front door that evening, Annie came quietly out of the kitchen and stood in the shadows, watching him shrug off his dark trench coat and hang it up.

Even now, she could hardly believe that this tall, rugged man with sun-bleached hair and piercing blue eyes was actually her husband.

For a while before she met him, Annie had almost given up on the notion of a husband. Oh, she'd had boyfriends, all right. There'd been Nick, the computer whiz; attractive enough in a slightly geeky way, pleasant enough when you could attract his attention, but so wedded to the virtual world that he could be physically in your living room without having a single particle of mental presence there. His passport should have been issued not by the United Kingdom, but the World Wide Web. Their relationship had ended abruptly one night when Annie ripped a handful of electrical plugs out of the wall in an effort to unglue his eyes from the computer screen.

Then there'd been Matty. Matty was too gorgeous-looking for his own good, her friend Henny said from the outset.

A smoking-hot man like that was bound to have a warped view of reality, she reckoned. Annie, of course, didn't pay any attention to Henny's warnings. After all, Matty wasn't a self-obsessed narcissist. Far from it. He was a man with a social conscience. Saving the environment was his explicit personal mission. (He believed everybody ought to have an explicit personal mission.) He'd managed to carve out a career for himself as middleman between people trying to sell green products and trendy young things with enough cash to buy them. He had a huge advantage in doing this. Just by association with his smoking-hotness, he could make any product under the sun seem chic and desirable – even automatic indoor composters.

In the end, what ruined things with Matty was his insistence on recycling ziplock lunch bags. Annie wasn't against recycling, per se. In fact, she was all for it. She just couldn't stomach his particular *method* of recycling, which involved throwing his old, mayonnaise-smeared lunch bags in with the laundry. The daily sight of these bags spinning around with his underwear gave her such an ominous feeling about life with Matty that, after a month-long experiment with 'living together', she asked him (apologetically but firmly) to shift himself and his stuff out of her flat. He didn't try to change her mind. It turned out that, for his part, he was thoroughly disillusioned by her lack of commitment to the worm farm he was cultivating in the corner of her kitchen.

Annie first laid eyes on Simon about a year after she'd broken up with Matty. She met him in Greece, on the final day of a holiday with her red-headed cousin Sarah – a massively self-indulgent few days spent reading paperbacks on the beach and perfecting her tan while Sarah went sailing.

As Annie and Sarah sat under an umbrella outside a restaurant in Lakka on the island of Paxos, waiting for their order of moussaka and spanakopita, a tall, blond man walked by, in earnest discussion with a shorter, broader man whose face Annie didn't even notice. When Annie caught sight of the tall man, her stomach swooped as if she'd hit an air pocket in a light aircraft.

'God! Look at that, Sarah!' she hissed, gesturing discreetly at the man. 'You're always asking me what my type is. Well, that's it. Right there. The tall bloke.'

Sarah obediently looked. Then, to Annie's consternation, she suddenly hailed the men in a loud baritone. 'Simon! Billy! Over here!'

The men turned and squinted their eyes at the pair sitting in the deep shade of the umbrella.

'Hey,' said the stocky man after a second. 'It's Sarah! Sarah Harleigh!'

The two of them made their way over to Annie and Sarah's table. 'Pull up a pew,' Sarah invited.

Annie felt a pleasant shiver go through her as she met the eyes of the tall stranger Sarah introduced as Simon Keeler. He had a stern, weather-beaten face, but his eyes were bright blue, and when he smiled – which he did just once during the whole encounter – they crinkled attractively.

Annie found herself completely tongue-tied, and Simon didn't seem to have much to say either, but Sarah and the other man talked nineteen to the dozen, in incomprehensible nautical language. Distracted as she was, Annie only caught snatches. '. . . Last saw Sarah when she was rail meat on a mono-hull off the Aegean islands ...' she heard Billy tell Simon.

'Yeah, the Meltemi was blowing that day, remember? We had one broach after another,' Sarah replied with gusto.

'But good sailing,' Billy insisted. 'Half the time we had to come in flying a chicken chute ...'

Annie didn't even try to understand what they were saying. She kept stealing glances at Simon, hoping that her blushes didn't show through her sunburn. When Billy at last stood up to go, Simon hastily pushed something across the table to Annie. It was a phone number written in pencil on a linen napkin. Annie still had the napkin to this day.

When Annie finally brought herself to dial the number on the napkin – three weeks passed before she could screw up the courage – she had no clue that Simon was a widower with a seven-year-old daughter. Of course, her cousin Sarah could have told her all this, and more, if Annie had only asked, but from the moment Simon walked away from the table, Annie had felt that gossiping about him with Sarah would be sacrilege.

In fact, she never mentioned him to Sarah at all. She even managed a casual, 'Nah' and a dismissive shrug when Sarah said, 'So Simon Keeler is your type, is he?'

By the time Annie was brave enough to call him, she wondered if he'd even remember meeting her.

But the question didn't come up. The minute she heard his deep, masculine voice on the phone, she dropped the receiver in abject fright, hanging up on him. It was a bit of a relief, really. What on earth could she possibly say to such a man, the solitary example she'd ever actually seen of the exact 'type' that turned her legs to jelly and made her heart pound like all those drums at the Beijing Olympics?

She'd be much better off going out for a drink with Sid Vole, the art director at *Rumour Has It*, the women's weekly magazine she worked for. The state of his hands was a bit off-putting, but she was almost sure the black under his nails was ink of some sort.

But within half an hour the phone rang, and it was him. Simon Keeler. He'd tracked Sarah down through his friend Billy, apparently, and asked for Annie's number. 'What made you do that, after all this time?' she asked when she found the breath to speak.

'Well, I had a crank call a few minutes ago,' he admitted. 'For some reason, before I picked up the phone I had this weird feeling that it was you. But it wasn't, of course. Just some heavy-breathing nutter who hung up on me. So much for sixth sense. But it made me want to talk to you.'

'Oh,' Annie said faintly. 'Um, can you excuse me a moment? I'll be right back.' She ran to her medicine cabinet and threw back an unmeasured dose of Rescue Remedy, her fingers shaking so much that she could barely get the bottle open. The trouble was, the bottle had expired years ago. She'd last used it when her dad died.

No man had ever upset her entire nervous system before, just by talking to her on the phone.

At first, Simon was a bit of an enigma. Something about his face – the stern, shut-off look she would surprise on it when she watched him from across a room – made her think she was mad to believe he fancied her at all. But then he'd catch her watching him, and his expression would dissolve into a lopsided, utterly irresistible grin, and she'd tell herself that he found her irresistible, too.

It was only on their third date that Annie found out about Lydia. It wasn't that Simon deliberately kept his daughter secret. He just didn't talk about her in casual conversation. Holding Annie's hand across the table of a dimly lit restaurant in Islington (close to her flat so that she could invite him back for their first after-date 'coffee' if she happened to feel like it), he confessed that he never quite knew how to explain his situation to new people. If he mentioned Lydia, then he had to mention his wife; and then, obviously, he had to explain that she'd drowned in a boating accident.

It was always a bit of a conversation stopper, he said.

'I'm so sorry,' she gasped, determined to keep the conversation flowing freely. 'What a terrible, terrible thing. When – when did it happen?'

'A little over a year ago. She went out alone on a boat in Cornwall. A storm blew up. She never came back.'

In the candlelight, she realised that his face wasn't stern at all. It was lined with grief.

'Can I meet your little girl?' she asked suddenly.

He raised his eyebrows. 'You really want to?'

'Yes, of course!'

He shrugged ruefully. 'I was thinking this would probably be the moment when you'd tell me goodbye, and thank you, and have a nice life.'

'I think it's too late for that,' she said, only half joking.

He stared at her very hard. 'Annie, I'm leaving for America in four months.'

Her heart gave a painful squeeze.

'On . . . on holiday?'

'No. To live there. My company's sending me to New York.'

She coloured. 'Oh. Well, then. Of course you don't want me to meet her. Obviously. I mean, what would be the point?'

'I do want you to meet her.'

She looked into his eyes. He held her gaze steadily. 'All right,' she said. 'I'd love to. If . . . if you think it's wise.'

'Wise?' he repeated blankly. 'What's wisdom got to do with it?'

Since wisdom wasn't a consideration, she took him back to her flat after dinner in the full knowledge that losing him to America would be altogether more wretched once she'd seen him naked between her sheets.

'Who's looking after Lydia?' she asked suddenly, at a point when she hadn't yet seen him completely naked but had checked out a fair amount of his bare skin at close quarters.

'Polish au pair,' he murmured between kisses. 'Very reliable. Can we just not talk about her now, though? She has a moustache.'

That very Saturday, Annie went round to Simon's big house in Kensington for the first time ever, clutching a gift for his daughter – a handheld puppet. 'I need something I can sort of *entertain* a seven-year-old with,' she'd told the spotty youth in the toy shop. 'Something interactive.'

He'd suggested an MP3 player or a Nintendo DS. 'Do

you have anything more ... I don't know, low tech?' she'd asked, staring doubtfully at the electronic offerings. He sighed, spat out his gum, and suggested a junior magician set – but she didn't fancy the idea of taking pound coins out of people's ears.

Then she spotted the monkey puppet. It was a luxuriant creature with soft faux fur and remarkably lifelike eyes – exactly the sort of toy she'd always hankered after, in vain, as a kid. In her day, she'd had to make do with paper dolls and the occasional home-made rag doll – her mother was a firm believer in creativity, thriftiness, and self-sufficiency.

Taking a quick look around the shop to make sure that nobody from the office happened to have wandered in off the street, she stuck her hand inside the puppet's body and made it perform a few experimental hand claps, bows and head nods. In a low voice, the monkey said, 'Hello there, folks, Peanut at your service.'

'I'll take it,' she told the spotty youth.

'Well, it's your decision,' the youth replied, eyeing the monkey with distaste.

Simon's daughter, as it turned out, was even less enthusiastic about the monkey than the shop assistant.

Lydia, small and blonde, ethereal as a dandelion, was huddled in a corner of a handsome leather sofa when Annie first laid eyes on her, wearing pyjamas and an expression of deep distrust.

'Lydia, this is my friend Annie,' Simon said a shade too heartily, drawing Annie into the room by the hand. The room itself was a little intimidating, Annie thought. It was what you'd call well appointed. The ceiling was high with lavishly adorned cornicing. The furniture – plentiful, dark and gleaming – bore absolutely no resemblance to her own eclectic collection of catalogue-bought, some-assembly-required pieces. It was all terribly solid and – well, *married* looking, whereas her own style was more student-meets-underpaid-magazine-writer.

'Look, I've bought you a present!' Annie found herself saying in a bright, sing-song voice. 'See? It's a monkey.'

The child stared at the proffered toy in absolute silence, making no move to accept it.

Bit of an awkward moment, really.

Simon, of course, tried to smooth things over. 'Come on, Lydia, take the monkey. He's really cute! You'll hurt his monkey feelings if you don't.' Then, as if on cue, his BlackBerry rang. 'I'm sorry, but I really must get this call,' he murmured, walking out and leaving Annie alone with Lydia and the monkey.

Quick as a flash, Lydia took a cushion and placed it in front of her, between herself and the newcomer.

'Hey folks, Peanut at your service,' Annie offered gamely, waggling the bright-eyed monkey. 'What's your name?'

Lydia said nothing.

Annie stepped over to an armchair and crouched down behind it so that Peanut was poking up over the back. Maybe Lydia would feel less threatened if she were out of sight. 'Can you guess what my favourite food is?' Peanut asked.

Apparently, Lydia couldn't.

'I bet your favourite food is, let's see now, Brussels sprouts?'

Lydia chose not to comment.

'How about I sing a little song for you?' Peanut was really struggling now. Annie wracked her brains, trying to think of a suitable ditty for him, but all that came to mind was Humpty Dumpty. Well, it would have to do. 'Humpty Dumpty sat on a wall,' she began. Only it wasn't a song, was it? More of a dirge, really. 'Humpty Dumpty had a great fall.' She snatched Peanut out of sight. 'All the king's horses and all the king's men couldn't put Humpty together again.' She eased her hand into view again and had the monkey drag himself along the back of the chair, groaning and moaning, as if gravely injured.

Loud clapping broke out!

Relieved, Annie stood up with a smile. 'I knew you'd . . .' She trailed off. The applause was coming from Simon. Lydia was still sitting in her corner, knees pulled up to her chin, arms folded around her legs.

'Daddy,' the child said clearly – and these were the first words Annie ever heard her say, 'can you please make the mad lady go away?'

Things had improved a lot since that first encounter, of course. Nowadays, Lydia spoke directly to Annie on a daily basis. She was never chatty, but at least they'd progressed beyond those early days when she spoke to Annie only through Simon.

Simon was kicking off his shoes when Annie came up behind him and put her arms around his chest, feeling the warmth of his skin through his fine-gauge woollen jumper. As he turned towards her she stood on tiptoe to kiss him on the lips – not a wifely peck, but a passionate, newly-wed, rip-my-clothes-off-now kind of kiss.

'Mmm,' he said, taking a step back and looking at her with his raffish grin. 'That was quite a welcome. What's with the apron?'

She looked down at the candy stripes (she was using a smock she'd bought that very day for Lydia's school art classes) and wrinkled her nose. 'I know, I'm not sure pink is my colour. It suits Lyddie much better. The thing is, I've been making spaghetti bolognaise, and I didn't want it spattered all over my clothes again.'

'Spaghetti bolognaise. Hmm.' His face went thoughtful.

'Don't worry, the mince isn't like bullets this time,' she assured him. 'I defrosted it first.' Cooking was not one of her strong points.

'Right. Sounds good. Hang on, I'll just run up and check on Lydia.'

While he was upstairs, she poured them each a glass of wine and turned on the gas fire, feeling very domesticated. It wasn't really cool enough yet to warrant the fire, but flames set a nice romantic tone.

'How is she?' she asked when he came back downstairs in old corduroy trousers and a T-shirt. He took his wine and sank down beside her on the sofa.

'Asleep. Looks like I'll have to take an earlier train if I ever want to see her conscious.'

'How was work?'

Simon was a rising young executive with ChefPro, one of Britain's top five food production companies. He and his team had been sent over to New York to investigate the viability of setting up a new chain of fast-food outlets, starting out on the East Coast and gradually expanding across America.

Simon shrugged. 'It was . . . interesting. We're processing results from the first focus group. They're not as decisive as we'd like.'

'So, which pie do they like best?' Annie asked, sipping her wine. 'I bet it's the chicken and mushroom.'

He put his glass down and stretched, yawning. 'That's the funny thing. If you don't tell them what they're eating, a surprising percentage like the steak and kidney.'

'New style or old style?'

In an initiative spearheaded by Simon, ChefPro was working on an updated version of its trusty staple, the meat pie. At Simon's urging, the test kitchens were developing lower-fat pies made with gourmet ingredients and fresh herbs. Disappointingly, the new pies were not finding much favour with the British market. Simon was counting on them going down a storm in America. 'Olde World made new' was the working catchphrase for the chain.

'Well, that's the problem. I don't think we've nailed it yet with the new-style pastry. The old recipe is winning hands down.'

'Oh dear. If only saturated fats weren't so bad for you.'

'Exactly. And if only wholewheat wasn't so chewy.' Simon shrugged and took a sip of his wine. 'Don't worry, we'll get it right. It just takes time.'

Later that night, as Simon lay sleeping, Annie slipped out from under his heavy arm and crept across the landing to the room known as the den. Closing the door softly, she turned on the light and looked around the snug room. She liked it in here, mainly because it was small and informal enough to feel comfortable. They had rented the house fully furnished, and the reception rooms downstairs were decorated with such rigorous professionalism that Annie always felt that she herself was a bit of a blot on an otherwise blameless landscape in her everyday jeans, T-shirt, and ponytail. Pyjamas and a ratty old gown, she felt, would be an absolute affront to the sensibilities of these rooms.

Annie's small flat in Islington had been bursting at the seams with clutter, but when her pictures and knick-knacks were spread across this large house in Connecticut, they virtually disappeared into the woodwork.

Unlike Annie, Simon had brought almost nothing from London; just clothes and a couple of photo albums that he buried under socks in his chest of drawers. Simon had encouraged Annie to go out and buy whatever she fancied to make the Connecticut house feel like home, but just at the moment she couldn't imagine what that would *be*. Books and a teapot, maybe? After all, she couldn't exactly change all the formal furniture for something a little more relaxed, could she?

Annie picked up the cordless phone, sank down onto the sofa and glanced at her watch. It was two in the morning. Safe, then, to call England.

But who to call? Her mum? She pictured her sixty-four-year-old mother jumping with fright over toast and tea in her Surrey kitchen as the phone shrilled out so early in the morning. No, she didn't want to worry Mum.

It had better be Henny again.

Henny Foster was married. She'd been married for ages. She even had children – one of whom was a little girl just a year older than Lydia. This, and the fact that Annie Harleigh and Henny Foster had known each other since they were ten years old, made Henny the perfect person to unburden herself to – not that she really had *burdens*, of course; just a touch of, hmm, would you call it homesickness, or was that too childish?

Henny picked up the phone after only a couple of rings. From across the Atlantic, her voice sounded surprisingly loud and robust. 'Hello?' she bellowed. '*Annie?* Do you know it's seven in the morning? I'm just trying to get Lulu through her flashcards for her spelling test. It's "i" before "e" except after "c". Go away and write it down a couple of times – receive, receive, receive. Right, I only have a few secs, Annie. What's going on?'

'I can't sleep again,' Annie said sheepishly. 'I just needed to talk to someone.'

'Why don't you wake up Simon?'

Annie played with the loose threads of her gown. 'I don't want to worry him,' she admitted.

'Is it about Lydia again?'

'Sort of. Have you – um, have you ever gone shopping and forgotten the kids at home?'

'Annie! You didn't!'

'Well, only for a few minutes. It really didn't take me long to realise I'd left her behind. But that was a hairy moment – you know, when I looked back and saw the empty seat.'

'Good grief. I bet it was. What did Simon say?'

'Do you know, I didn't actually tell him. I mean, it wasn't

a big deal. And I'd hate him to go off to work thinking maybe it wasn't safe to leave Lyddie with me all day.'

'Yes, I see what you mean.'

'It's Lyddie's first day of school tomorrow. Well, *today*, I suppose. I'm a bit stumped about what to make her for lunch. She doesn't like ham or cheese, and she's not allowed to have peanut butter because of allergies. I thought I'd give her Marmite but they've never even heard of it at the supermarket.'

'Annie, you've called me at seven in the morning to ask what sandwiches to make?'

'No, of course not. It's just ... I felt like talking to someone, that's all. Plus I wanted to ask you, what do you normally do when the children are at school? I'm ... you know, just trying to plan my day tomorrow. I mean, what is it most mums *do* all day?'

There was silence on the other end of the line for a moment. Then Henny burst out, 'Oh, for God's sake, Annie! Don't you know that's just about the most insulting thing you could ask me?'

'Look, you know I'm not trying to insult anybody! It's a perfectly valid question. I'm used to getting up, putting on my clothes and going out to work!'

Annie had been features writer for *Rumour Has It*, the women's weekly best known for never allowing the truth to get in the way of a good story.

'Well, it's the same thing now, for heaven's sake! Except your work is at home.'

'You mean – housekeeping?'

Henny sighed. 'Well, houses do need a certain amount of

keeping, that's for bloody sure. The dishes and the laundry and the vacuuming. Changing sheets, making beds, cleaning loos, scrubbing bath rings, sweeping bloody floors.'

'The thing is,' Annie said a little self-consciously, 'I don't have to do as much of that as you'd think. Simon thought we should have a cleaning service, since the house is so big. They did a massive clean-up after we moved in, and they're going to come in twice a week. And all his shirts go out to the dry-cleaner.'

'Well, even so, you're cleaning up after Lydia all the time, I'm sure.'

'Um, not really. She's a very tidy child. Doesn't really have many toys. Makes her own bed.'

'OK,' said Henny evenly. 'I'm trying to sympathise, I really am, but right now I'm a bit short of time because I've got to go and strip a wee-soaked bed, make three lunches, write a note to the teacher, make sure everyone has their trainers, and ice a batch of fairy cakes for the school fete.'

Annie sniffed. 'Oh God, I sound spoilt rotten, don't I?'

'No,' said Henny. 'You sound bored and lonely. I suppose it's not nearly as hectic, dealing with just the one child. Have you thought about getting a part-time job?'

Annie sighed. She'd thought about getting a part-time job, all right. She'd had lurid, feverish, just-short-of-erotic dreams about getting a part-time job. New York, the Big Apple, was just a tantalising hour away by train. She could only imagine what fabulous opportunities awaited an ambitious journalist in the *actual* city of *Sex and the City* fame.

'Can't do it,' she said, trying to keep the hollow regret out of her voice. 'Don't have the right paperwork. I'm here as a spouse, that's all. I tried to set up some freelance work before I left the UK, but it didn't pan out.'

If Annie had never in her wildest dreams imagined she'd marry a man who would whisk her away to a fully furnished mansion in a foreign country, she had also never imagined she'd marry a man with a fully furnished family. She'd never imagined she would wind up sacrificing her career to be a mum before she'd even had a baby.

Given the choice, she would have liked to get a bit of practice on a dog or a cat first. She'd had a goldfish once, a few years back. Goldfish were pretty fragile, it turned out. Little girls were much more robust; or so she hoped.

So here she was, thrust all unprepared into a stage of life she had always thought of as very distant, possibly even unattainable.

She'd been handed married life on a platter: husband, daughter, house, garden, cleaning lady, landscaping service, credit card. And it was great. Of course it was. Only sometimes she walked into the beautiful house, sat down in the fabulous stainless steel and granite kitchen, and wondered exactly what she was supposed to do next.

'Well – well, you'll just have to get involved with the school then,' Henny said decisively. 'Offer to shelve books at the library, that sort of thing. Look, I really must go. Shoe crisis. Talk to you soon.'

What sort of a shoe crisis? Annie wondered. Knowing Henny, it wouldn't be something simple, like a lost shoe. No, it would be a shoe stuck halfway down the Labrador's throat, or the three-year-old using his boots as boats in the garden pond.

Annie reached for the chenille throw draped fetchingly over the sofa, and wrapped it around her body. She was getting a little cold. So. Volunteering at the school. She pictured herself arranging flowers for the school secretary's desk. Or – or helping the lunch lady dole out chicken nuggets. Or sharpening all the pencils in the second-grade classroom. Or holding a lollipop sign and helping kids cross the road. Or something . . .

'Would my lady care for a cup of tea?'

Annie opened her eyes reluctantly and sat up. Looking around, she realised she was in the den, and fingers of light were filtering in through the window.

'Was I snoring then?' Simon asked mildly. He towered over her in his dark suit, freshly showered and shaved and really quite fragrant, briefcase in one hand, a steaming mug in the other.

Annie accepted the tea and took a tiny sip. 'No, of course not. You only do that if you've had too much whisky. I just couldn't sleep, that's all.'

Simon raised his eyebrows. 'Something on your mind?'

'Not really. It was just – you know, jet lag.'

'Jet lag? After a whole week?'

Annie laughed a little uneasily. She didn't want Simon catching wind of her homesickness, or boredom, or whatever it was. He had enough on his plate, worrying about his New Age pies, and about Lydia's adjustment to their new life. 'I have a very sensitive internal clock, as it happens,' she told him. 'It has to do with the fluid in your inner ear, apparently.'

'Really? Hmm. Well, feel free to wake me next time your inner ear starts playing up. I'm sure we'll think of something to do.' He leaned in to kiss her, and she felt the familiar rush of blood to various parts of her anatomy, including her face. He tasted quite deliciously of tea.

She pulled away reluctantly. 'Hey, you'd better get a move on or you'll miss your train.'

'I could miss it just once,' he said, putting his briefcase down with a clatter and lowering himself onto the sofa. Just as he was sliding his hand into the warmth of her dressing gown, raising a trail of goose-pimples, his BlackBerry gave its strident ring.

'Bugger,' he said, fishing it out of his pocket and glancing at the screen. 'I forgot the teleconference on the bloody train. Sorry, love, got to go after all.' He turned to look her smack in the eyes. 'You're not worrying about anything, are you? I don't like waking up to find you gone. Much prefer to see you drooling on the pillow.'

'Bloody cheek!' She grabbed a cushion and he stood up quickly, grinning as he backed away from her. 'I don't *drool*!' she cried. The cushion caught him smartly in the small of the back just as he exited the room.

Chapter Two

Bradley Elementary School was a five-minute walk along wooded streets from the Keelers' house on Maple Tree Ridge. Annie had taken Lydia over to explore the playground several times already, to familiarise her with her new stomping ground. Normally the walk was punctuated with groans and moans from Lydia: 'Why do we have to go? I was playing a game. I don't *want* to go on the swings.' But today they walked in silence, the shiny pink Hannah Montana backpack rattling slightly with every step Lydia took.

As they stepped through the double doors into the school's front lobby, Annie glanced at the little girl, trying to gauge how she was feeling. Her head was down and her fair hair fell over her face, making it impossible to see her expression. 'Lyddie? You OK?'

Lydia nodded without looking up.

'So like I said, I put in a plain butter sandwich, but there's also one of those mild mini cheeses that you like. If you eat them both, then bingo! You've eaten a cheese sandwich.'

'OK.'

'Let's see ... I think the second-grade wing is this way. Funny how empty the place is. We're early, I suppose.'

After a few false turns, they found Miss Scofield's room and verified that Lydia's name was on the list of students pinned to the door.

'You can go now,' Lydia said, her face very white and set.

'What, and leave you standing out here in the corridor? You've got to be joking. Come on, let's see if Miss Scofield's in there yet.'

She knocked on the door, and a voice asked them to come in.

'Right,' said Annie, tucking Lydia's wayward hair behind her ears, 'let's go and introduce ourselves.'

Lydia pulled her hand out of Annie's grasp. 'I don't think you're supposed to come in with me.'

'Rubbish,' said Annie. 'Miss Scofield will be happy to meet me. Come on!'

She pushed the door open and walked in, smiling at the woman behind the desk, who blinked up at her in surprise. 'Hi, I'm Annie Har— Keeler and this is Lydia. We've just moved here from England.'

'Right. Good to meet you, Mrs Har-Keeler. I'm Melissa Scofield. Hi, Lydia, great to meet you.'

Lydia looked very hard at the floor.

'So, we're early.'

'Yes, you are. That's OK. Lydia can find her desk and do a little colouring while she waits. Look, Lydia, this is where you hang your backpack.' Miss Scofield showed her a hook with her name underneath it, and Lydia duly hung up her bag.

While the teacher settled Lydia at a desk, Annie looked

at the displays on the bulletin boards. 'This is all very bright and cheerful,' she remarked.

'We try to make it a happy room,' said Miss Scofield. 'Now, Mrs Har-Keeler, I assume you've had your package from the school secretary? We do have a parents' evening in a couple of weeks when you get to come in and hear about the curriculum.'

'Yes, thanks, I got the letter.'

'Good.' Miss Scofield stood and smiled at her.

Annie smiled back.

'So . . . walkers normally stay out in the playground until the whistle blows,' the teacher said. 'They all line up by grade outside once the buses have arrived.'

'OK,' said Annie.

'No real need for moms to come inside at drop-off,' Miss Scofield added.

Just then a scuffle of feet and a hum of voices broke out in the corridor.

'Here they come.' Miss Scofield walked over to the door and threw it open.

Children began to pour into the room, chatting excitedly as they searched for their designated coat hooks. Lydia, seated at her table, stared fixedly at the piece of paper in front of her, but didn't make any pretence of actually colouring in.

When the children had all hung up their backpacks and found their seats, Miss Scofield clapped her hands briskly.

'Girls and boys,' she said in a carrying voice, 'good morning and welcome to second grade. I'm Miss Scofield and I'll be your teacher this year.'

A boy raised his hand. 'Who's that?' he asked, pointing at Annie.

'Um ... that's Mrs Har-Keeler, Lydia's mom. Lydia is new to Bradley this year. Boys and girls, say hello to Lydia, please.'

'Hello, Lydia,' the class droned.

Lydia didn't look up from her piece of paper but the tips of her ears, visible because Annie had tucked her hair behind them, were seen to go very pink.

'Oh, and we have another new pupil in the classroom this morning,' the teacher went on. 'Let's all say hello to Hailey.'

'Hello, Hailey,' the boys and girls chorused. A plump girl with a mop of dark hair gave a jaunty wave.

Miss Scofield crossed the room to where Annie was standing. 'Thanks for coming in,' she said pointedly.

'Right. No problem. I'll ... I'll be on my way, then.'

'Probably a good idea. We do encourage moms to come into the classroom, by the way, for specific volunteer opportunities. I guess you'll be heading over to the second-grade coffee at the cafeteria to put your name down for some of those.'

Annie smiled. 'Oh yes. That's at nine, I think. I'll get out of your way, then. Bye, Lyddie. Have a good day.'

Lydia glanced up at her briefly but didn't return the kiss she blew.

It wasn't worth going home, Annie decided, before this 'coffee' thing, so she gave herself a little tour of the school, glancing in at the library, the gymnasium, and the art room.

A few minutes before nine, she found her way to the cafeteria, a big, clattery room with a linoleum floor and rows of long metal tables with attached benches. Women were buzzing around a table laden with boxes of doughnuts and cartons of coffee, greeting each other with air kisses and shrieks of joy.

Annie looked at them with interest. Almost to a woman, they had long blonde hair, deep tans, sunglasses perched on their heads, and good pedicures displayed by colourful flip-flops beneath bright Capri pants. The only make-up they seemed to be wearing was a hint of lipgloss. They looked as if they were all on holiday at some island resort. In her 'meet-the-teacher' outfit – a favourite black skirt, closed-toe heels, and a fitted white blouse – Annie felt like a penguin among birds of paradise. Her own Greek tan was long gone, by now.

'Hi, I'm Susie Stein, room mom for Miss Scofield's class.' A tall woman with a blonde ponytail was standing before her holding out her hand. Annie took it and was engulfed in a firm handshake. 'I don't recognise your face. Are you one of the new moms?'

Annie laughed. 'Is it that obvious? Yes, I'm a new mum.' In more ways than you can imagine, she might have added.

The woman looked at a list in her hand. 'So, let's see, I bet you're Annie Keeler?'

'That's right.'

'Great! Love the accent, by the way. Here, there's someone you should meet.' Susie's eyes raked the room with a predatory look. 'Ah, there she is. Come on!'

Feeling faintly apprehensive, Annie followed Susie as she

snaked through the crowd. Reaching a small knot of women, Susie stopped and tapped someone on the shoulder. A woman with a cloud of dark hair spun around, eyebrows raised.

'Hey, Heather. I want you to meet Annie Keeler. She's new to the school, just like you, and guess what? She has a daughter in Miss Scofield's room, too.' With an encouraging smile to both of them, Susie Stein sailed away on other important business.

Annie and Heather eyed each other silently for a moment.

'So,' said Heather, 'that's sorted us out, hasn't it?'

Annie gave a snort of surprised laughter. 'Right, except we probably have nothing in common and won't have a word to say to each other.'

'Yeah, and then Susie will have to come back and tell us to play nice.'

'Oh God, you're right. We'd better look like we're chatting. So. Heather. Pleased to meet you. You really have a daughter in Miss Scofield's class?'

Heather grinned. 'That's right. Hailey. And you have Lydia.'

'How do you know?'

Heather glanced down at the booklet in her hands. 'It's in the directory. You'd better get one – over on that table. By the way, have you heard the scoop on Scofield yet?'

'No. I hope they didn't stick all the new kids in with the dud teacher.'

'Oh, she's not a bad teacher. Word is, the kids love her but she doesn't go down that well with parents. She doesn't tolerate helicopters, you see.'

'*Helicopters?*'

'Moms who hover. You know, the overprotective types. If she had her druthers, she'd have no mom volunteers at all in her room.'

'Oh God! I think I was hovering this morning! We came in early and I hung around, you know, just to make sure Lyddie was going to be OK . . .'

Heather pulled a sympathetic face. 'She has separation anxiety?'

Annie had a brief flash of Lydia's disgusted face as she blew her a goodbye kiss. 'Not exactly,' she said. 'But it's a whole new country for her, never mind a whole new school. I felt I should stick around as long as I could.'

'Hey, did you sign up for mystery reader yet?' Susie Stein was back, waving a piece of paper at them. 'We also need more volunteers for math games.'

Heather drifted away as Annie took a look at the sign-up sheets, and she didn't see her again until she was walking home. As she was approaching the pedestrian crossing at Shady Oak, she noticed a familiar-looking figure standing with folded arms, waiting for the light to change. It was hard to mistake Heather's cloud of dark hair, even after such a brief meeting.

Annie felt a grin breaking out as she caught up with her. 'Hello again,' she said. 'You're a walker too?'

'Yes, we're on Tulip Street, right across from the school,' Heather said, pointing with her chin at the street sign on the other side of the road. 'So no bus for us.'

'And you're new in town?'

'Yeah. We moved in over the summer. Just from Westport, though, so no culture shock.'

'Westport. That's a few miles north of here, right?'

'Yeah. We've shaved five minutes off my husband's commute. He crunched the numbers to see how much time that would buy him over the course of a year, and figured the move was worth the hassle. You guys moved from England?'

'That's right. About a week ago, so we're still settling in.'

The traffic light changed and they began to cross the street together.

'So what do you think of all this?' Heather waved her hand to encompass the wide street with its pretty, wooden-framed houses set well back from the road, each with a rolling green lawn that ran down to the pavement, one or two bordered by a low stone wall or white picket fence, but most simply open to the world. Trees towered over the houses, casting a luxurious shade.

Annie shrugged. 'It's gorgeous, of course. But I'm still getting used to it. I mean, I grew up in a village, but for the last ten years or so I've been in the thick of things in London.'

'Yeah, it was tough for my husband too, when we first moved in from the city,' Heather said. 'I grew up around here, so it seems pretty normal. As a matter of fact, I don't miss the city at all.'

'Which city?'

Heather gave her a strange look. '*The* city. You know. New York.'

'Oh, right.'

'Yeah, we made the trek to suburbia a couple of years

ago, when Hailey was ready to go to school. I was happy because it meant I could keep a horse again. I was crazy about horses, growing up. Still am. Do you horseback ride at all?'

'*Horseback* ride?' Annie felt her stomach plummet.

'There's this really good barn just up the road – another reason why we moved to Norbury. I've had my horse there for some time, and it was a real pain driving over from Westport every day. Anyway, if you're interested in riding, you should get your name in front of them as soon as possible. They don't have a lot of openings for new riders.'

'Actually, horses aren't my thing. I've never been on one in my life, and I'm not sure I want to.'

'Pity,' said Heather with a shrug. 'I guess Lydia doesn't ride either?'

'I don't know. I don't think so.'

Heather raised her eyebrows in confusion. 'You don't *think* so?'

Annie shrugged. 'I'm pretty sure she doesn't – but then, I'm not her mum.'

'You're the nanny?' Heather asked, looking thoroughly confused.

'No, no, the stepmum. Um ... look, my house is just around the corner. Do you ... do you want to come in for some tea?' She felt suddenly as nervous as if she were asking some man out on a first date.

To her relief, Heather grinned with real pleasure. 'Sure, but I'll have coffee, if that's OK,' she said. 'The coffee at the meeting was lukewarm by the time I got to it. I could use another cup.'

'Great!' Annie resigned herself to drinking coffee too, although she'd never liked it much.

Annie took her guest through the garage into the kitchen. The front door seemed too imposing for casual use. As Annie fussed with the coffee maker, Heather settled herself on a bar stool and looked around the room with interest. Annie remembered how she herself had first reacted, standing in this huge, sunny room beneath the cathedral ceiling, gazing with open mouth at the curvaceous custom cabinetry, the Viking gas stove built in to look like an imposing country fireplace, the generous granite island in the middle of the room. She was pretty sure Heather wouldn't be half as impressed. She probably lived in an even grander house.

But, shaking her head, Heather gave a small whistle of appreciation. 'I'm having a major attack of kitchen envy,' she said. 'This is a great space.'

Annie grinned. 'Isn't it? I can't take credit for the decorating. It came this way – French chateau style, apparently.'

'Well, that explains all the toile, anyway. Did you look at many other houses before you bought this one?'

Annie bit her lip. 'Well, no,' she said. 'And we didn't buy it, actually. It's a rental – part of our ex-pat deal. It was the first place the relocation lady took us, and we didn't think we could do better. My husband really loved the idea of Lyddie walking to school.'

'God, I wish our house-hunting had been half as quick,' Heather said. 'We must have looked at forty, fifty houses before we found something in our budget that we could work with. That was before the bottom fell out of the property market, of course. But then, we were only moving locally; we had all the time in the world. You probably had just a week or two to find a place.'

'Three days, as a matter of fact,' said Annie, remembering their flying visit at the beginning of the month. 'But we were sort of on honeymoon so we didn't want to waste it house-hunting.'

'On *honeymoon*?'

'We got married just weeks before we moved,' Annie explained.

'Sounds very whirlwind.'

'Oh, more like a rollercoaster,' Annie admitted. 'It was only four and a half months from the time we met to the time we married.'

'Four and a half months!' Heather sounded incredulous. Annie was used to incredulity. Almost everybody she knew had been incredulous when she and Simon announced their plans. Nobody got married after four and a half months, people told her. It simply wasn't done.

'There's no law against it,' she'd told a number of people, including Simon's risk-averse brother, John, and Annie's reckless cousin, Sarah.

'If there isn't, there should be,' Sarah responded in no uncertain terms. 'After four and a half months, everybody's still on their best behaviour. You've only seen the tip of the *tip* of the iceberg, after four and a half months. You want to see what he's like after a year. That's when he'll let his guard down and stop waxing his back.'

'He doesn't wax his back!'

'Well, how the hell would you know?' Sarah demanded. 'Which proves my point.'

The trouble was, Annie knew that people weren't just incredulous. They were also cynical.

Annie had overheard her friend Henny making a little crack to Sarah on the very day she and Simon tied the knot at a register office in Islington. Henny and Sarah had walked into the cloakroom at the pub where they were all having a celebratory lunch, both a bit tipsy, neither of them realising that Annie was in one of the cubicles. 'You have to hand it to Simon; he doesn't mess about,' Henny was saying loudly as they came in. 'Sacked the nanny already, has he?'

Annie heard Sarah's hoot of laughter. 'Yeah, I bet. But it's a win–win situation, don't forget. I mean, our Annie was probably starting to fret about her shelf life. She's not like me – God knows, I don't care if I never get shackled. Still, Simon's a good bloke. Nanny be damned, he wouldn't be doing this if he didn't fancy her rotten.'

Then Henny said, 'Yeah, they can't keep their eyes off each other. Or their hands, for that matter. But I just hope he's not kidding himself, that's all. If he lets her down—'

'We'll chop his balls off,' said Sarah. And they'd both roared at their own wit.

Annie's mother wasn't incredulous or cynical, though. Far from it. In fact, she thoroughly approved of the speedy courtship. 'Sensible to get married as quickly as you can, if both parties are willing,' she said. 'Think of the money you'll save on heating and rent. Why keep two homes going when you can make do with one?'

*

Annie nodded at Heather. 'That's right, four and a half months. We probably wouldn't have moved so quickly, only Simon had this job lined up in New York. And I had to get my visa sorted out.'

'Hmm.' Heather was staring at her with curiosity. 'But when you know, you *know*, right?'

'Exactly,' agreed Annie. 'People dilly-dally so much about tying the knot these days, it's ridiculous.'

'Oh, absolutely,' Heather agreed. 'Rob and I were like that. Four years in, we still hadn't set a date. All that time wasted when we could've been making babies. Who knew we'd have fertility issues? But God, I wish I'd gotten him to freeze his sperm back when it was healthy.'

Annie was speechless for a fraction of a second. 'Well, there you go,' she said faintly. As she busied herself pouring milk into a jug, she was thankful that her hair had a habit of flopping forward and hiding her face. She didn't want Heather to catch her pressing her lips together to suppress laughter. Surprise sometimes took her that way.

'So what does your husband do?' Heather asked after a moment.

Annie felt her eyebrows shoot up. She was used to a bit more beating about the bush. 'Um ... he works for a big food company. Do you take milk and sugar?' She didn't want to sound evasive, but neither did she want to come right out and say that he was VP: Development for ChefPro. Her mother (not to mention her father, her teachers, and every other adult who'd ever had any authority over her) had drilled into her a dread of seeming boastful.

'Really? Mine's an executive with one of New York's

top ad agencies specialising in digital media. They're pretty much on the bleeding edge.' No false modesty here, apparently. Heather waved aside the milk. 'You don't have any fat-free half-and-half?'

'Sorry, I don't even know what that is.'

'I'll take it black then, and no sugar. Thanks. So, you were saying about Lydia?'

Annie pressed her lips together as she handed Heather her mug. 'Yes. Lydia. Um. Where to start . . . Her mother – her mother, well, she drowned in a boating accident.' Annie blinked quickly. She could never tell this story casually.

Heather's eyes widened and her hand flew to her mouth. '*Drowned?* Oh my God.'

'I know. Lydia was five.'

The two of them stared at each other, instinctively observing a moment of silence.

'How did it happen?' Heather asked at last, with a sort of fascinated horror.

Annie told her what she knew – the bare bones of the story. She herself had filled in so much – the worry that must have grown into fear when Beth Keeler didn't come home; the barely contained panic as the coastguard made its search; the stunned disbelief when the boat could not be found; the flat-out agony when nightfall forced the search party to postpone its activities until dawn.

'They were on holiday in Cornwall,' she said. 'They always went there in the summer time – they were both mad about sailing, you see. Beth went out on the water alone one day and got caught in a storm. The boat went under.'

Heather's hand was at her mouth. 'No! Did they find her body?'

Annie nodded. 'It washed up eventually.'

'Jesus. The poor kid. I mean, it had to be pretty bad for your husband, but that's a kid's worst nightmare: Mom just goes off one day and never comes home. How's she dealing with it?'

Annie shrugged. 'So-so,' she said non-committally.

'Does she accept you as a mom?'

'Well, sort of. She doesn't call me mum or anything. And she won't let me hug her.' Annie thought ruefully of the many fruitless attempts she'd made to fold Lydia's stiff little body in a warm embrace. The last time, the child had all but headbutted her. 'The most I can do is pat her head. But, you know, things are getting better. At least she speaks to me now.' She was determined to sound bright and breezy, but somehow a catch had crept into her voice.

Heather patted her hand. 'Don't worry, Hailey doesn't do hugs any more, either. It's the age, I think.'

'Yeah, probably.' Annie fell silent, thinking.

Motherhood was supposed to come naturally to women, and yet she found herself second-guessing almost every 'motherly' thing she did. Perhaps she was missing some vital maternal gene? Or maybe you had to go through the whole pregnancy thing first, before the nurturing instincts kicked in properly?

Right now, she felt like an impostor among the Bradley Elementary mothers: an undercover journalist posing as a mum. But she wasn't undercover. This was all real. Nobody was going to send her home to write a punchy story about stay-at-home-motherhood among the prosperous commuter towns of south-western Connecticut. No. She wasn't here to find out how the other half lived.

She was here to live with the other half.

It was all a bit disconcerting.

'So how's Lydia with her dad?' Heather asked, bringing her back to the moment.

Annie thought about that. 'They're very close,' she said after a while. In her mind's eye she saw the two of them on the plane trip from Heathrow, their heads bent over the colouring-in book the air hostess had supplied, the crayon very small and out of place in Simon's big, tanned hand. 'They seem to have a special kind of bond. They've been through some tough times together. Sometimes . . .'

'Sometimes what?'

'Oh, nothing.' She wasn't going to say out loud that sometimes she felt a bit left out, a bit excluded. She was ashamed of that thought, quite honestly. But as vigorously as she squelched it, it always seemed to pop back up.

Instead, she blurted out, 'Do you mind if I ask you something, Heather? I mean, it's a weird question, really. I just want to know: as a real mum, do you – well, do you *like* the job?'

Heather did a bit of a double-take.

'Oh, I don't mean do you love your *daughter*. Of course, you do. God, you'd probably jump in front of a bus for her. I mean, do you like the actual, you know, *work* you have to do as a mum? Cooking and cleaning the kitchen and making packed lunches and helping with homework and all that? You're not supposed to say, are you, but looking after kids

. . . it's sort of – boring. You're *busy* all right, you're just not – not mentally occupied.'

'Actually, I love it,' said Heather. 'I like being my own boss, coming and going as I please, planning my day to suit me, getting things done on my own schedule. Hey, it's hard work – *manual* work, a lot of the time. Carrying groceries, cleaning windows, folding laundry, weeding borders. But it's varied, that's what's so great. Except in the afternoons, when it's mostly driving. But I don't envy the poor bastards stuck in their cubicles all day, I can tell you.'

'So you don't sort of wonder why you bothered to go to uni? I mean, when you're scrubbing soap scum rings off the bath tub?'

'Uni? You mean college? Well, it's good to be able to explain quantum physics, when they ask.' She laughed and shook her head. 'Look, staying home with the kids isn't a life sentence. I was out in the workplace before I had Hailey, and I'll be heading back when she's older. These kids, they'll be all grown up in a New York minute, that's the scary thing. But right now I'm living in the moment.'

Annie looked at her with respect. A spark of hope flared inside her.

'It helps to get a hobby,' Heather added. 'I'm into the horseback riding to keep me sane. Other people play bridge. Tennis is a good one too, so I hear.'

Annie pressed her lips together. 'A hobby, huh? Well, I couldn't do riding. I'm terrified of horses. And I was never much good at tennis. I *suppose* I could try bridge. It just sounds so old-ladyish.'

'You could always be one of the ladies that lunch,'

Heather suggested. 'You know, get into the social network by joining a couple of charities. Calamities International was huge back when the tsunami hit, of course, but right now Hand-Me-Down is the hot one in town. People like it because of the ball. Big black-tie event at one of the country clubs.'

'I was thinking of doing something at the school, just to start with,' Annie said.

'Good idea; they're always looking for help. Oh, look at the time, I have to go.' Heather set her mug down. 'Got to run over to the barn real quick. Thanks for the coffee.'

Annie stood at the kitchen window, watching her new friend hurry home along the street. There she went, the woman who was her own boss and could arrange her own schedule. Annie felt a smile breaking out. It was amazing what a change of perspective could do for your state of mind! She now felt quite cheerful and upbeat about scheduling herself to go to the supermarket to restock the fridge.

The next morning, after she had walked Lydia over to school, Annie had a brilliant idea. She would take the train in to New York and surprise Simon with a visit! Why on earth not? There was nothing to stop her.

She hadn't set foot in his offices yet, and she was dying to see the view of Central Park from his twenty-fourth-floor window. She was also eager to say hi to his team of five. She'd met a couple of them in London and they seemed like a nice bunch. They were young and single, and living in apartments in Manhattan. Lucky things, a disloyal part of her brain murmured; *they* hadn't been exiled to the suburbs.

In anticipation of wandering along Madison Avenue and peering into designer shop windows, she hurried home and threw aside the Capri pants, flip-flops and T-shirt she'd put on that morning in a bid to fit in with the Bradley Elementary mums. Instead, she pulled on her favourite knee-high leather boots and a long-sleeved jersey-knit dress. She piled her hair up in the chignon she'd worn almost daily to work, back in London, and added dangling earrings. Ah. Now she felt better.

She took an eye pencil and drew in the dramatic line she liked to wear on her upper eyelid. Round here, she felt like Amy Winehouse if she applied her usual London make-up; but in New York, she reckoned, she could get away with it.

Feeling all charged up, she drove the minivan to the train station and managed to park it without scraping anything. (Simon hadn't noticed the marks on the back bumper, and she hadn't felt the need to tell him about her close encounter with a pole at the supermarket. After all, a person who hadn't driven anything larger than a Renault 5 in her life needed time to get to grips with the outsize dimensions of a monster like the minivan.)

She felt an intoxicating sense of freedom as she jumped onto the train, holding her polystyrene cup of tea and a newspaper. God, this was like the old days, she thought, settling down in an empty seat and turning to the entertainment section of the paper where she ran a knowing eye over the gossip pieces. She could pretend she was on the Victoria line, going in to work. She'd be going to the weekly brainstorming meeting, and she'd suggest a story on . . . let's see, on this woman who'd had eight babies with fertility treatment, despite having no husband, because she felt so alone in the world. Or on the divorcing couple who were suing each other over a kidney he had donated to her way back when they were happy. God, both those stories seemed so sad and so, well, *personal*. Maybe she could find something a bit more upbeat, like a celebrity cat fight.

Hang on. She didn't actually have to find a story! She wasn't actually going in to work. She could sit back, relax, and enjoy the ride.

When the train pulled in to Grand Central Terminal, Annie stepped off onto the crowded platform with a sense of exhilaration. After the humming silence of her big, empty kitchen, it felt good to be jostled by a stream of people all striding purposefully towards unknown destinations in this great city. She felt as if she was back in the engine room of life again, back where things happened and news was made; yip, she was pumped full of adrenalin and ready to take on the world.

Finding her way onto Madison Avenue, she decided to walk a few blocks north, and then catch a taxi to Simon's building on the Upper East Side. Standing at the traffic light with several hundred other people beneath towering steel and glass buildings that blocked out the sun, breathing in the gasoline fumes and listening to the honking of horns, Annie had a sudden image of the quiet traffic light outside Bradley Elementary, where the only things towering over you were trees.

Gosh, she was glad to be here, absorbing the energy and general oomph flowing all around her.

A car swept past, cutting the corner so tightly that she and several other pedestrians had to jump backwards to save their toes from being run over.

So invigorating!

She was enjoying the hustle and bustle so much that by the time she decided to flag down a taxi, her feet were aching in her high boots, and she was sure she had developed a blister on her left heel. Just a few days of wearing flats, she reflected bitterly, and her feet had gone soft.

ChefPro's corporate headquarters in New York were housed in an impressive building within spitting distance of Central Park. As Annie stepped into the lift, she found herself grinning happily at the worker bees sharing the tiny space with her. Nobody grinned back, but that didn't dampen her spirits. She couldn't wait to see Simon's face when she walked into his office!

As it turned out, she was going to have to wait.

The woman behind the desk in ChefPro's lobby told her in a low voice that Mr Keeler was in a meeting, and wouldn't be available for at least half an hour.

'Oh? That's too bad. Never mind, I can wait.'

The woman raised her eyebrows. 'Is he expecting you?' She was paging through a book, apparently looking for any sign of an appointment.

'No, but—'

'He really is very busy. I'm not sure he'll be able to see you without a—'

'I'm Annie,' she burst out. 'You know – his *wife*. Annie.'

The woman, about fifty years old but trying to conceal

the fact beneath a layer of white foundation, allowed herself a small smile. 'Oh, that's different then. I'll show you to his office. You can wait there.'

He had a corner office, Annie was pleased and proud to see, complete with a big desk, and a new-looking leather couch in front of a glass coffee table. 'Can I get you a coffee?' the woman asked.

'Oh, no, that's OK. I'm just going to sit here and enjoy the view. Gosh, look at those treetops down there.'

The woman walked out quietly and closed the door.

The couch was very comfortable. After a few moments, Annie decided that it wouldn't hurt to lie down. She was rather tired, actually. Insomnia was becoming a bit of a nightly menace. Maybe she really did have a malingering case of jet lag.

She sank back into the soft leather, but couldn't get comfortable, mainly because her feet hurt. She wondered if she had a blister or just a tender spot. Might as well check, while she had some privacy. Glancing at the closed door, she slipped her boots off and had a look at her heel. She couldn't really see it properly through her tights, so, after a tiny hesitation, she pulled them off. There. Now she could see what was going on. Her heel was bright red, but as yet there was no sign of an actual blister. She stretched her feet and twirled her toes. Ah. Bliss!

No harm in leaving the boots off, just for a bit. After all, she had about half an hour to kill. Maybe she'd close her eyes and do a bit of meditation.

Seconds later, or so it seemed, she felt somebody shaking her by the shoulder and calling her name.

She opened her eyes and found herself looking up into Simon's face. He looked a little wild around the eyes.

'Annie? Annie? Are you OK?'

'Is she OK?' another voice asked.

Annie sat up, rubbing her eyes. 'Of course I'm OK.'

There seemed to be several people in the room, all of them staring at her.

'Pull your skirt down,' Simon whispered urgently.

Annie looked at her lap. Her dress seemed to have ridden up quite a lot higher than was decent. She adjusted it hastily, smiling at the small crowd. She recognised a couple of faces but couldn't think of names. 'Oh, um, hi,' she said brightly to a blonde woman who looked especially familiar. 'How are you liking New York? Settling in nicely? We must really have you all up to Norbury for lunch or something.'

The woman smiled a cool, amused smile. 'The name's Cindy,' she said.

Simon straightened up and ran his fingers through his hair. 'OK, everybody,' he said. 'How about you all go back to your desks, for now, and start putting your thoughts on paper. We don't want to lose the momentum, but obviously we can't get down to brass tacks right this minute. Why don't we reconvene in an hour?'

'Right,' people mumbled and began to shuffle out, some of them taking a last glance over their shoulders at the fascinating sight of their boss's wife, standing there all groggy and rumpled in her bare feet.

The minute the door closed, Simon pointed at something on the floor. Annie followed the line of his finger to the small puddle that was her tights.

'Oh shit,' she said, scooping them up and tucking them under her arm. 'I'm sorry. God, I wonder what your minions are thinking?'

'Annie, what's going on? Why are you here?'

Annie was feeling her chignon, which seemed to be falling out and flopping down her back. 'Surprise! I came to take you to lunch.'

'Lunch? But it's past two.'

'It's – what? But I got here at eleven!'

'Crikey. You must have been sleeping for hours.'

'I didn't mean to go to sleep. I . . . I was meditating.'

To her great relief, he burst out laughing. 'Meditating? You were in a REM cycle, my love, eyelids twitching like crazy. So where's Lydia?'

'Well, she's at school, of course.' Some vague uneasiness was beginning to stir in Annie's still fuzzy brain.

'At school? But doesn't she get out at three?'

Annie felt the blood drain out of her face. Her mouth was suddenly so dry she could hardly talk. 'Um,what did you say the time was?'

He looked at his watch. 'It's after two. You don't have a hope in hell of making it back in time.'

'Oh God. Oh Jesus. What do we do now?' She was picturing Lydia standing outside the school, waiting for her stepmother to show up. All the other walkers would leave. All the buses would leave. The car park would be deserted. The teachers would lock up and go home. And Lydia would just keep standing there, lost and alone, an obvious target for kidnappers and child molesters.

Or, no, she might decide to walk home by herself. Yes,

that was what she'd do. She'd wait for a while, and then when Annie didn't show up, she would try to go home alone. She'd walk over to the traffic lights, and of course the crossing guard would be long gone, and, being just seven years old, she might or might not have sense enough to wait for the light to change.

Annie shook her head against an image of a car flying down Shady Oak towards the intersection just as Lydia lifted her foot to begin crossing.

'Is there somebody you can phone?' Simon's voice was hard and cold.

'Um – somebody? Well, the thing is, I don't actually— Hang on.' With a sudden surge of hope, she remembered the school directory. At the urging of the PTO woman who was selling them at the second-grade coffee yesterday, she'd bought two copies: a big one to keep at home, and a small one to keep in her bag. 'I have a directory! A school directory! I'll phone and ask somebody to pick her up.'

'Who?'

'Um – this woman! This woman I met yesterday. Her name is Heather. She has a girl in Miss Scofield's class and they live on Tulip Street. She's nice. Remember, I told you she came in and had coffee with me? I bet she'd take Lyddie!'

'OK,' he said briskly. 'Do it.'

She went over to his desk, sat down on his throne-like swivel chair and began paging through the directory. 'The thing is,' she said in a quivery voice, 'I don't actually know this woman's surname. I mean, I know she's called Heather and her daughter is Hailey, and she's in Miss Scofield's class, but the names for the whole school are listed alphabetically by bloody surname.'

'Oh, for God's sake. Here, give it to me.' He took the directory from her shaking fingers and paged through it himself, running his eyes down the columns of names.

'Here,' he said. 'Heather Gibson, 7 Tulip Street.'

'Thanks,' she whispered, and dialled the number.

After five interminable rings the phone connected to Heather's voicemail. 'You know who we are and you know what to do,' a child's voice told her precociously.

'She's not home,' she told Simon, putting the receiver down. 'Oh God, let me see if I can call someone else ... Maybe that Susie woman ...'

'You'd better call the school,' Simon said. 'Ask them to keep her there until you get back.'

Annie paled at the thought of phoning up the superior-looking school secretary and revealing the shameful news that, just minutes before pick-up time, she was miles away in New York City with absolutely no plan in place.

She glanced desperately at the directory again. 'Hang on! Heather's mobile number is listed, too. I'll try that!'

Simon was pacing the room now, his face grim.

'Please pick up, oh please pick up,' Annie was whispering to herself when Heather's voice suddenly spoke into her ear.

'Hello? Who is this?'

'Um ... Heather? Heather, it's me, Annie Keeler.'

'Annie who?'

'Annie Keeler. From the second-grade coffee morning yesterday.'

'Oh. Right. Annie. Of course. How's it going?'

'Fine, fine. Well, not that great actually. The thing is, I'm . . . well, I'm in New York right now and I'm not going to be able to get home in time to pick Lydia up from school. So I wonder if you could do me a huge favour and take her for me?'

'You mean, like, today?'

'Yes, today. If you could. If at all possible.'

'Oh geez, today isn't that great for me. I'm sorry but—'

Annie's eyes flew to Simon. He was frowning at her and mouthing something. The sternness of his bright blue eyes unnerved her. She turned away from him and said, very low: 'Please! It's an emergency. I don't know anyone else to ask.'

There was a moment of silence. Then Heather said, 'OK, I'll do it. Just call the school and let them know, OK? I'll be in my car today, not walking. Have the teacher tell her what's going on so she won't think some strange lady is kidnapping her.'

'Of course. Thanks! Thanks so much. I'll see you around four.'

'Seven Tulip Street,' Heather told her. 'Don't worry, she'll have a blast with Hailey.'

Annie hung up and turned to Simon with shining eyes. 'It's OK,' she said. 'It's all organised. Heather will take her home. I just have to call the school and fill them in.'

He nodded curtly, his mouth still tight. 'Good. Better get your boots on, too.'

Minutes later, as Simon rode down in the lift with her, she quipped, 'Well, at least Lydia gets her first play date out of the whole thing.'

Simon, head down, hands in his pockets, glanced up. 'This is no joking matter,' he said in a tone she'd never heard before. 'I know you're new to the whole parent thing, but you can't slip up like this, Annie. It's just not on. The stakes are too damn high.'

She gulped. 'I know. I'm sorry. But to be fair, it's not as if I just forgot about Lyddie. If I hadn't fallen asleep I would've had more than enough time to go to lunch and get the train back in time for pick-up.'

He clenched his jaw, making the muscles pop out. Clearly, he was livid, biting back words. He didn't say another thing until he'd flagged down a taxi and was holding the door open for her. By then, he seemed to have regained some control.

'We'll talk about doing lunch another day,' he said, his voice strained. 'But for God's sake, no more surprise visits. I don't have a lot of wriggle room just at the moment. The schedule's very tight if we're going to launch on target.'

'Sorry. I should have known you probably couldn't just drop everything and go out. And I'm so sorry about Lydia.'

He shrugged. 'No harm done. See you later.' He slammed the door, tapped the roof of the car, and stepped back onto the pavement.

She looked back as the taxi nosed its way into the traffic, half expecting to see him still standing there, waving. But he was hurrying back towards his building, and he had disappeared through the glass doors even before the taxi pulled away from the first set of traffic lights.

Chapter Three

By the time Annie arrived at Heather's house, she had managed to convince herself that the day hadn't really been a total disaster, despite the unfortunate turn of events at Simon's office. After all, she had accomplished quite a lot – received a much-needed shot of urban energy, seen the truly spectacular view from Simon's window, shown him that she took an interest in his career, and demonstrated crisis-solving skills in her capacity as stay-at-home mother. She had also, as a spin-off benefit, organised a play date for Lydia.

The fact that she'd been caught snoozing on the office couch with her dress hiked up and her tights in a heap on the floor – well, you couldn't really put a positive spin on that, but in the big scheme of things a little mistake like that didn't do anybody any harm, and it had probably given Simon's team a bit of a chuckle and, who knew, maybe even drawn them together in a morale-building sort of way.

Anyway. The long and the short of it was, one of these days she and Simon would go out to lunch in Manhattan in a calm, civilised, pre-organised fashion, and they would laugh their heads off at the way her surprise visit had misfired; because one of her strong points, and probably one of the reasons Simon loved her, was that she *could* laugh at herself.

She took a tissue out of her bag, dabbed her eyes, blew her nose hard, and rang the doorbell of 7 Tulip Street. Moments later, the door inched open a crack and Annie could make out Heather on the other side, peering at her through her cloud of hair, which seemed to be hanging over her face in its entirety today.

'Oh, it *is* you.'

'Yes, it's me. Thank you, thank you, thank you for taking Lyddie. You absolutely saved my bacon. Did everything go OK? Lyddie didn't freak out or anything?'

'Oh no, everything was absolutely fine. They're down in the basement right now, watching a movie. Look, Annie, are you in a rush? Do you have a minute to come in?'

'Sure.' Annie began to look at her watch, but Heather reached out and almost yanked her over the doorstep.

'This way,' she said, striding off into the house. Slightly confused, Annie hurried after her.

When they reached the kitchen, Heather lifted the hair away from her face in a big, handheld ponytail, and turned to look at Annie.

'Now you know why I didn't really want to take Lydia today,' she said.

Heather looked as if she'd gone a few rounds with a prize fighter. The right side of her face was bruised along the cheekbone, and she was all swollen and slightly bloody around the mouth.

Annie felt her eyebrows shoot up. She opened her mouth to say something and then snapped it tightly shut.

Somebody had beaten Heather up. That was the only possible explanation for her battered appearance. You didn't get injuries like that from walking into a lamp-post. And, of course, it could only be her husband, because if there'd been a mugging or a burglary, surely somebody would have mentioned it to her already.

So Annie shut her mouth and shook her head mutely.

With a short sharp laugh, Heather pulled out a kitchen chair and dropped into it. 'Hey, don't look at me like that,' she said. 'It's not what you think. Sit down a moment and I'll explain. I haven't been smacked around by Rob, I promise you. I've just been to the doctor, that's all.'

Annie pulled a face of disbelief. 'The *doctor*?'

Heather giggled like a schoolgirl. 'Dermatologist. See, Rob's away for a couple of weeks, and I – well, I decided to try some surgical beauty treatments. This is the Botox.' She pointed to the bruise on her cheekbone. 'And this is the filler.' She indicated her swollen and bloody mouth.

Annie's mouth fell open. 'What?'

'Come on, you know what I'm talking about. You must have wondered about this kind of stuff yourself.'

Annie ran her finger nervously over the faint frown line between her brows. 'Yes, maybe, but—'

'Anyway, I decided now's the time to do it. Just to see if it freaking works. Please don't tell Rob, though. Or anybody else.'

'Of course I won't tell Rob. I've never met him.'

'Oh yeah, that's right. See, this is a birthday present for Rob, but he's never going to know about it. Not the details, anyway. He's a real visual kind of guy. He likes me to look my best. It makes him happy, so I'm doing what I can. OK, that's my confession and you'd better freaking keep quiet about it. Not a word to anyone, do you promise? I know these stay-at-home moms. They live for gossip.'

Annie felt a sudden rush of affection towards this woman. 'Who would I tell?' she asked with a little laugh. 'I hardly know a soul.'

'That's why you're the perfect person to help me out.' Heather nodded her head briskly.

'But why does it have to be a secret? Shouldn't you just be brazen about it? I mean, doesn't everybody do Botox?'

Heather shrugged. 'Maybe. But nobody advertises it, do they?'

'I suppose not. Come to think of it, I don't see people walking around looking as if they've had a punch-up all that often. Is it usual to bruise and swell like that?'

Heather jumped off her bar stool and began to rinse dishes at the sink. 'Apparently not,' she said. 'Apparently I have aberrant blood vessels around my eyes.'

'What?'

Heather tilted her face to one side. 'See? Here? Aberrant blood vessels. Apparently I have such expressive eyes that I've developed this huge muscle just to create extra crow's feet, and the huge muscle needs to be fed by extra veins that normal people don't have in their faces.'

Annie could feel her mouth twitching.

'Go on, laugh. I'd laugh too but it hurts too much. It's the gunk he shot into my naso-labial grooves. He told me it was going to be a quick fix, instant gratification, but then he didn't know I was a sweller.'

Annie found herself snorting into her hand. 'I'm sorry,' she gasped. 'I'm really very sorry. It can't be that funny from where you're standing. Look, is there anything I can do to help out?' She was thinking along the lines of doing a small grocery run for Heather, or maybe walking Hailey to and from school for the next few days.

Heather stopped her frantic dish-rinsing. 'As a matter of fact, I was hoping you could do a couple of things for me,' she said. 'It's … it's a lot to ask, I know, but you're the only one who's seen me like this and I'd kind of like to keep it that way. The fewer people who know about the surgery, the better. Could Hailey walk to school with you guys for a couple of days?'

'Good grief, of course!' said Annie. 'I mean, after what you did for me today …'

'Great! I drove in to pick the girls up today, and it was OK because my windows are tinted, but I was real nervous in case somebody came up and tapped on the glass. Oh – and there's another thing. Any way you could go to the, um, barn and, um, sort out my horse for me?'

Annie took an involuntary step backwards. 'Go … *where*? Hang on. Didn't I tell you I'm not a horse person?' Shocked as she was, Annie still had her wits about her enough to notice a flash of navy blue in the far corner of the kitchen. Lydia had sneaked into the room and was trying to hide under the table.

'I'm not asking you to actually handle the horse,' Heather said quickly. 'I'll send Hailey with you. She can put the halter on and walk Pompom to and from the paddock. She'll help with the mucking out too. She knows all about it.'

'Mucking *out*?' Annie's head was reeling. She needed a friend in this new life of hers, but did she need one this badly?

At that moment, Lydia crawled out from under the table.

'Oh, hi, sweetie,' said Heather. 'Is the movie over?'

Lydia didn't answer. Instead, looking at Heather with a directness and intensity Annie had never seen in her before, she asked, 'Is Pompom a horse?'

'Yes, Pompom is a horse,' Heather said quickly. 'A big chestnut mare with beauty-queen legs and one white hock. She's a sweetheart, old Pompom. Your mom doesn't need to be scared of her.'

Lydia looked curiously at Annie. 'You're scared of horses?'

Annie shrugged. 'They're not my favourite animal.'

'I'm not afraid of horses,' declared Lydia.

Lydia hadn't volunteered this much information about herself, ever. Annie's pulse picked up a bit of speed.

'You've been around horses?' asked Heather.

Lydia frowned. 'I think so. Long ago. In the old days. Can we see Mrs Gibson's horse, Annie?'

Oh no. What was she going to do now? She couldn't agree to look after some whopping great brute with sharp hooves and yellow teeth. She couldn't muck out a stable! She imagined a small room full of enormous piles of dung, guarded by a vicious quadruped.

'There's really nothing to it,' insisted Heather. 'Just take Pompom to the paddock, shovel out the wettest sawdust, change the water, fill the feed basin and stuff some hay into the hay net. Don't even bother to groom her. Hailey could practically do it all herself, except she can't drive over there.'

Annie drew breath to say no, she couldn't possibly take it on, Heather would have to phone up someone else, or – if she didn't know anybody else well enough to ask such a preposterous favour, which was quite possible since she was new in town – then she'd have to find some service that could do it for her. There must be such a service here in New England; flyers had been piling up in her mailbox for everything from picking up the doggy-do in your backyard to helping you organise your closets.

Then she felt a small hand sneak into her own and give it an urgent squeeze.

Lydia had never initiated physical contact with Annie in her life.

'OK,' Annie rasped. 'I'll do it. Just this once, mind. You'll have to find somebody else to take care of it tomorrow.'

Heather beamed at her, her swollen face contorting strangely. 'I knew you'd come through for me,' she said. 'There's a guy over at the barn who would probably do it for me, but I'd feel kind of weird asking him to help out. I mean, I'd have to lie about why and everything. Listen, you'd better hurry. I'm normally over there by now.'

'Right,' said Annie, 'it's facing the wrong way. How do I get it to turn?' She was staring at the big gleaming rump of Heather's socking great horse. Lydia and Heather's daughter, Hailey, were too short to see over the stable door.

Hailey, a stocky, forthright child with short, dark hair and no discernible gap between her eyebrows, suddenly reached up and undid the bolt on the door.

'Hang on!' cried Annie, quickly slamming the door shut. 'What if it runs out?'

'Don't worry, Mrs Keeler,' said Hailey. 'Pompom doesn't do that.'

'Be careful of its rear end!' Annie cried as the child opened the door a crack and slipped into the stable. 'They kick if you go up behind them!'

But Pompom didn't kick. Hailey touched the horse gently on its rump, then slid her hand along its side as she approached the business end, all the while crooning some sort of horse baby-talk. Suddenly the creature lifted its head and lurched around in the narrow box, clacking its hooves together as it went. Annie shrieked, convinced Hailey was about to be trampled underfoot, but the child stepped nimbly out of the way and then actually manoeuvred herself in front of the horse's broad chest and reached an arm up around its neck.

'Pompom, good *girl*, Pompom,' she sang, holding her hand out flat. When the horse dipped its head to nuzzle her palm, Hailey expertly slid a halter over its long nose and buckled the strap that went behind its ears.

'There,' said Hailey. 'Good, good girl. Can you open the door again, Mrs Keeler?'

Annie unbolted the door, which she'd fastened in panic the minute Hailey entered the stable.

'Stand back,' said Hailey, and without further ado led the horse out into the brick courtyard.

Yes, Annie remembered horses all right, and she hadn't got it wrong. They were just as big and lethal-looking as they'd been when she was ten, and her friend Henny had dragged her along to the stables near Guildford to observe one of her riding lessons. Annie's introduction to horses hadn't gone well. She'd been standing at Henny's elbow, watching her adjust the belt-like thing that kept the saddle on, when the peevish school pony whipped its head around and savaged her in the arm. Horses didn't have sharp teeth, but what they lacked in edge they made up for in brute force. Annie's arm had been bruised for weeks.

Her heart was in her mouth now as she calculated what damage the creature could do to chubby little Hailey if it suddenly got a bee in its bonnet and decided to skitter off, kicking aside obstacles to its escape. What nonsense to think that this child, who (though robust) couldn't weigh more than five stone, would be able to restrain the pea-brained thousand-pounder if it suddenly stopped cooperating.

'Lydia! Keep back! Don't touch!' Annie said. Lydia had stepped up beside Hailey and was now standing directly in the monster's bolt path.

'It's OK,' said Hailey. 'Pompom is a big softy. She won't hurt anybody. Do you want to hold the rope, Lydia?'

'NOOO!' yelled Annie. Everybody jumped in fright, including the horse.

'Um, Mrs Keeler, horses don't really like shouting,' Hailey said soothingly. 'Don't worry, everything will be OK.' Annie didn't know if this horse-whispery tone was meant for herself or Pompom. 'Come on, Lydia, let's just walk her to the paddock, shall we?'

The girls walked off, Pompom nodding her enormous head as she tapped along delicately behind them. Annie brought up the rear, rather distantly so as to be out of range of the deadly back hooves. As their small procession made its way to a pathway outside the stable yard, a woman with a hose trained on a muddy horse box gave them a perky wave. 'Hi, Hailey, where's Mom today?' she called.

'She's home,' Hailey called back, making the horse jump again. 'She doesn't feel good so Mrs Keeler is helping.'

The stranger, elegant in navy jodhpurs, riding boots and chaps, raised her eyebrows at Annie in her yoga pants and white sneakers threading her way gingerly along the muddy path. Annie found herself thanking her lucky stars she'd changed out of the jersey knit dress and high-heeled boots. She gave the woman a brisk wave back. No wonder Heather hadn't wanted to show her face around this place. Annie hadn't given much thought to horsy people, but at the back of her mind she'd supposed they were non-threatening types, tending towards buck teeth and big behinds. But if this stylish blonde woman was anything to go by, she'd been dead wrong.

At that moment Pompom lifted her tail, gave a few perfunctory blasts, and dropped a big pile of steaming dung in Annie's pathway.

'Wasn't it lovely?'

They had already dropped Hailey home and were heading back to their own house. Annie, exhausted and muddy, nursing a sore shoulder that she seemed to have put out while shovelling muck, felt a rueful smile break out.

'It was smelly,' she said. 'And cold. And I can't *believe* I said I'd do it again.'

That evening Simon came home well after eight, but when he went up to Lydia's room to kiss the top of her head he found her wide awake, waiting in the dark for him. 'She scared the living daylights out of me,' he reported, crashing down on the sofa next to Annie, 'suddenly rearing up under the duvet when I crept in. Looks like she's had quite a day. First the play date, then the horse jaunt.'

'I'm guessing she's been around horses before,' Annie said, giddy with relief because the grim mood he'd been in at the office seemed to have lifted.

'God, yes, the holiday place we used to rent in Cornwall was on a farm. There was this field full of muddy little ponies. Shetlands, I think they were. Lyddie loved them. Beth used to ...' He paused and cleared his throat. 'Lydia used to ride one of them round the field.'

Annie was silent a moment, picturing a mother and child in a green field, the mother with her hands wrapped in the rough mane of a shaggy pony, her other hand holding the little girl steady on the animal's back. Perhaps Simon would have been leaning up against a gate, shouting encouragement as Lydia bounced along.

Annie burrowed closer to Simon's warm body, listening to the rhythmic thump of his heart, wanting to make him smile again. 'You should have seen her this afternoon, filling the hay net and spreading sawdust. She was in her element! Almost makes me glad I messed up and couldn't get to school in time for pick-up. Hey! Maybe I should look into riding lessons for her!'

Simon froze a moment. Then he drew slightly away from her.

'Steady on,' he said. 'I mean, I'm happy with her going over there to see the horses – but *lessons*? I don't know.'

'I thought you wanted her to be busy and get lots of exercise?'

Simon took her hand. 'I do,' he said. 'But she isn't even *asking* for riding lessons. I'd rather she did something more active – some sort of ball sport. Riding is just sitting on your bum, when you get right down to it. What do the girls play around here. Hockey?'

'Soccer, apparently,' Annie said. 'But do you really think—'

Simon interrupted by leaning in for a kiss. Just before their lips met, she saw the corners of his mouth tug up into a smile.

'What are you grinning at?' she mumbled against his lips.

'You,' he murmured back. 'You're wearing this fabulous perfume. Eau de dung, perhaps?'

She pulled away quickly, dismayed. 'Oh no! I meant to have a shower but I didn't get the chance.'

'Never mind.' He drew her back towards him. 'I need one too. We can scrub each other's backs.'

'Couldn't you give her some aspirin?' Annie asked Heather over the phone three days later.

Heather had phoned to break the news that Hailey had

a fever and wouldn't be able to help Annie muck out the stable that afternoon.

'Annie, it's strep throat, it's infectious,' Heather said. 'You won't want Lydia to be around her. Oh, and you should *never* give a kid aspirin, by the way. Look, I know you're a bit nervous to do it on your own, but surely you can see that Pompom is a doll?'

A *doll*?

'But ... but your face is nearly normal now,' Annie protested.

'The bruise on my cheek is a freaking rainbow. You saw it yesterday! It didn't just disappear overnight. Look, I promise to send Hailey out with you tomorrow. Overnight on the antibiotics and I know she'll be up to it. I hate to ask you, but no *way* am I going to the barn like this. I mean, I can get away with doing the school run in the car now, but the barn is different. You've seen the women over there. Freaking queen bees. And it's not as if I can explain myself to them. How could I? Just walk up and say, Oh, by the way, this is Botox, not a black eye?'

Annie could see her point. All this week she'd been noticing the sort of people who frequented the barn. Something about these elegant and moneyed women with their sharp eyes and careful hair was just plain scary.

'OK,' she groaned into the phone. 'I'll do it.'

'Just think how thrilled Lydia will be!'

'Oh yes. She'll be doing backflips, I'm sure.'

Taking a deep breath, Annie opened the stable door a crack and eased herself into the dragon's lair.

'Whoa, girl, whoa,' she called. She must have spoken too loudly or in the wrong tone of voice, because Pompom immediately stopped ripping at the hay net, threw her head up, then flung her whole body round in a tight circle, narrowly missing standing on Annie's foot.

Annie pressed herself against the stable wall, cursing beneath her breath. Really, this went way beyond the call of duty. Heather was going to be paying Annie back for the rest of her life, and possibly well into her afterlife.

'Whoa, girl,' she called again, trying for a low, crooning note.

'Are you OK?' Lydia asked from the other side of the door.

'Fine,' Annie called back.

The horse flattened its ears but otherwise didn't react. Annie stretched out one hand and connected gingerly with Pompom's shiny rump, just as she'd seen Hailey do. The animal threw its head up and did that abrupt circle again before returning to the methodical savaging of the hay net.

Annie decided she'd dispense with the foreplay. Gritting her teeth, she crept towards Pompom's head, body pressed against the wall, heart pounding so loudly she was pretty sure the horse could hear it. When she finally got within striking distance of her target, she cleared her throat and held out her hand, the way she'd seen Hailey do. 'Come on, Pompom, come on, come on, girl.'

Pompom nodded her head rapidly and rolled her eyes at her.

'Come on, you bloody great monster, come and eat out of my hand like you're damned well supposed to.' This she murmured between her teeth, aware of Lydia on the other side of the door.

The horse stamped her hoof and sidled towards her. Then she extended her neck and bumped her nose against the outstretched palm. 'Ha!' Annie yelled, and lunged at the horse with both arms, trying to catch her around the neck.

Pompom snorted and jerked away, slamming her considerable backside into the wall. 'What's happening?' Lydia's voice cried out.

'Nothing, nothing, everything's fine,' Annie called back with false calm. Her blood was up now. There was no way this animal was going to make a fool out of her in front of her stepdaughter.

After giving them both a moment to get over the excitement, she began sidling up towards Pompom's head again. 'Come on, girl, come on, look what I've got for you.' Why hadn't she brought a carrot or something? Why had Hailey gone and made it look so easy?

In desperation, she snatched some hay from the net. 'Come on, girl, look here, nice hay.'

It turned out that Pompom wasn't that bright a spark, after all. She didn't seem to realise she was being tricked as she curled her lip out towards the stolen handful of hay. While the horse's head was down, Annie managed to throw the rope around her neck, and once she'd done that, Pompom seemed to know she was beaten. With wisps of hay hanging out of her mouth, she allowed Annie to slide the halter over her nose and fasten it. Annie was amazed. Didn't the brute know her own strength, then? She could have thrown Annie aside with a quick jerk of the massively muscled neck, but apparently now that she was tethered, she was quite prepared to behave herself.

Flushed with pride, Annie called to Lydia to open the stable door. She had a momentary feeling of panic, as she pulled the horse into motion, that Pompom might take the opportunity to knock her down and make a run for it, but the horse had apparently resigned herself to business as usual.

'Here, you can hold her too,' Annie told Lydia as she led Pompom out of the stable yard. Smiling, Lydia took the end of the rope.

'She's a nice horse, isn't she?'

Although Annie was still shaking with stress after her ordeal in the stable, she responded with an enthusiastic yes. When you got right down to it, this horse was worth its weight in gold; because Lydia only smiled for her dad.

They set off towards the paddock, Annie beginning to feel almost confident. The worst was surely over. Catching Pompom to bring her back to the stable might present a problem, but Hailey had never had any difficulty. In fact, Pompom, knowing that her evening feed awaited, had always come trotting over to be caught.

As they rounded a bend, they approached what Hailey had described as the lungeing arena. It was a circular area neatly fenced to shoulder height with wooden palings. Just the day before, Hailey had taken Pompom in there and made her trot around in circles at the end of a long rein for about twenty minutes, for exercise.

Today there was a horse in the lungeing arena, but it wasn't being exercised. It seemed to be exercising itself, though, running up and down the fence with an arched neck and flared nostrils. The moment Pompom caught sight of this horse, she stopped in her tracks, raised her head, and gave an almighty bellow that nearly deafened Annie. It didn't sound like a whinny or a neigh, or any noise that a horse was supposed to make. It was a loud, quivering blast of anguish, and Annie nearly fell over with fright. Out of the corner of her eye, Annie saw Lydia freeze in confusion.

'It's OK,' Annie said bracingly into the pulsating aftermath of Pompom's cry. 'It's OK. Everybody calm down. It's just another horse. Don't worry, Pompom, the bad horsy can't get out. We just have to walk by. Everybody will be OK. Come on, let's just walk on by.'

She was trying to sound both calm and authoritative, and Lydia certainly looked a little reassured, but Pompom didn't seem to have caught her tone. In fact, Pompom's eyes seemed in danger of popping out of her head. Her nostrils now appeared as wide as Martini glasses, and her head was up in the air at an unnatural angle that pulled the rope taut in Annie's hand.

Annie gave the rope a little tug. 'Come on, Pompom, let's go,' she begged.

Pompom took a deep breath and bellowed again. This time, the horse in the lungeing arena bellowed back and began to gallop in earnest around the circumference of the fence.

Annie's heart banged hard against her ribs. She yanked at the rope again. 'Come on, you stupid, *stupid* beast.'

'Don't talk to her like that,' cried Lydia.

And then Pompom reared up and tore the rope out of Annie's and Lydia's hands. Snorting and kicking up her heels, Heather's precious mare clattered off towards the distant car park, trailing the rope behind her. Annie gave a scream of pure panic. She had a sudden mental image of the beast with its iron hooves kicking out at all the parked Hummers and SUVs. An even worse scenario popped into her head. What if a car suddenly pulled in at speed, and there was a collision, and the horse's long legs were snapped at the knee, and the car was a write-off, and a child inside broke its neck . . .

Just as Pompom seemed about to do her best to turn these horrors into reality, the horse had a sudden change of heart. Annie and Lydia were halfway across the grassy field by now, in hot pursuit, when Pompom gave a joyful buck, turned around, and began galloping at breakneck speed back towards the lungeing arena.

Annie switched directions to run after her, lungs screaming for air.

Pompom raced up to the other horse, screeched to a halt, and stood nostril to nostril with it for a moment. Then both horses squealed and did some jumping about. Then the big sand-coloured horse in the arena stretched its head out, flattened its ears, and appeared to bite a chunk out of Pompom's neck. Pompom did the screaming whinny, reared in the air, and clunked one hoof against the fence.

Oh dear God, something bad was bound to happen soon. Annie hadn't realised horses were so aggressive. Would it be like a dog fight, with one of them lying dead on the ground at the end? Could they rip each other's throats out with their grass-eating teeth?

Annie felt in her pocket for her phone – but who to call? Surely in a situation like this, Heather would throw caution to the winds and come flying over to help, despite her rainbow-coloured face and strep-infected child? Or maybe she should dial 911? She pictured the commotion of sirens blaring and lights flashing as the entire Norbury police force pulled into the barn's car park, closely followed by the fire engine. The police never seemed to go anywhere without the fire engine, she'd noticed. If the huge shiny truck didn't drive Pompom over the edge, nothing would.

'Having trouble, ma'am?' a voice drawled.

Phone in hand, Annie glanced over her shoulder. A man who looked remarkably like a cowboy out of a spaghetti western stood behind her, complete with hat, narrowed eyes and tasselled leather chaps worn over jeans. He lacked only a bandanna and a cheroot to be picture-perfect for a role in a John Wayne classic.

'The brown one's mine,' Annie replied. 'Well, not mine. My friend's, but I'm supposed to be looking after it. I don't know whose bloody horse that is in the arena but it's taunting Pompom like anything. Took a bite out of her neck just a moment ago.'

'The palomino?' said the cowboy. 'He's mine.'

'Well, get over there and bloody stop him, can't you? I don't know what he's been saying to Pompom, but he's really giving her the heebie-jeebies. She's ready to go for the jugular. Quick, do something before they hurt each other!'

The horses were squealing back and forth in a loud, threatening fashion, the sand-coloured one rearing up and slamming his chest into the fence.

To Annie's outrage, the cowboy laughed.

'They're not trying to hurt each other. Pompom's in heat,

is all. My boy's just been gelded but she ain't picky, I guess. Reckon his brain hasn't figured out his balls are gone.'

Annie felt her face flush, and she glanced at Lydia. The child was staring at the stranger with wide eyes. 'Can you keep it clean,' Annie hissed at him.

His face broke into a lazy smile. 'Sure I can,' he drawled. 'Here, you need help getting that mare away from Stanley?'

Relief made Annie weak at the knees. 'Oh yes, yes,' she said. 'Please! I know almost nothing about horses, you see, and to be honest I find them a bit . . . intimidating.'

'You don't say.' The man sauntered off towards Pompom, making some kind of clicking noise with his mouth as he went. Pompom could barely take her eyes off the palomino, but she had the humans covered with her peripheral vision. As the man moved closer, she gave a contemptuous snort and danced off sideways, still keeping her eyes on the prize. The man began to move very slowly, perhaps an inch at a time, his hands at his side. Pompom watched and snorted and danced. It was clear that she wasn't planning to let him get within spitting distance of her.

But she'd forgotten the lead rope hanging from her halter.

Before she'd figured out what he was up to, the cowboy was standing on that rope with both of his boots. Feeling the resistance, Pompom tried to lunge away, but the cowboy bent down quick as a striking snake and took the rope in his hands. Then, still clicking his tongue and talking softly, he began to reel her in.

He made it look so easy.

Within seconds he was holding the halter at the metal

ring and marching an unrepentant Pompom away from her wildly protesting would-be lover. Annie ran to catch up with them, and Lydia followed.

'Oh, thank you so, so much,' Annie panted. 'Can you put her in the first paddock? We just have to muck out her stable. We'll do it really, really fast. And then – I wonder if I can ask you – I mean, I'm not sure if you were planning to leave right away, but—'

'I'll bring her back past Stanley for you, no problem,' he said. 'No sense getting everybody all worked up again.'

Back in Pompom's stall, Annie rolled up her sleeves and got busy shovelling and raking as fast as she could. She just wanted to get the job over and done with so they could go home. Lydia didn't seem to sense the hurry. She moved about in a leisurely fashion, unhooking the hay net, tipping out the last of the water in the bucket.

'What does "in heat" mean?' she asked just as Annie was about to set off for the compost heap with her wheelbarrow.

Damn.

Annie clung to the handles of the wheelbarrow with white knuckles. 'Um ... it sort of means Pompom wants to ... to find herself a boyfriend. A horse boyfriend, of course.'

'Oh,' said Lydia, and went back to spreading clean sawdust with no further sign of interest. Annie lingered, feeling she should explain things better. Wasn't this, after all, what those parenting books called a 'teachable moment'? Lydia hardly ever offered such moments, because she hardly ever said anything at all.

But Annie flinched as she thought of ways to develop the theme. She could explain that Pompom wasn't angry with the other horse, just excited to see him, and that was why she'd acted like such a lunatic. She could explain that Pompom really wanted to be in the lungeing arena with the other horse so they could make babies. She could explain further that this would be a futile exercise because the boy horse lacked the necessary equipment.

Or she could just move on by with her wheelbarrow.

After a moment of reflection, she just moved on by with her wheelbarrow.

On their way home, Annie stopped off at the drugstore on the town's oak-lined main street. 'Do you have anything for somebody who has a bad, um, you know, mark on their face?' she asked the woman behind the counter. Lydia, toying with a small stand of key rings, seemed entirely uninterested in the conversation.

'A mark? You mean, like a birthmark?'

'Yes. Like a birthmark.' Annie fluttered her hand around her cheekbone. 'Sort of a multicoloured birthmark.'

'I'll show you what I have.'

Twenty minutes later, Annie was ringing Heather's doorbell. When Heather cautiously opened the door, lurking well back in the shadows of an unlit hallway until she saw who it was, Annie thrust a brown bag into her hands. 'This is for you,' she said. 'It's make-up. You put the green stuff on first, then the thick paste. It's supposed to be really good. Slap it on with a spatula if you have to. But I can't go back to the stables tomorrow. I'm sorry. I just can't.'

'Jesus, Annie, what happened?'

'Your horse,' Annie hissed. Then she looked down at

Lydia and swallowed back a few choice expletives. 'Your horse is in *heat*.'

According to Heather, the cowboy at the barn was Dan Morgan, a well-known personality in these parts, well nigh a celebrity. Although he looked and acted as if he'd been out riding fences all his life, he was in fact some sort of oil tycoon who'd moved east for mysterious reasons, and spent much of his free time (of which, like Annie, he seemed to have an abundance) dispensing horse wisdom at the barn. People came to ask his advice about horses that wouldn't box, horses that refused to jump, horses that reared, crib-biters, wind-suckers, bolters, buckers, even horses with bizarre diagnoses such as emotional dissociation and sensory overload.

Beneath his rustic speech patterns and aura of countrified simplicity lurked a deep and complex personality, Heather reckoned.

'I don't know about that,' said Annie, 'but it's funny how you notice a man's bum when he's wearing those leather legging thingies.'

'I think you mean butt,' said Heather. 'A bum is a homeless person sleeping in a cardboard box in a doorway.'

Annie shook her head. 'You're wrong! A butt is the tail end of a cigarette.'

'It's a tail end, whichever way you look at it,' Heather laughed.

Annie wondered briefly if she could persuade Simon to wear a cowboy hat, jeans and leather legging thingies. She rather thought not. Shabby old corduroys were more his style.

Chapter Four

'She had this trip to the south of France lined up, but then she broke up with the chap who was organising it, and he's taking someone else instead,' Annie told Simon that Saturday afternoon as they walked around the nature trail at Fairacres Park with Lydia.

Simon raised his eyebrows, looking faintly amused. 'Which chap was this? I can't keep up with Sarah's boyfriends. I wonder why she'd want to come here? It's not really her kind of place. I don't think there's a singles scene in Norbury at all. It's just families, as far as I can tell. Of course, she could take the train in to Manhattan and go clubbing.'

'She's coming to see *me*, of course,' said Annie.

Annie and Sarah were very close, for cousins. They were like sisters, without the rivalry. Because her parents travelled abroad a lot, Sarah – the youngest in her family by far – had spent countless weekends and school holidays with Annie's family in Surrey. Conveniently, the weekly boarding school she attended was only about an hour's drive from their home. Annie, an only child, had practically worshipped the ground her older cousin walked on.

'Anyway, she enjoys meeting all kinds of new people,'

Annie said. 'Not just men. We should have a dinner party or something for her.' They could see Lydia ahead of them, poking at things with a long stick, and then running on a few strides to make sure the grown-ups didn't catch up with her.

Simon smiled down at Annie. 'A dinner party. Wow. Do we know anybody to invite yet?'

Annie gave him a playful kick. 'Idiot. Of course we know people. There's Heather, and I wouldn't mind asking this other mum who lives on our street, Jennifer Miller. She's a bit prim, but I've got a feeling she could be a different person altogether after a glass of Pinot Grigio. And maybe we could invite a chap for Sarah.'

'A chap? What chap?'

Lydia waved a hand. 'I don't know. Don't you have any single blokes on your team?'

Simon gave a sudden snort of laughter. 'Well, yes, there are a couple – but I wouldn't want to introduce any of them to Sarah Harleigh! I'd never live it down.'

'Sarah's not so bad!'

'Sarah's great. She's a hoot. But even you have to admit, she's a bit of a rough diamond.'

'You'd be embarrassed to introduce your colleagues to her?'

'Bloody right I would. If she takes a fancy to somebody, next thing you know she's clubbing him over the head and dragging him off to her room by the ankle.'

'Rubbish!' She kicked him a bit harder, but still playfully. With lightning reflexes, he grabbed her foot and held her hopping and helpless.

'Look, we don't have to be pimps for Sarah,' he said. 'She's tough. She can take an evening of being the only single woman in the room. Or we could just scrap the whole dinner party idea.'

'No, no, I want the dinner party. Whoooa,' she yelled as she began to topple over backwards. Simon released her foot and leapt into action, managing to catch her before she fell. For a moment she lay in the tight band of his arms, looking up into bright blue eyes that seemed to be chinks of the crisp autumn sky itself. Then he dipped his head to kiss her.

Annie felt somebody tugging urgently at the back pocket of her jeans. Delicious though it was to be tasting Simon's cool lips, she drew away from him. Lydia was standing nearby with an unreadable look on her face, arms crossed over her narrow chest.

'Daddy,' she said in a louder voice than usual. 'Why are you doing that? Why was Annie kicking you? Is she in heat?'

There was a stunned silence. Simon turned speechless eyes on Annie. Annie shrugged helplessly. Simon cleared his throat. 'Darling, Annie's not a horse,' he said. 'We were just . . . just having a little fun.'

'I don't like you doing that,' Lydia said, glaring up at him. 'It's stupid.'

He squatted down next to her. 'Come here, sweetie.' He held out his arms and after a small hesitation she slumped into them. Annie could see her petulant face resting on his shoulder. He looked up at Annie. 'Will you give me a minute to talk to her?' he asked.

She nodded and walked away from them quickly down the trail. They didn't catch up with her again – she made sure of that by breaking into a run as soon as she was out of sight around a corner.

She'd never been on a nature walk in a park with her own dad. He wouldn't have been caught dead in a park – he reckoned they were riddled with druggies and dog poo. But he used to play cards with her, when she was growing up. Gin rummy, cribbage, even poker. He made her win her pocket money off him, and the truth was she often found winning the money more fun than spending it.

As she waited at the car, watching Simon and Lydia draw closer, a strange melancholy came over her. They were chatting away, engrossed in each other's company: the tall blonde man and his skinny blonde daughter. They didn't look anything like her dad and herself at seven years old. Her dad had been of average height and slight, and he had always worn a tie, even when he was on holiday. His hair had been the same colour as Annie's own – plain brown. Yet, in some inexplicable way, the sight of these two reminded her almost unbearably of herself and her dad, whose face she hadn't seen since he died of a heart attack when she was in her early twenties.

'Ah, *there* you are,' Simon said, lifting his head and looking straight at her.

She unpeeled herself from the car and waved at them.

Their approach was slow and awkward now, because Lyddie was holding Simon's right hand in both of hers and jumping forward every few steps with curled-up legs, so that she could swing from his arm.

'Come over and give me a hand with this monkey, will you?' Simon called.

Annie felt the smile breaking out on her face as she ran over to join them.

'Lyddie, take Annie's hand and we'll both swing you,' Simon suggested.

Lydia tightened her two-handed grip on Simon's hand.

'Go on,' said Simon. 'Trust me, this is one of those things a dad can't do alone.'

'Yes, you can!' Lydia threw her weight onto his hand to prove her point. He let her dangle a moment, then lowered her to the ground.

'But not very well,' he said.

Annie held out her hand. Lydia detached one of hers and slid it reluctantly into her stepmother's grasp.

'OK, here we go,' said Simon. 'One, two, three ... *up*!'

Lydia flew so high into the air that for a moment Annie had a glimpse of her pink trainers against the blue sky. As she swung up, she shrieked with glee.

Inspired by the idea of throwing a dinner party, Annie thought she'd better try to kick-start Lydia's social life a bit, too. 'Is there anybody you'd like to have round to play, other than Hailey?' she asked one evening while Lydia was brushing her teeth. They had already returned Heather's favour and had Hailey round. It hadn't been a particularly successful play date. Hailey had spent the entire time kicking a ball about outside with Annie, while Lydia played with her bald doll up in her room.

'No,' said Lydia. 'I like playing by myself.'

'Yes, I know, but ... Look, who do you sit next to in class?'

'This girl called Courtney.'

So Annie looked up the name in the school directory and cold-called Courtney's mother. Mrs Phelps sounded a bit surprised to hear from her, but duly agreed to send her daughter over.

To prevent Lydia from hiding away in her room again, Annie decided to take the girls to Dogwood Park, where there was apparently a very nice playground.

And it *was* a very nice playground, as it turned out. The only trouble was, it seemed to be entirely made up of activities that were best tackled alone. You didn't need a companion when you were rock climbing or balancing your way over a wobbly rope bridge or hurtling down a tubular slide. In fact, a companion during these feats of derring-do was a bit of a liability, or so she gathered from the way Lydia and Courtney shot off in different directions the moment they set foot in the place. But that was OK. They were probably bonding, nonetheless. Common experiences brought people together, everybody knew that; even if they ignored each other while experiencing them.

Annie settled down on a bench and looked around with interest at the other adults in the park. She noticed a tired-looking woman with dark hair tucked behind her ears walking around behind a bandy-legged toddler. Standing up slowly, Annie stretched in a nonchalant way and ambled over towards the woman. She didn't want to look like a stalker, but she was in desperate need of adult conversation. She hadn't spoken to a soul all day. She'd never really thought, before, of the solitary nature of the life of a stay-at-home mum. The truth was, she'd never thought *at all* about the life of a stay-at-home mum.

She waited till the dark-haired woman glanced her way, then smiled and said, 'You'd think they'd have a see-saw at a big playground like this, wouldn't you?'

The woman looked a little startled. 'See-saw?'

'Yes. Didn't you just love see-saws when you were little?' She demonstrated an up and down motion with her hands.

The woman frowned. 'Oh, you mean a teeter-totter? They don't put those in parks any more. Too much liability.'

'Liability?' Annie echoed, but the woman was waving to somebody across the playground.

'Gotta go,' she said, giving Annie a polite smile as she hauled her toddler up onto her hip and crossed the wood chips towards her friend.

Annie watched her walk away, feeling wistful.

This was one of those moments when she felt as if she'd give anything to be back inside the fuggy offices of *Rumour Has It*, at her familiar desk in her familiar cubicle, surrounded by the motley crew she'd worked with for four years. Oh, she'd spoken to them by phone a few times since she left, and her friend Amanda, the copy editor, kept sending her silly email jokes, but it wasn't the same thing as being in the office with everybody.

With a brisk shake of her head, Annie put her old life out of her mind. She'd given up her job at the women's weekly without a moment's hesitation, despite predictions that she was shortlisted to fill the shoes of the retiring assistant editor. She hadn't felt a single pang as she cleared her desk and emptied her half-shelf in the office fridge. Indeed, she'd even handed over her top secret Ideas file to the incoming staff writer.

Yes, she'd been on the up and up at the magazine, but no, she didn't regret leaving, not for a moment – even though she'd been planning to springboard off her position as assistant editor into a magazine with slightly more credibility than *Rumour Has It,* which was a bit of a bottom-feeder in the industry, if she were honest. Something like *Marie Claire* would have done nicely.

The truth was, she'd always been ambitious – a fact that her career path didn't really reflect, at first glance. Early on, she'd found that there were far too many girls fresh out of university willing to work for *Tatler* for almost nothing. But Annie was cunning. When the direct route to women's magazine stardom seemed to be blocked off by congestion, she'd decided on the road less travelled.

So she'd taken a job first with a magazine for doll's house and miniature collectible enthusiasts, then with an online aquarium hobbyists' journal. Her lucky break had come when she'd heard through the friend of a friend that *Rumour Has It* was looking for a general dogsbody. She did that for about a year, until one of the copy editors suddenly threw in her job in order to follow her boyfriend to a Buddhist retreat in India.

Without fanfare or fuss – without even a pay rise – Annie took over the vacant desk and the unfinished proofreading. Her considerable talent for idea generation (i.e. for reading competing magazines and mining their stories) soon emerged. And the rest was history.

But she would have given up a lot more than her career to marry Simon Keeler.

As a matter of fact, she *had* given up a lot more than her career to marry Simon Keeler. She'd given up her flat, her ancient Mini, her handmade curtains, her hand-picked furniture, the land of her birth. Not to mention her friends, her family, and her gym membership.

But it wasn't the adrenalin-rush of working in media that she missed. It wasn't even the perks (although it *was* hard to live without the cosmetics samples, free books and other small bribes that streamed in almost daily). It was being in a place where people knew (and cared) that she took her tea weak with one spoon of sugar and a dash of milk.

Annie gave herself a mental shake and surveyed the playground, looking for Lydia's white shirt and Courtney's purple one. Lydia was on the swings and Courtney was . . . oh no, Courtney was running up to another little girl who'd just arrived. They were squealing with excitement, hugging, and generally acting like long-lost lovers. And now they were glancing over at Lydia and talking in low voices. Annie felt her heart begin to thump. Lydia looked back at the girls, then dropped her eyes and slumped down in the swing. The girls giggled and ran off together, hand in hand.

For a few minutes, Annie watched Lydia dangle on the swing, shoes stirring up wood chips, while Courtney ran around noisily with the newcomer. Then she stood up and walked casually over to her stepdaughter.

'Can I give you a push?' she asked.

'No thanks.'

'Are you sure? It's more fun if you go a bit higher.'

'I don't want to go higher.'

A shrill cry caught their attention. Courtney was screaming with laughter as her friend tried to catch her.

'Is that other girl in your class?' Annie asked.

Lydia shrugged.

Annie looked at her watch. It was only four o' clock. Courtney's mother was coming for her at five thirty. An hour and a half. Eternity. 'You know what?' she said suddenly. 'I think we should head on home now. I've had about enough of this park for one day.'

'All right,' said Lydia. Annie couldn't even tell whether she was relieved or disappointed.

Thankfully, Courtney came away from her friend obediently when called. 'See you tomorrow, Samantha,' she yelled to the girl through the open window as they pulled away.

'Does Samantha go to Bradley?' Annie asked in a bright voice.

'Yes, and she lives on my street, and she's my BFF,' said Courtney.

Bully for you, Annie thought. 'That's nice,' she said. Lydia said nothing at all. You couldn't blame her, really.

'So – what games do you play at recess?' Courtney asked Lydia after a moment. She was obviously a girl who couldn't abide dead air.

Lydia didn't reply.

Annie glanced in the rear-view mirror at Courtney's confident, slightly sneering face, her heart sinking. She stole a look at the small, clenched face of her stepdaughter. Lydia was staring out of the window, one shoulder raised protectively.

'I never see you on the blacktop,' Courtney continued.

'Do you go over to the monkey bars? *We* always play on the blacktop in the corner near the portables. We play ponies. Sometimes we play tag, but mostly it's ponies. I play with Samantha and McKenna and Brittany. Who do *you* play with?'

Annie looked at Lydia's face again in the rear-view mirror. She was still staring stonily into the distance.

'Can you do the monkey bars, Courtney?' Annie asked hastily. 'Lydia can. She's really good. She can go from one end right over to the other side. I've tried it myself, but I can't do more than a couple of bars.'

'Sure, I can do the monkey bars,' said Courtney. 'Everybody in second grade can. But we pretty much don't bother with the monkey bars any more.'

'Really?' Annie cursed silently. She'd thought Lydia's unexpected prowess on the bars would give her a bit of an edge. But no. The bars were passé, apparently. Good grief, they were a tough bunch these Norbury second-graders, agile as monkeys and nonchalant with it.

'Can we take the bikes out?' Courtney asked when Annie pulled up outside the house.

'Bikes? Um . . . we don't have bikes,' Annie said.

Crikey. She didn't even know whether Lydia could ride a bike. That was something she needed to fix.

'How about scooters, then?'

'Sorry, no scooters.'

'Trampoline?'

'No trampoline.'

'So what do you guys have?' Courtney asked, looking genuinely curious.

'Um ...' Annie was stumped.

'We have TV,' said Lydia.

The girls spent the rest of the afternoon slumped in front of *Sponge Bob*.

'It went very well, I thought,' Annie said staunchly as they waved goodbye to Courtney from the driveway.

'It totally sucked,' said Lydia, uttering her first Americanism.

'This is effing unbelievable,' said Sarah, staring out of the car window at the pastel-painted wooden-framed houses on their artfully landscaped grounds. They were driving through Norbury, on their way back from the airport. 'Look at the picket fences! The rolling lawns! The stars and stripes all over the place! I thought this kind of thing was a figment of Hollywood's imagination.'

'No, it's real,' said Annie proudly. 'You won't see any pebble-dash here, let me tell you. And no terraces. People aren't into sharing walls.'

'And the gardens are huge!'

'Not gardens, backyards. Yes, around here they're all one or two acres.'

'And look – hay bales and pumpkins all over the place! It's a seasonal extravaganza. Slow down, I want to look at that scarecrow. Crikey. Is that a cashmere scarf he's wearing? God, maybe I could nip out and nab it. Just kidding,' she added as the minivan leapt forward in sudden haste. 'Can you imagine people at home bothering with all this? It's a paradise for kids, isn't it? I can see what Simon was thinking when he moved, now.'

'Yeah, well. It's a bit of a paradise for mums, too. It's all about convenience, you see. Every kind of appliance you can imagine. And so much space everywhere! You never have to battle for parking. Nail salons on every corner. Big supermarkets with plenty of room to turn your trolley in the aisle. Trolleys with wheels that work. And if you don't have time to take care of something, like – I don't know – walking your dog or ironing your shirts, you just call up a service.'

Sarah settled back in her seat and gave a low laugh. 'Yeah, nice for some. Where do the real people live, the ones who are going to be repossessed?'

Annie pulled a face. 'Don't know, really. Want to see the beach?'

The town's private beach was deserted this school morning. Annie and Sarah put on their jackets and took a seat on a bench, looking out at the calm water of Long Island Sound and listening to the gulls.

Sarah examined the distant boats, bobbing at anchor, with beady-eyed interest. 'Wow, Annie,' she said musingly after a while, 'you've gone and landed with your bum in the butter, haven't you?'

Annie felt a slight prickle of resentment. 'Things aren't always as cushy as they look,' she said with a shrug. 'And that's butt, not bum.'

'It's bum to you and me, my girl. How hard can it be, looking after one kid in a big mansion, with all kinds of help laid on? Look, I'm not taking a dig at you. I'm happy for you, that's all.'

Annie was silent.

Sarah gave her a shrewd look. 'What's going on?' she asked after a moment. 'Is there a serpent in paradise?'

Annie stood up briskly and walked off towards the water's edge. Staring out at the distant shape of Long Island, she was appalled to feel tears forming in her eyes. After a while, Sarah came and joined her.

'You're homesick,' Sarah said. 'Settling into a new place must be hard. No friends, no family.'

'No job,' added Annie. She dashed her hand across her eyes. 'God, listen to me. I'm not normally so pathetic. It's just ... seeing a familiar face, you know. I'm actually very happy here. Very.'

Sarah grinned and ran her hand through her springy red hair. 'Look, love, you don't have to convince *me*. I'm bloody green with envy. Of course you're happy. I mean, you've got all this,' she gestured at the beach, the bobbing boats, the distant houses with their lawns running down to the water, 'and the lovely Simon Keeler to boot.'

Annie smiled and blushed with pleasure. 'He is lovely, isn't he?'

'Yeah, and he's not just a pretty face. I've sailed with him. He's a good man in a squall.'

Annie nodded. 'I bet he is.'

'Why isn't he sailing any more?' Sarah asked abruptly. 'It's a crying shame. He ought to be out on that water! He tells me he hasn't even joined a club.'

Annie clicked her tongue and stared out over the water. 'I don't know,' she said after a moment. 'I certainly haven't pressurised him to stop, if that's what you're thinking. Maybe he just doesn't want to take away from family time.

There's little enough of it, as it is.' She leaned over, picked up a smooth pebble and turned it around in her hand. It was a beautiful stone, flecked with orange and green. Studying it as if she was going to have to draw it from memory, she asked suddenly, 'Did you know Lydia's mother?'

Sarah picked up a couple of pebbles too. She didn't look at them, just weighed them in her hand then threw them far out across the water, making them skip over the surface with the practised ease of a teenage boy. 'Beth? Yeah, I met her a few times. Never got to know her very well.'

'So? What was she like?'

Sarah began to walk towards the rocky outcrop that marked the end of the beach. Annie followed, still holding her pebble.

'Oh. You know. She was thin and blonde. White eyelashes. Looked frail, you wouldn't have thought she weighed enough to be rail meat.'

'For God's sake, what *is* rail meat?'

Sarah glanced at her in mild surprise. 'Well, it's the people who sit on the rail to balance the boat when it heels, of course. But Beth was stronger than she looked. One of those wiry women with muscles like steel cables.'

'Different from me, then.' Annie glanced at her own arm. Muscles like steel cables did not lurk beneath her jumper, she knew for a fact.

'Of course. And you should be glad of that. Wouldn't like to think he was looking for a clone, would you?'

'Good God, no, now you put it that way. But . . . it's just hard. Dead people are a bit intimidating, aren't they? They can never put a foot wrong.'

Sarah gave a snort of surprised laughter, then shook her head in disbelief. 'Oh Annie . . . Does he go on about Beth, then?'

'No, the opposite. He hardly mentions her. Do you think he loved her very much?' Annie asked wistfully.

'I would hope so. He loves *you* very much, that's pretty obvious.'

'I know he does,' Annie said, fiddling with her pebble. 'But – sometimes in the middle of the night, when I can't sleep, I go into a bit of a cold sweat. You see, I can't help thinking I'm in over my head with all the mum stuff. I mean, I don't mind teaching myself to cook and all that. It doesn't matter if a casserole gets overdone or a cake flops. But you don't want to be overdoing or flopping a *kid*.'

Sarah shook her head. 'Come on, Annie. Don't be so hard on yourself. Lyddie has to be better off with you than she was with the nanny. Just keep doing what you're doing and everything will sort itself out in the long run. I mean, of course you'll make mistakes, but you'll never go too far wrong.'

'How can you possibly know that?'

'Well, because you care enough about all this to worry, in the first place. Your heart's in the right place. And that makes up for almost everything else.'

Annie gave a sniff. 'It had better,' she murmured. Then, brushing the sand off her hands briskly, she added, 'Anyway, let's move this tour along. I want to show you the real centre of Norbury life.'

Fifteen minutes later, they stood on the shiny marble floor of the Fairfield County Leisure Store, looking at the displays of hundred-dollar ribbon belts, indecently expensive flip-flops, and 'resort wear' embroidered all over with tiny dolphins or elephants, like a bumpy fabric rash. Everything seemed to be either hot pink or lime green, or both.

'Bit chilly for this sort of gear,' remarked Sarah.

'Not if you're flitting off to St Kitts,' Annie explained. 'Oooh, look at the lovely tennis outfits. I have to confess, I've bought one of these already.'

Sarah squinted at the lycra skorts and sports bra tops. 'Why would you buy a tennis outfit? You don't play, do you?'

'No, of course not, but *everybody* in town wears them. I'm sure they can't all be playing, either. They're cute, aren't they?'

Sarah shook her head austerely, and they moved on.

'Look at this lot,' said Annie when they reached the children's section. 'The unofficial school uniform of the town. The right footwear is the foundation stone of any respectable winter wardrobe, of course.' She pointed at a rack of slipper-like sheepskin boots.

'Those things? Oh my God! Look at the price of them! I'd never spend that on a pair of boots for myself, let alone a kid. You didn't buy these for Lyddie, did you?'

Annie wrinkled her nose. 'Not yet. Oh, these are the backpacks. You get them monogrammed and they have matching lunch boxes. I didn't know about them when I got Lydia's, so she's walking around with a Hannah Montana backpack, poor girl. Of course, I can't bring myself to replace it – what a crying waste of money, and what on earth would Mum say?'

Sarah chuckled. Annie's mother was known to be such a scrimper and saver that she'd keep the wax from cheese to make home-made candles.

'Oooh, look, these are the must-have North Face jackets.' Annie pointed excitedly at a colourful rack. 'Lydia *does* have one of those, I'm proud to say. I got the last one in her size. I'm not sure teal is her colour, but still.'

Sarah picked up a jacket and squinted at the tag. 'Annie, this thing costs more than a hundred dollars. And she'll be out of it by next year, right?'

Annie shrugged. 'I know. Mum would just faint with horror. But Sarah, I want Lydia to have a fighting chance out there. She wouldn't have a hope in hell if I sent her out in some geeky anorak. I mean, these kids have their own embossed stationery, their own monogrammed bath robes ... They go into Manhattan to get their dolls' hair done, for God's sake.'

'I don't know,' said Sarah, shaking her head. 'Kids seem to get too much, these days. Put them all out on the water on a Sun Fizz, that's what I say. That'll soon teach them a bit about real life – sail too close into the wind and over you go.'

'Sarah, you're sounding like somebody's grandfather. Come on, let's get out of here. I shouldn't have brought you in, really. I'll take you down the road to Target. You'll like it much better.'

Three days later, Annie pushed the last napkin through its beaded napkin ring and stood back to admire the table. She'd decided on a sleek, simple look, with pillar candles down the centre of a table-runner in jewel tones.

As she tweaked a place mat, she heard a muffled cry from the kitchen. 'Hang on, I'm coming!' she called back.

For once, she wasn't too worried about the actual food component of the dinner party. Sarah had offered to make the shrimp cheese balls that she was so justly famous for in Kilburn, plus they had some mini pies from ChefPro, and Simon was roasting a leg of lamb with rosemary potatoes and a colourful tray of autumn vegetables. Between them, they'd agreed to let Annie boil up some peas and make a green salad. Dessert was ready-bought cheesecake jollied up with a scattering of fresh blueberries; not exactly gourmet fare, but a good, hearty meal of the English Sunday lunch variety.

In the kitchen, Simon stood at the open door of the fridge, running his eye over its contents. 'Do we have any mint?' he asked urgently.

Mint! She knew she'd forgotten something. 'I don't think so,' she said with a rueful grimace. 'Do we really need it?'

Simon's eyebrows went up. 'Well, yes, given that we're making leg of lamb with mint sauce. Look, I'll dash out and get some.'

'But . . . but people will be here in twenty minutes,' Annie protested. 'Sarah's already gone up to change!'

'I'll be quick,' he said firmly. 'Lamb without mint is like . . . I don't know, coffee without milk.'

'Some people like it black!'

'Not me.' His tone was decisive. 'Don't worry, I'll be right back. You won't even miss me.'

'Can I come, Daddy?' Lydia's voice surprised them. They

hadn't noticed her, sitting quietly in the bow window. Simon cocked an eyebrow at Annie.

'I wanted to get her ready for bed,' Annie said. 'But OK, if you're quick.'

'Don't forget to turn off the oven if I'm not back by seven,' Simon called over his shoulder before slamming the kitchen door.

Annie stood alone for a moment, listening to the car start up and drive away. She pulled a little face at herself. She couldn't remember ever feeling this panicky about a dinner party – and normally she had a lot more *reason* to panic, because normally she was the cook, and normally she was cooking something complex and way beyond her limited abilities, like Fricassee de Mer.

But tonight her nerves had nothing to do with the food. The truth was, she felt a bit like an old-fashioned debutante, launching herself on society in the hope that she would 'take' and find herself accepted into fashionable circles.

Although Heather was a newcomer to the town, she'd lived in the Connecticut suburbs long enough to understand how things worked, and she'd already warned Annie that if she wanted Lydia to be on the birthday party circuit, she'd better get out and do some networking. Happily, it turned out that her neighbour, Jennifer Miller, was one of the queen bees in town. If Annie impressed Jennifer, then she might be admitted into the inner circle of school mums, and Lydia's social life would prosper accordingly.

Annie glanced at her watch. Time was ticking on and she'd better get herself showered and ready to 'receive'.

But she was still in front of the mirror, hair damp, trying

to choose between a ribbon of beads (creative, playful) and a solid gold rope of a necklace (sophisticated, bold), when the doorbell rang. 'I'll get it,' Sarah foghorned as she thundered down the stairs.

Oh no. This wasn't how she'd pictured her first dinner party in Connecticut; her first dinner party as a married woman, really. She hadn't for a moment imagined that her husband would be out, nor that her cousin Sarah – all very well in the right context, but rather rough and ready for a formal sort of evening – would be welcoming people at the door.

She took a steadying breath. If her fledgling friends were put off by Sarah's frank, no-nonsense style, then they could jolly well bugger off home again.

Still, she hoped it was Heather at the door, not Jennifer Miller. She couldn't imagine Heather being fazed by anything or anybody – or being judgemental, for that matter.

As Annie descended the stairs, careful not to trip in her heels, she heard Sarah's voice: 'Let's see, are you the horsy one or the posh neighbour? I'm the London cousin, of course. Lord and lady of the manor are still hosing down. Here, hand that wine over, I'll take it to the wet bar and let it breathe. As for the flowers, you'd better hold onto them till Annie comes down. I wouldn't know where to find a vase in this place.'

When Annie got there, Jennifer and a nondescript man with blondish hair, presumably her husband, were still standing in the hallway, but Sarah was nowhere to be seen. The Millers were dressed impeccably, like mannequins from the Fairfield County Leisure Store. Annie tweaked at her pencil skirt, suddenly aware that its cut was probably more suitable for the office than for dinner at home. She should have bought herself something with box pleats, like Jennifer's.

Jennifer's face formed a small, polite smile as Annie came into view.

'Annie, how nice to see you. Your cousin let us in. She's gone off to decant the wine, I believe. This is my husband, Drew.'

Drew held out his hand, and Annie took it automatically. He had a light, very dry grip. 'So pleased to meet you,' she murmured. 'Come on in and sit down. Oh, these are for me?' She took the bouquet of flowers and buried her nose in them. They had absolutely no scent. 'I'll just find a vase.'

As she spoke, the doorbell rang again. 'Why don't you go through,' Annie told the Millers, gesturing at the formal living room, 'and I'll be right back.'

Still clutching the flowers, she opened the door on a small crowd. Heather was in the forefront, with two men hanging slightly behind her. One of them was Dan Morgan, the cowboy, and the other – dark-haired and handsome in a TV-anchorman way – was presumably Heather's husband.

'Heather! How lovely to see you! Dan! So glad you could make it!' It had been Heather's idea to invite Dan, to even up the numbers. Apparently, she knew him well enough to approach him with an invitation on a friend's behalf.

'And you must be ...' Annie looked at Heather's husband in a hostessy way. To her great surprise, he returned her polite glance with a scorcher of a look that drew an involuntary blush up from the soles of her feet to the tips of her ears.

'Rob,' he replied, holding out his hand for her to shake. Even his voice was ridiculously attractive. 'I'm delighted to meet you. I've been hearing "Annie this" and "Annie that" for the last couple of weeks.'

Annie nodded awkwardly, aware of her cheeks still burning away. She hoped Heather hadn't noticed her sudden rosiness. 'Yes. Well. I've heard a lot about you, too. Anyway, come on in. I'll introduce you to the others.'

As she walked into the living room, holding the flowers like a bouquet, she was stopped in her tracks by the sight of Sarah handing around nuts.

Now, Annie had always adored her cousin Sarah. She'd looked up to her when she was just a little girl, and Sarah an adolescent, with something like hero worship, because Sarah had always seemed so confident, so outspoken, so chummy with boys and men, so comfortable in her own skin. But Sarah had never known how to dress, and it looked as if her sartorial skills had now slipped askew entirely.

She was wearing a tiny, body-hugging tie-dyed T-shirt over a pair of loosely fitting combat pants. The T-shirt looked vaguely familiar. With a jolt, Annie realised it was the shirt Lydia had dyed at school for second-grade field trips. For God's sake! It was a shirt for a seven-year-old! If that weren't enough, when Sarah turned to put a bowl of olives on the table, Annie was mortified to see her cousin's lime-green G-string rising up over her hips out of the baggy pants.

As Sarah straightened up, her earrings caught Annie's eye.

They seemed to be mini Navajo dreamcatchers, complete with beads, shells and feathers in unlikely colours.

Annie's eyes flickered in growing disbelief to Sarah's feet. Oh no! Clunky brown Doc Martens. Annie hadn't seen a single soul, not even a teenage boy, wearing boots like that in these parts.

'Sarah!' Annie cried in an artificially bright voice, 'I want you to meet Heather and her husband, Bob.'

'Rob,' said Heather's husband in his throbbing voice. Annie was surprised to see that his eyes were fixed on Sarah with the intensity of a lion spotting a really juicy-looking wildebeest. She prayed Heather wouldn't turn around and catch that look.

'Right. Rob.' Annie cleared her throat. 'And everybody, this is Dan Morgan, a friend of Heather's.'

'A family friend,' Heather said quickly.

Dan Morgan smiled lazily around the room. He was hatless, but clad in jeans and boots as if he might be called on to mount a mustang at any given moment. Even indoors at night, he had the squinty-eyed, weather-beaten look of a man used to spending most of his time out on the range. Jennifer Miller gave everybody a small wave with her fingertips, and Drew stood up to offer the newcomers his dry handshake.

Gosh. They were a bit of an ill-assorted group, now Annie came to think of it. What on earth would they talk about?

'Where's Simon to do the drinks?' Sarah demanded. 'Give him a kick up the backside if he's still in the shower. Tell you what, I'll start mixing the Bloody Marys. Everybody has to get one down the hatch in the first five minutes. House rule.'

'Steady on, Sarah!' Annie protested, tossing the flowers down on a table. 'There's no house rule, of course,' she added brightly to the company at large. She'd read that Americans didn't drink nearly as much as English people, and she didn't want her household to be known for forcing the demon alcohol upon the fine, upstanding citizens of Norbury.

Moving closer to her cousin, she hissed, 'Simon's buggered off to buy some mint, so let's just keep them occupied till he gets back. Maybe give them your shrimp cheese balls. Oh, and the mini pies.' Aloud, she said, 'Anybody care for an Evian? I also have iced tea, orange juice . . .'

'I think I'll have that Bloody Mary you mentioned,' said Jennifer Miller, dipping a carrot in guacamole.

'Sounds good to me,' Drew chimed in. 'And make it bite.'

Annie's eyebrows rose. Clearly, whoever had written the culture-shock book on America hadn't spent much time in this particular part of Connecticut.

Before long, everybody had a lethal red cocktail in hand, and conversation was becoming quite general and relaxed. Annie was just beginning to enjoy a chat with Drew (who turned out to have a dry sense of humour) about his many peculiar experiences on the 5:37 back from the city, when – with a stab of alarm – she realised it was nearly eight o'clock and there was still no sign of Simon. 'Excuse me a moment,' she told his surprised face, and darted upstairs to call Simon on his mobile.

When the mobile began to ring loudly from his bedside table, she threw her own phone onto the dressing table in disgust and forced herself to go back downstairs into the fray.

By eight twenty, she was pretending to listen to people with a fixed smile on her face, barely able to concentrate on a word they were saying. At least the party was going with a definite swing. Nobody had asked her where on earth her husband was, or why dinner was still not served, and she couldn't help feeling desperately grateful to Sarah for her steady flow of cocktails from the wet bar, not to mention her prawn cheese balls, which people were wolfing down with alacrity. But still; it was only a matter of time before it became clear that mine host was definitely not among them.

At 8.27, Annie abruptly slammed down her glass and hurried off to the kitchen, in the middle of a story Dan Morgan was telling about a neurotic horse with a passion for a billy goat. She'd suddenly remembered the lamb roast, all unattended for the last hour or more.

The smell of burning reached her in the dining room. Luckily, it hadn't yet snaked its way into the formal living room. That was one of the advantages of a big house. Chaos and disaster could be contained.

The kitchen itself was full of an oily black cloud that had Annie coughing and grasping her chest. Clearly, the smoke alarm had a flat battery.

In a panic, she switched on the extractor fan and flung windows open. Wrapping a dishcloth around her lower face, she eased open the oven door.

The bright red and green peppers had turned into pepper-shaped ashes. The potatoes looked uncannily like charcoal.

The leg of lamb itself had shrunk down to the size of a tennis ball and was profoundly black.

Oh! She was going to murder Simon with her bare hands. Why hadn't he put the oven timer on?

And what in God's name was she supposed to do now, with six people expecting to sit down to some sort of cordon bleu meal within minutes, and the host still AWOL?

The cloud of smoke had dispersed and Annie was on the phone when the back door opened and Simon erupted into the room on a cool breeze, carrying a bunch of mint and looking full of suppressed energy.

He opened his mouth to speak, but Annie hushed him fiercely and continued to read out her credit card number to the person on the other end of the line.

When she'd given the last details, she put the phone down and looked at Simon.

'How's it all going?' he asked. 'Everybody here yet? How's the roast?'

She gestured wordlessly at the oven. He went over and peeked inside. There was a pregnant pause as he took in the sight of the cremated remains of his hearty feast.

He straightened up and closed the oven door gently. He turned to face her, still holding the bunch of mint. He opened his mouth, but no words came out.

'I've ordered pizza,' she said into the silence. 'I tried to get Chinese, but the kitchen was closed.'

He was shaking his head now, and pressing his lips together. 'I take it you forgot about turning off the oven?' he managed to utter after a moment.

For God's sake. He was trying not to laugh. The bastard was trying not to *laugh*.

And then, without warning, she felt the laughter welling up inside her too, like a violent need to sneeze. She choked it down relentlessly. If she started laughing now, she wouldn't be able to stop. 'Of course I forgot to turn the bloody oven off,' she said. 'But I don't suppose it matters. Everybody's getting sozzled on Sarah's concoctions so they probably don't care about dinner any more. Hang on – where's Lydia?'

Simon hesitated a moment. This seemed ominous to Annie. He wasn't a hesitant sort of man. Then suddenly he walked over to the kitchen door and called out, 'You'd better come in now, Lyddie.'

The child staggered up the stairs into the kitchen, carrying some sort of heavy, awkward bundle wrapped in a towel.

For heaven's sake. It looked like – but it couldn't be – it *looked* like the body of a dog.

Oh no. It *was* the body of a dog. The thing's head hung down at an impossible angle, and its blackish tongue lolled out of its slack, open mouth.

Lydia lowered the dog's floppy body to the floor and squatted down beside it. No rigor mortis as yet, Annie noticed with some part of her brain that was still capable of thought; that would make it easier to shove it into a cupboard, at least. Oh, she was forgetting the basement. They could stash the body down there.

'I'm sorry, Annie,' Simon said ruefully. 'I know this is the last thing you want on your doorstep tonight.'

'Understatement of the bloody year! Who goes out for

a bunch of mint and comes back with a dead dog?' The laughter was boiling up in her again, but she was tamping it down.

'He's not dead,' said Lydia fiercely.

'Of course, he's not dead,' said Simon. 'Why would I bring a dead dog home?'

'I don't know – to give it a decent burial? Are you sure it's not dead? I don't see it breathing. And the way its head was hanging down . . .'

'Look, he's very much alive, take my word for it. We found him in the car park at the supermarket, cowering near the trolleys.'

'Was this before or after you bought the mint?'

'Well, *after*, of course. His leg was all matted with blood and he was out of his mind with fear. We thought he might've been run over, but the vet—'

'The vet?'

'We rushed him to an emergency vet. That's what took the time. The vet says it's probably an injury from a dog fight. He had to have stitches. Poor chap doesn't have a collar or a chip under his skin, so we couldn't contact anybody. He's out for the count because the vet gave him something to calm him down. A tranquilliser.'

'Good grief, poor thing. Can we tuck him away somewhere quiet? I mean, just while we're trying to throw this dinner party? He does look exactly like a dead dog—'

At that moment, a posse led by Dan Morgan burst into the room. 'Everything OK in here? We heard voices . . .'

Simon caught Annie's eye and she bit her lip hard to keep from folding up with hysterical laughter. 'Don't worry, everything's fine. Everybody' – because everybody did indeed seem to be in the kitchen – 'this is Simon. Oh, and Lydia. Lydia, say hello to everybody.'

Lydia didn't even look up. She was still bent over the dog, stroking him gently, whispering in his ear.

'What's up with your dog?' asked Jennifer. 'Is he OK?'

'They don't have a dog,' said Heather and Sarah together.

'It's a stray,' Annie told them with a helpless shrug. 'They found him at the supermarket. He's not dead, by the way, just looks it. Anyway, sorry about the hold-up, everyone. Dinner will be ready any moment. Did I mention, we're doing this sort of ironic new thing where you order pizza and serve it on your best china with a green salad?'

Sarah looked at her sharply, but no one else showed the slightest flicker of interest in the status of their dinner. They were too busy talking dogs.

'We have a Golden,' Jennifer was saying. 'Great breed, but our Sunny is a little hyper. We could never get her crate-trained so now she just has her own room. I mean, the guest bedrooms just stand around empty all the time; we figured, why not use one of them? It's the one place in the house she never poops.'

'Goldens are OK, but you can't beat an American Indian dog,' declared Dan. 'Now, there's a thinking breed. Gutsy, too.'

'I've been told there *is* no such breed,' Drew interrupted. 'We looked into them, ourselves. They're supposed to be hypoallergenic, right? But most reputable dog breeders will tell you they're extinct.'

'Bullshit,' said Dan. 'You come over some time and see my dog, Blue. Then you try telling me the American Indian dog is extinct!'

'You're extinct, too, cowboy, but you don't know that either,' Heather's husband muttered under his breath. Annie, who was standing close enough to hear, gave him a startled look. He grinned back at her and closed one eye in a slow wink. She looked hastily away.

'Hush, everybody – he's coming round,' said Simon.

The dog huffed loudly a few times, then unpeeled his tongue from the hardwood floor and retracted it into his mouth. Annie pushed her way through the crowd and squatted down beside Lydia. 'Careful, now,' she told the child. 'He'll be confused and scared. He might try to bite.'

Lydia gave her a contemptuous look.

The dog, still woozy, began to scrabble at the floor with its front paws, presumably trying to stand up. Just then the doorbell rang, and to everyone's surprise and consternation, the dog began to howl. The hound of the Baskervilles probably never made half as much of a racket.

Showing remarkable aplomb, Simon hastened to the door to forestall any further ringing. Moments later, he came back into the kitchen, followed by a man in a red uniform bearing four large boxes of pizza.

'Looks like dinner is served,' Simon announced. 'And, um, does anybody have cash for a tip? He's telling me I can't put a gratuity on a credit card.'

The men reached into their pockets, pulled out their wallets, and began rummaging for dollar bills.

*

'You have to give me the recipe for those cheese balls,' Jennifer Miller trilled to Sarah as she and her husband left the house some time after midnight.

'You guys sure know how to throw a party,' Dan Morgan added, pumping Simon's hand and then surprising Annie by leaning in to kiss her cheek.

'We had a blast,' Heather chimed in, holding onto Rob's arm a little unsteadily. Rob merely grinned and winked his agreement.

Annie felt as if she were floating on a cloud as she, Simon and Sarah moved between the rooms, clearing up. Who cared if the evening had been a bit unconventional? Anybody could throw a perfect party, but it took an inspired few to throw an unforgettable one.

And then Simon walked into the kitchen with a silver tray. One look at his face and Annie knew that something was horribly wrong.

'The mini pies,' he announced, proffering the tray for inspection. 'They barely touched them.'

Annie glanced at the plate. 'That's not true,' she said staunchly. 'There were more than a dozen on the tray to begin with—'

'There was a baker's dozen,' Simon said. 'Four steak and kidney, four chicken and mushroom, five steak and pepper. That's how they come in the wholesale box.'

'OK, so thirteen ... That means, let's see,' she counted pies quickly, 'five people tried them.'

'Tried and *rejected* them.' He was pointing to a small stack of plates on the counter, unmistakably mounded with the remains of several pastries.

‘Well, you have to realise that women often don’t finish things they put on their plate because they’re always dieting,’ Annie said.

‘They didn’t leave a crumb of my cheese balls,’ Sarah put in. Annie gave her a black look. ‘I’m just *saying*.’ Sarah shrugged and sauntered out of the room.

Annie went over to Simon where he stood staring at the nibbled-at leftover pies, his arms crossed over his chest.

‘One pie,’ he said hollowly. ‘That’s all they ate, between the lot of them.’

She slipped her hand into the crook of his arm. ‘They’re just not *used* to pies, that’s all,’ she said. ‘It’s . . . it’s a case of education.’ She gave a little laugh, hoping to lighten the atmosphere. ‘Maybe we should’ve started them off on pies stuffed with shrimp cheese balls.’

At that moment the dog, who’d been lying quietly in the corner of the kitchen looking dead again, scrambled to its feet and vomited violently. Annie grabbed a paper towel and set to work hastily to clean up the mess. The dog had obviously bolted down its food without bothering to chew it. She fervently hoped Simon hadn’t noticed the distinctive fluted edges of pastry crust.

Chapter Five

Annie woke the next morning with a horrible jolt, head throbbing, vision strangely sharp, filled with a vague sense of unease. Instinctively, she reached a hand out for Simon, for the sheer physical comfort of his warm body beside her, but he wasn't there.

Pulling on her dressing gown, she wandered downstairs, hoping Simon had put the kettle on. She was suffering the after-effects of too many of Sarah's Bloody Marys, and was sorely in need of a cup of tea. As she opened the kitchen door, the dog looked up from a mess of half-chewed pizza boxes, wagged its tail with joy, and came skittering over to her, leaving a trail of wee droplets on the stone tiles.

Of Simon there was no sign.

She was about to move on to the family room when she spotted a note on the counter. She grabbed it and read it at a glance. It was pithy, to say the least: 'Emergency call from the big boss in London. Had to go into work. Please feed and walk dog. Sorry about pizza boxes. Simon.'

'He works on Sundays?' Sarah sounded incredulous a little later as she sat at the counter eating a piece of dry toast.

'Not usually,' Annie said, wishing Sarah wouldn't talk quite so loudly.

'You know, sometimes you wonder if it's all worth it.' Sarah stood up, yanked her G-string (purple, this morning) into a more prominent position above her low-slung tartan pyjama bottoms, and made a sweeping gesture that took in the kitchen, the house, the yard, the whole of Annie's new world. 'The eighty-hour weeks, the long commute, the weekend hours. I mean, I know Simon's pretty high-powered, but wouldn't it be better to have a less demanding job and spend more time with his family?'

'He's really committed to his career,' Annie said defensively. 'ChefPro has given him a huge responsibility, and he takes it very seriously. You have to, if you have a top job.'

At that moment Lydia walked in, trailing the dog, which she'd christened Patches despite the fact that it was a solid yellowish colour without a single patch to speak of unless you counted the pink battle scar on its nose.

'Where's Daddy?' she asked. 'I've looked all over. He said we'd take Patches to the park.'

Annie paused in the act of refilling a bowl with water for the dog. 'Sorry, love, but Daddy had to go in to work. We can still go to the park, though.'

Lydia scowled and folded her arms over her chest. 'He always has to go to work,' she said, her voice wobbling. 'I never see him any more. All I ever see is stupid old *you*!' She ran from the room and back upstairs. In the distance, they heard a door slam.

Sarah raised her eyebrows at Annie. 'God,' she said, 'somebody's got an attitude.'

'You'd have an attitude too if your mum had died when you were five,' Annie retorted. 'And it's true. She doesn't get to see him very much.'

'Maybe so, but you shouldn't let her speak to you that way, Annie. It makes me want to give her a good ticking off. She has no *idea* how lucky she is to have you as a stepmum.'

'You're dead wrong. Turns out I'm not that great as a stepmum.'

'Rubbish, you're brilliant.'

'Ha, that's what you think. But then you weren't here the day I went shopping and left her at home. Or when I took the train to New York and couldn't get back in time to pick her up from school. Or when I forgot to go into the classroom for maths games. Or when I slept late and sent her to school without lunch. Or when I—'

'Annie. Stop. Those things don't *matter*. What matters is that you're trying your best, really throwing your back into it.'

At that moment the dog spat out a masticated mess that Annie recognised as the remains of her contact lens case. With a jolt it dawned on her that she'd slept in her lenses, which explained the uncannily clear vision and horribly dry eyes. Perhaps she'd go up to her room and have a little cry, in the interests of rehydrating the things. She would never peel them off her eyeballs, otherwise.

It was Monday morning, elevenish, and traffic was relatively light on the I-95. Sarah sat in silence beside Annie, watching her drive. As they approached the exit for the

Whitestone Bridge, Sarah said, 'I heard Simon come in last night. Must've been close to midnight. What time did he leave this morning?'

'Around six thirty.'

'God. No wonder I missed him. Will you tell him goodbye for me?'

'Of course. But you might just see him in the next couple of days, you know. I told him to look you up if he had time.'

'What – are you saying he's going to be in London?'

'Yip, that's right. He flew out earlier this morning.'

'Talk about sudden!'

'Yeah, well. He was in talks with the big boss all of yesterday. He's going to consult with the research people in the test kitchen. He has some serious concerns about the texture of the lower fat pastry.'

'Crikey. I never knew the pie business was this intense. So why don't you and Lydia come out too? Hop on a plane? Auntie Gladys would love to see you.'

Annie shook her head regretfully. 'God, I wish I could. But Simon and I agreed we can't take Lyddie out of school. She's just settling in and we don't want to risk whisking her off home on a flying visit and getting her all homesick. Besides, she has her first soccer practice this week, and Simon doesn't want her to miss it.'

'That's too bad,' said Sarah. After several minutes of silence, she stole a glance at Annie. 'Good party on Saturday night, wasn't it? Did that bloke try to feel you up? Your friend's husband?'

A car pulled sharply in front of Annie, narrowly missing

the nose of her minivan, and she jammed both hands down on the horn. The driver stuck his hand out of his window and gave her the finger. She hooted again. At this rate, she'd provoke a drive-by shooting.

'No, of course he didn't try to feel me up!' she said when the other car had darted off out of sight at high speed.

'Really? Well, he tried it on me.'

Annie glanced at Sarah, her mouth hanging open. 'Are you *sure*? Rob Gibson tried to feel you *up*?'

Sarah laughed. 'Sneaky bugger twanged my G-string when I squeezed by his chair to go to the loo.'

Annie shook her head. 'Oh God, poor Heather.'

'Oh, I don't think he means anything by it,' Sarah said. 'It's just *noblesse oblige* or something.'

Annie snorted. 'What kind of *noblesse* would that be?'

Sarah shrugged. 'You know. Chivalry. Gallantry. His way of acknowledging a single woman.'

Annie shook her head some more and lapsed back into silence. She didn't want to cast aspersions on Sarah's credibility, but she was having a difficult time believing Rob Gibson would twang a G-string right in front of his wife.

As they approached the airport, Sarah said, 'Look, don't park the car and come in. Just drop me at the door and bugger off home. I'll go and find a coffee.'

'No, I'll come in and see you off.'

'Please don't. Honestly. I sort of fancy being alone. I hate goodbyes, anyway, especially long-drawn-out ones. And you've got to get back anyway; that dog's probably tearing down the curtains by now.'

Annie nodded. 'Well, OK – if you're sure. I hate goodbyes

too. Did you have an OK time? I mean, it wasn't the south of France, but . . .'

'Oh, it was great. That bloke at the dinner party did my ego no end of good.'

'I hope you didn't encourage him, Sarah. I think Heather has a bit of a hard time keeping him in line.'

'No, I don't mean him. The cowboy bloke.'

'Oh?'

'Yeah. We ended up having a bit of a snog in the loo.'

'Sarah! You're *impossible*!' Annie was surprised at how irritated and out of sorts she felt to hear this news. After all, what right did she have to feel proprietorial about a man just because he happened to have rescued her from a couple of amorous horses?

Sarah chuckled. 'You need to loosen up a bit, Annie. You're getting quite prim and proper. Soaking up the puritanical New England spirit like a bloody sponge.'

Annie grinned back at her. 'You're right, I should get a grip. Nothing wrong with a bit of snogging in the loo at a dinner party.'

Still, a certain sense of relief was mingled with the regret Annie felt as she watched her cousin drag her battered rucksack out of the boot of the car and stomp away in her Doc Martens.

'Let me see if I can make him smile,' Lydia said later that day, after school. She was sitting behind Patches, holding him still so that Annie could take a photo with the digital camera. She leaned in now and pulled the sides of his mouth up, exposing black lips and yellowing teeth.

'Maybe not,' said Annie. 'His owners might not recognise him if you mess with his face.'

'No, no, please! Take it like this!' Lydia insisted, pulling the dog's lips up even higher.

'Oh, all right, then. But he looks really weird.' Annie took a couple of shots and looked at them doubtfully in the viewfinder. 'Come on, let's see what we've got.'

She and Lydia spent a happy afternoon printing out posters advertising the fact that they'd found Patches, and then attaching them to lamp-posts around town.

'Is it usual to offer a reward to the owner for *claiming* a lost dog?' Jennifer Miller asked, stopping her Hummer to read the poster that Annie was stapling to the tree trunk at the end of their street.

'Maybe not,' said Annie, 'but these are special circumstances.' And she rolled her eyes towards the dog, who was lying on the pavement at the end of his leash, savaging a stick.

Jennifer smiled. 'Gotcha,' she said.

'We put an ad in the paper too,' Annie told her.

'Well, good luck to you!' Jennifer trilled as she pulled away.

Whenever the phone rang over the next few days, Annie ran to pick it up, half expecting it to be the dog's grateful owner. But mostly the calls were from Simon, sounding tense and stressed, telling her that he needed to stay in London for just a few more days.

Then one morning the phone rang and her caller ID told her that the Board of Education wanted to talk to her.

She picked up the receiver with sweaty palms. She'd

never been called up by a Board before, and frankly she felt a bit apprehensive.

But it was only Lydia's teacher, Miss Scofield. 'Mrs Har-Keeler? Melissa Scofield here.'

'I've been meaning to say, it's actually just "Keeler".'

'You dropped the double-barrel, huh? Look, there's no problem in the classroom. I'm just calling to ask if you could come in at ten o'clock on Friday for Lydia's show-and-tell slot? I don't usually ask the mom to come in, but in this case ...'

'Um – in which case?' asked Annie. 'I mean, of course I'll come in – but why, exactly?'

'Well, because Lydia doesn't speak.'

'Doesn't – speak? Well, I know she's a bit quiet, but—'

'Oh dear. I thought you were aware ... Are you saying Lydia used to speak at her old school?'

'Well, I don't really know, to be honest. I met her during the summer when she wasn't *at* school.'

There was a brief silence.

'You *met* her?' Miss Scofield's voice was faint.

'That's right. I'm her stepmum,' Annie explained. She had wanted to send the teacher a letter, outlining Lydia's home life, but Simon had thought it might be good if Lydia just went to school like any other child from a normal nuclear family. He'd thought that she might cope better if people treated her the same as all the other kids in the room. At her school in London, apparently, the whole staff had been very aware of her 'situation' – and Simon reckoned all the walking around on eggshells (they'd banned any talk of Mothering Sunday in her classroom, for example) hadn't actually been that helpful.

'Oh, I see,' said Miss Scofield in a speculative sort of way. 'Was it by any chance an acrimonious divorce? I only ask because I want to understand how Lydia's mind is working.'

'It wasn't a divorce,' Annie said. 'Her mum died in a boating accident.'

'Ah,' breathed Miss Scofield. 'That explains a lot.'

'So you want me to come in on Friday?'

'Yes, and could you please help her choose something to show the class, something special to her in some way.'

'No problem,' said Annie. 'I'll be there.'

'I don't *have* anything special,' Lydia said that afternoon, folding her arms over her chest and glowering at Annie. Suddenly she narrowed her eyes. 'Why is your hair *grey* today?'

Annie shook back her hair self-consciously. She'd just come from the salon where, in the 'when-in-Rome' spirit, she'd taken a deep breath and asked for highlights.

'It's not grey. It's ash blonde.' She felt a bit dubious about the colour herself, but the colourist had assured her it was a very popular shade. 'But never mind my hair. You *must* have something special. Everybody does. How about ... Oh, I don't know, a photo of Daddy?'

'I don't want to take a photo in. You have to pass it round the room, and people *breathe* on it.'

'Well, how about a toy, then? Your doll?'

'I'm not taking my doll.' Her lower lip was beginning to stick out mulishly.

'Why not?'

'They'd laugh at it.'

'Would they? I'm sure all the girls in your class have dolls.'

Lydia pulled a strand of hair into her mouth and began to chew ferociously. 'My doll is *bald*, and she has those holes in her head where the hair goes in.'

Annie shrugged. 'Fair enough. So – what about, I don't know, a book? Maybe we could read them a little story or something?'

Lydia got up and left the room without a word.

Annie phoned Henny on Thursday morning to see if she had any suggestions about what Lydia should take in. 'It has to be something that means a lot to her,' she said. 'But she won't take her doll, or even a book. Do your kids ever have show and tell?'

Henny's laugh reverberated down the phone. 'We took a kitten in when Lulu was in Reception. What a bloody disaster! The bloody thing got scared, scratched up a boy's arm, and hid behind the radiator. We couldn't get it out until the end of the day, when all the kids had gone home. It mewed piteously all morning. The teacher was ready to kill me.'

Annie paled at the thought. It had crossed her mind to ask if they could take in Patches. 'Right, so no live animals. Any other ideas?'

'Oh, the boys like to take in trading cards. Lulu once showed her grandad's stamp collection.'

'OK. So some kind of collection. That's a good idea. Except, dammit, we don't collect things. I mean, other than Simon's ties, or my shoes.'

'Take it easy, Annie. This isn't a boardroom presentation. It's show and tell. It really doesn't matter what she takes in. As long as she can say a couple of words about it . . .'

'Well, no hope of that either,' Annie said. 'She's gone schtum at school. Won't talk at all. I have to go in and say her piece.'

'Oh. That's not so good.'

'I know. God, I wish I could wave a magic wand and make everything OK for her. If only she had a sidekick at school . . . I mean, there's this girl, daughter of a woman I know, and they've had a play date, but when I asked Lyddie if she wanted to invite her back, she said she would rather not.'

They were both silent for a moment, thinking of the horrors of school without a sidekick.

'Is she homesick?'

'She doesn't say. She's not a big talker even at home.'

'Did she have a best friend in London?'

'I've heard some talk of a girl called Emily.'

'Maybe she could write her a letter or something?'

Annie perked up. 'Yes, that's an idea. But in the meantime, what about the bloody show and tell?'

'Leave the ball in her court,' Henny advised. 'She'll come up with something.'

In the end, Lydia said she'd take in a plastic teaspoon.

'A plastic *teaspoon*?' Annie asked, incredulous. It was Friday morning and they were running late.

'Yes, I keep this spoon in my backpack,' she said. 'I got it in the cafeteria.'

'And it's *special* to you?'

But Lydia only shrugged.

Annie turned up at the school at ten o'clock in some trepidation. The children were already sitting cross-legged on a brightly patterned mat in readiness for show and tell, and they all turned to stare as Miss Scofield greeted her. Lydia was seated in front of the class on a small chair. Her face was as white as chalk.

Right. Annie certainly wasn't going to let the little monsters scare Lydia. Or her, for that matter. She strode confidently into the room and sat down on the empty chair next to Lydia.

She looked over at Miss Scofield, a small, plump woman with shoulder-length brown hair. Miss Scofield gave her a firm nod.

Annie glanced back at the children. Their faces were upturned in expectation. She cleared her throat. Gosh, there were a lot of them. 'Good morning, girls and boys. My name's Annie Keeler and I'm Lydia's stepmum. I've come to help her do show and tell.'

Several hands shot into the air. Annie smiled at a boy with ears like open car doors. 'Yes?'

'Why are you talking like Harry Potter?' the boy asked.

Annie went on smiling. 'Because I come from the same place Harry Potter does.'

'Hogwarts?' he asked excitedly.

'No, I meant England.' She nodded her head at a girl with pigtails.

'What's a stepmom?' the girl asked.

'Um.' Annie looked desperately over at Miss Scofield who raised her palms and gave a discreet shrug.

'A stepmum. Well, a stepmum didn't give birth to you, but she's married to your dad.'

'What's give birth?' another voice demanded.

'Where's her *real* mom?' somebody else chimed in.

Miss Scofield stood up and clapped her hands. 'Boys and girls,' she said ominously. 'We need to remember our manners. Do we shout out in class? No, we don't. We raise our hand. We wait to be called on. Think about the choices you're making, boys and girls. OK?' Then she sketched a bow in Annie's direction. 'Please go on, Mrs Keeler.'

Annie thought she wouldn't take any more questions just for the moment. 'Right, let's get on with the programme, shall we? So. Lydia has chosen to bring in a . . . um . . . well, a plastic spoon, as a matter of fact. Could you show them, Lydia?'

She held her breath, waiting for a huge eruption of laughter. Strangely, it didn't come. Lydia pulled the spoon down out of her sleeve and held it up with a hand that trembled slightly. Annie gave a sigh of relief. It wasn't just an ordinary plastic spoon, after all. Lydia had drawn a face on the round surface, and the handle had been transformed into a narrow dress, skinny legs, and shoes.

Hands shot up again. With her spoon, Lydia pointed at Hailey Gibson. 'Where did you get the spoon?' Hailey asked.

Lydia leaned over and whispered in Annie's ear, 'Cafeteria.'

'She got it at the cafeteria,' Annie reported.

Lydia selected Courtney Phelps next. 'What's its name?' Courtney asked.

'Doesn't have one,' Lydia hissed, her hand shielding her mouth, perhaps in case anybody in the audience could lip-read.

Annie nodded. 'She hasn't named the spoon just yet. She's still thinking about it.'

'Why is it sad?' somebody else called out.

The spoon's expression was miserable, it had to be said. Its mouth was an upside-down U, and there was even a tear trickling down next to its nose.

Lydia shrugged and stuffed the spoon up her sleeve again.

'Let's take one last question,' said Miss Scofield.

Annie glanced at Lydia, but her head was down, her hair falling like a curtain across her face. Hastily, Annie pointed at a boy who was stretching his hand as far into the air as it would go.

'Isn't it stealing to take a spoon from the cafeteria?' he asked triumphantly.

'Of course it's not,' snapped Annie. 'It's a plastic spoon. Disposable. I bet you throw away two or three of them every day.'

'No, I don't,' said the boy. 'I eat a packed lunch from home and I bring my own *fork*.'

Suddenly Lydia tapped Annie on the shoulder, then whispered in her ear, 'Tell him I got it out of the bin.'

'For your information, she says she got it out of the rubbish bin,' Annie reported.

'She means the garbage,' somebody cried.

'Eeeewwww!!'

'Gross!'

'Yech.'

Miss Scofield was on her feet, clapping as hard as she could. It wasn't applause. 'That's enough, boys and girls. Let's say thank you to Mrs Keeler for coming in.'

As they chorused a thank you, Annie ruffled Lydia's hair, but the child wouldn't look up and meet her eye.

Chapter Six

'Your hair – it's different,' Simon remarked on Friday night as he rifled through Annie's purse looking for cash so he could tip the taxi driver, all the while fending off Patches, who was overjoyed to see him.

'Yes, I had highlights. You know, it's virtually the law around here; you have to be blonde.'

'Ah, I see. It's – yes, very nice. But I think I prefer your natural colour.'

'You like brown? Plain brown?'

He took a strand of her hair in his hand and considered it. 'It wasn't plain,' he said. Then he pulled her into his arms. 'I missed you,' he murmured against her lips. 'It's been a *long* five days.'

'I missed you too. It's weird in this place without you.'

But the romantic mood didn't last long. By the time Simon had dragged his suitcase upstairs, it had burned off like morning fog.

'I thought that damn dog was sleeping in the kitchen.' Simon jerked his chin at the laundry basket in the corner, now doing duty as a dog's basket.

'Oh, he howls and scratches the door if you leave him in

the kitchen,' Annie explained. 'As soon as that tranquilliser wore off, he started getting very exacting about house rules. He reckons the kitchen is no place for a dog to sleep.'

'In that case, the sooner we find his owner, the better.' At the tone of Simon's voice, Patches – still capering about with excitement – slunk back to his corner and settled down.

'Well, we're trying. But I thought you liked dogs. I mean, you went to all that trouble to rescue him.'

'Yes, I like dogs, but I wouldn't have gone out and chosen a . . . a cringing yellow cur. I brought him home for Lyddie's sake.'

'Gosh, you sound – tired,' Annie said, flinching at his tone of voice. 'Was the flight OK?'

Simon shrugged as he twiddled with the combination lock on his suitcase. 'Oh, it was fine – but I'm pretty knackered. It's been one bloody meeting after another for days.' He shook his head and with a visible effort tried to switch gears. 'But how are you? And how's Lyddie been?'

He had been into Lydia's room already. Annie had glanced in on him standing there, lit up by the night light, gazing down at the top of his daughter's head with a rather vulnerable expression on his face. She had walked away quickly, not wanting to intrude on the moment.

'Oh, she's been fine! Very helpful with Patches. You know it's her first football – I mean, soccer game tomorrow, right?'

She said this a little anxiously. It wasn't an exaggeration to say that Lydia was actively dreading this first game. The child had attended one practice under protest, and Annie had let her skip the second one when she said her tummy hurt. The stomach ache had disappeared miraculously once the threat of soccer practice went away, but that was going to be their little secret. In any event, Annie thought that two practices a week was a little intense for seven-year-olds.

Simon's strained-looking face lit up. 'Her first game? Great! I'm really looking forward to it!'

'I wouldn't get too excited,' Annie said. 'She doesn't seem all that keen on playing, as a matter of fact.'

'She's probably a bit nervous. Perfectly normal to be nervous your first time out.'

'Maybe, but I'm just not sure soccer is going to be her thing.'

His face stiffened. 'Let's just wait and see, shall we? I reckon being part of a team will be really good for her. Help her make friends and build up her confidence.'

'I think you only make friends and build up your confidence if you're actually any *good* at the sport involved,' Annie muttered. She spoke from personal experience, but she wasn't about to treat him to anecdotes about her brief career in hockey, that was for sure.

'What did you say?'

'Oh, nothing.'

He looked at her with narrowed eyes for a moment. 'All right. I'm going to hop in the shower now.'

He disappeared into the en suite bathroom, then stuck his head back around the corner. 'Don't feel you have to wait up any more. It's late.'

Annie looked across the room and met the dog's eye. Curled up in the basket again, he looked strangely downcast.

Brooding on the idea that he was a cringing yellow cur, no doubt.

With a sigh, Annie climbed between the sheets, but when she heard the shower running, she got out of bed, shrugged off her nightie, and tiptoed towards the bathroom. She would take him by surprise in the shower; see if he could keep up his bad mood while she lathered his back!

He didn't notice when she slid the frosted glass door open. He was standing beneath the powerful jet with his eyes closed, hands hanging at his sides, his head raised to receive the needles of water directly on his face. The sound must be drumming in his ears like the Niagara Falls, drowning out everything but his thoughts.

She stood and stared. Something about his attitude was deeply disturbing. He looked like a man trying to wash away some terrible misfortune. He looked like a man who needed to be alone.

She took a deep breath and stepped back quietly, on her way out. He need never know she'd seen him like that, in such an attitude of despair.

But at that moment he turned his head and opened his eyes. 'Annie?'

'I – I was just using the loo,' she said quickly, covering her bare breasts with her arms. 'Thought I'd . . . you know, take a peek at you before heading back to bed.' Oh, very good, Annie. Now he had this attractive image of her perched naked on the throne, perhaps ogling him through the frosted door before giving in to her peeping Tom impulses.

He frowned for a moment, his expression bleak. Then, in an instant, his face cleared, his eyes lit up, his mouth twitched, and she could almost believe she'd imagined the grim look in his eyes. 'Heading back to bed?' He held out a dripping arm to her, the hairs all flattened against his skin. 'Not bloody likely. Come on in, the water's lovely.'

With a fair imitation of a surprised laugh, she allowed him to pull her into the spray. It *was* lovely in the shower, all steamy and warm. Quite interesting, too. Kissing, for example, presented a bit of a challenge because the shower-head was set to such a high pressure that if you turned your head the wrong way, the water could catch a lip and peel it right away from your teeth. Or—

'Ouch!' Simon yelped as Annie snapped shut her mouth and leapt away from him, coughing and spluttering. 'God, I think you bit my tongue!'

'Did I? Oh no! Sorry,' she coughed. 'Water ... went straight up my nose. Down my throat, too. Felt like I was drowning. Can you turn the shower to a softer setting?'

Simon was trying to look at his tongue in the shaving mirror. 'It's only a nick,' he said with evident relief. 'Tongues are oversensitive, apparently. I thought you'd bitten a chunk out of me. A softer setting. Let's see, now.' He fiddled around a bit and managed to control the flow. Gratefully, she moved back into his wet embrace, telling herself that she didn't feel squeamish about kissing someone with a bleeding tongue. Just as they had worked up a bit of a lather between them, Annie felt a soft, brushing sensation against the backs of her knees. She had no idea how Simon was managing to reach down there, not with his hands where they were right now. Suddenly, something sharp and distinctly outside her idea of foreplay dug into her back at waist height.

She swirled round with a horrified yell.

'Oh! For God's sake! It's the bloody dog.' Patches, hair plastered down on his muzzle so that his head looked too small for his body, took this is a shout of encouragement. He jumped up a second time, this time catching her on the bare stomach with his claws. He must have nosed open the sliding glass door. 'Aaargh! Get him *out* of here.'

With admirable speed, Simon nipped out of the shower, slung a towel around his waist, grabbed the dog by his collar, and dragged him away from the scene. Annie heard the thump of the bathroom door closing, and he was back.

Right. Somehow they seemed to have taken two steps back and were obliged to start all over again. At this rate, they'd drain all the hot water before they got to the crux of the matter.

But hello, things were actually progressing with a bit of speed now. Gosh, that was rather nice. Mmm. Yes, the water was definitely at just the right pressure now.

Abruptly, they sprang apart as a cacophony erupted in the bedroom: muffled crashing and clanging sounds mingled with the high-decibel frenzy of a dog barking at the top of his vocal range.

'*Bloody* animal!' Simon dashed out of the shower again, this time not pausing for a towel. Annie followed hot on his heels, wondering how on earth a dog could actually *make* so much noise.

The state of the bedroom indicated exactly how. Patches, obviously distressed at being shut out of the fun, had upturned the round table in the corner (the crashing), which held a decorative pewter wash basin and pitcher (the clanging), barking like mad all the while. The moment his new owners burst out of the bathroom, he fell silent, flattened his ears in an ingratiating way, and wagged his tail.

'Oh, for God's *sake*,' said Simon, setting the table back on its legs. 'If we throw him out of the room altogether he'll probably go ballistic and wake up Lyddie.'

Annie was shivering now. Wet and bedraggled, she stepped into the walk-in closet and retrieved her dressing gown.

'Maybe we should just go to bed,' she said, throwing a towel in Simon's direction. 'My skin's getting all wrinkly.'

'Yeah, mine too.' Simon began drying himself vigorously. 'My parents' dogs don't behave this way,' he said after a moment. 'They just fetch sticks and chase rabbits and lie about the place asleep, like animal skins. They don't *bother* anybody.'

Simon's parents lived on the outskirts of Carlisle in Cumbria, in a substantial country house set among fields. His dad was a doctor, and his mother made a career of being flamboyant and arty. When Simon drove Annie up to meet them, she was charmed by the easy, bucolic rhythm of their life – a fire in the grate every night, wine glasses on the table, dogs all over the place, Simon's mum's glazed pots adorning every surface, a succession of casual dinner parties with red-faced neighbours. In retrospect, the dogs had been very self-effacing. She'd only noticed them as a sort of background motif. Not once had any one of them forced its way into a shower cubicle and jumped all over her.

'I suppose he feels all unsettled, poor thing,' Annie said, glancing at Patches. He looked up at her with mournful eyes and wriggled his behind in an ingratiating way. 'You're a bad boy,' she told him severely. He wagged his entire body at her. 'Oh, Lord,' she said, turning to Simon. 'I think we left the shower on.'

When she came out of the bathroom after turning off the tepid water, Simon was already under the covers. She slipped off her dressing gown and climbed in beside him, nuzzling up against him.

'Annie,' he said, inching away from her, 'it's nearly one in the morning and I'm knackered. Let's just give it up as a bad job, shall we?'

Annie got out of bed the next morning with a feeling of foreboding. Simon was up already, in the kitchen making tea and reading the *New York Times*, now delivered daily. He was humming as Annie drifted downstairs in her dressing gown. *Humming!* After all his doom and gloom last night!

'You sound happy,' Annie said.

'Here, have some tea.' Simon pushed a mug towards her. 'I'm planning to go outside and kick the ball around with Lydia when she comes down. Get her warmed up for the game a bit.'

'Hmmph. You'll be lucky,' Annie said, but so low that he didn't hear.

Even when Simon saw Lydia's fed-up face as she trailed downstairs in an enormous white T-shirt that came down to her knees, almost entirely hiding her red shorts, he wasn't downcast.

'How about some porridge to line your tummy?' he suggested. 'You need some decent fuel if you're going to crush your opponents to smithereens.'

'It's not really about crushing your opponents,' Annie said quickly, seeing sheer fright take over from long-suffering misery on Lydia's face. 'You know, at this level they don't even keep score. No goalies. No positions. No offside rules. It's just about getting out there and having fun.'

'Ah, that's what they tell you,' Simon said, sprinkling sugar on Lydia's porridge. 'But it's *always* about crushing your opponents. Here, get this down you and we'll go outside and practise passing.'

Lydia slumped down over her bowl, hair trailing in the cereal. She ate so slowly that Simon was pacing the kitchen floor by the time she was ready to go out with him.

Ten minutes later, they came trooping back inside.

'That was quick,' observed Annie.

'No point tiring her out before the game,' Simon replied, listening to the distant thump of Lydia stomping her way back upstairs. He looked a lot less enthusiastic and a lot more thoughtful than he had earlier.

'Simon, do you really think we should insist on the soccer?' she asked, sensing that this might be a good time to press her point home. 'I mean, given how much she seems to hate it?'

Simon folded his arms across his chest and propped himself on a bar stool. His face was serious. 'Annie, she needs to get out of the house. She needs to be busy and do something outdoorsy. Every week there's some new article in the paper saying that kids today aren't getting enough exercise. Lyddie spends far too much time holed up in her room; it can't be good for her health. Besides, how do we know she hates it? She's never even played a game.'

'Would – would Beth have wanted her to play soccer?'

Simon froze for a fraction of a second. Then he shrugged. 'I'm not sure, to be honest,' he said slowly. 'Lyddie was only five when ... The whole sport thing hadn't come up, at that stage. But, you know what, that was *then* and this is now. Lydia needs something to get her blood pumping. Don't you think?'

An image of Lydia's pale, drooping face popped into Annie's mind. She found herself nodding. 'OK,' she said. 'You have a point. The soccer might sort of energise her, I suppose. Hey, guess what? I think this is what they call "tough love" in the parenting books.'

Over at the middle school field, they found Heather already set up on a folding chair, holding a giant Styrofoam mug of coffee and reading *People* magazine.

'Too bad Rob isn't here,' Heather said. 'He's on one of his eternal business trips.'

Annie hadn't thought to bring chairs, so she and Simon were obliged to stand on the sidelines, looking unduly prominent.

After the first few minutes, though, Heather was on her feet too. It turned out that Hailey had the killer instinct on the soccer field. Annie found herself screaming wild encouragement alongside Heather as the little girl tackled child after child on the blue team, stealing the ball from between their feet with consummate ease, and running it down the length of the field with a turn of speed that left everyone else eating dust, one elbow at the ready in case anyone dared challenge her. Nobody did. In the first ten minutes she scored three goals.

Lydia had something of a different game plan, naturally.

'She's obviously playing defence,' Simon said staunchly. She could be seen at the inactive end of the field, wandering about near the goal posts, kicking at clumps of grass, squatting down to pick dandelions, sucking her hair (possibly there was still some cereal in it), and at one stage lying on her back, apparently gazing at the sky.

It was while she was sky-gazing that a member of the blue team managed to wrestle the ball off Hailey and give it a huge kick that sent it flying unimpeded towards Lydia's end of the field.

'Lydia, get up!' yelled Simon. 'Get up and get ready! Clear the goal! Come on, come on, get *up*!'

Lydia must have heard her father's desperate cry. She got to her feet in a leisurely fashion, brushing blades of grass from her T-shirt. A bit of a titter broke out among the spectators. As she adjusted her clothing, she happened to glance at the ball, still rolling towards the goal, but beginning to lose steam. Then she looked at the pack of girls stampeding towards her, all intent on the ball.

Unhurriedly, she walked up to the ball, got behind it, and gave it a tentative kick. Her cleats seemed to catch on the top of the ball, and her legs shot out from under her. Down she went onto the turf again, but all of a sudden she seemed consumed with a sense of urgency. She sprang back to her feet, glanced in a panicky way over her shoulder, and kicked inexpertly at the ball a second time. Her toe caught it with just enough impetus to send it rolling slowly towards the goal post. It trickled into the net just as the pack caught up to her.

It was a goal. Definitely a goal.

Annie punched the air in triumph, and turned to hug Heather, who didn't look as excited as Annie would have expected.

Simon was doubled over, hands in his hair.

'Own goal!' shouted the umpire, and the titter erupted into a generalised guffaw.

'Oh,' said Annie. '*Own* goal. I suppose that's not good.'

'Not so much,' said Heather, pressing her lips together.

'Well, she had the right instincts, wanting to score,' Simon said, recovering his composure with visible effort. 'I just need to spend some time explaining the rules to her. Maybe we can watch a couple of Premier League games together. She's bound to get the hang of it.'

'You're right,' said Heather, a shade too heartily. 'This is her first game. So she made a mistake? We all make mistakes. She'll be unrecognisable by the end of the season, you'll see.'

'You don't think we should just let her give it up?' Annie asked.

'What, tell her that now we've seen her play we agree she's a no-hoper?' Simon asked, incredulous.

'He's right,' Heather said. 'If you take a fall, the worst thing you can do is walk away. Got to get back up on that horse again.'

Gosh, Annie thought, being a parent was a pretty brutal business. All her instincts were telling her to grab Lydia off the field, whisk her away home, throw the ugly soccer clothes into the rubbish bin, and tell the child that she never had to go back. Obviously, she had a lot to learn.

Chapter Seven

If Saturday's soccer game was a bit of a downer, Sunday was going to be great – because Annie had decided to surprise Simon with a family day on a rented sailing boat.

Sarah had planted the seed of the idea in her mind, when she'd asked whether Simon was doing any sailing.

Sailing had been a huge part of Simon's life when he was married to Beth. Annie knew this because she'd seen the photos in the albums he kept in his underwear drawer.

Boats were the backdrop of every second photo she looked at. Simon and a smiling, freckled Beth seemed to have spent their honeymoon sailing. They seemed to have entered sailing races together. They seemed to have drunk a lot of champagne while sitting on top of white hulls. If there was a picture of them standing next to a car, then the car was hooked up by a tow bar to some kind of boat on a trailer. And all the while, they seemed to have been deliriously happy. Simon didn't look bleak and brooding in a single one of the pictures.

The only pictures without a nautical theme were those of Lydia; Lydia in nappies, lying asleep in a white crib, plump and bald; or toddling around the London house half-dressed, grinning over her dimpled shoulder in delight at whoever was taking the snapshots.

The photos screamed the truth. Sailing hadn't just been a huge part of Simon's life. Sailing had *been* his life. She suspected he'd given it up on her account. It was true she'd never expressed much interest in being out on the water, but she was game for anything. He should have known that!

Why exactly Annie wanted the sailing expedition to be a surprise, she wasn't sure, but she kept picturing Simon's face as he stepped out of the car and first caught sight of the boat. He'd be bowled over, delighted, touched, enthusiastic as a little boy. He'd turn to her and kiss her hard – a big, sloppy smooch that would make Lydia groan and roll her eyes. Then he'd help her and Lydia on board, and they'd sail off into the sunshine with Simon at the steering wheel – or whatever it was called. She could hardly wait.

Not having the slightest idea of how to go about renting a boat, she had enlisted the help of Heather and her neighbour, Jennifer Miller, both of whom, as it turned out, knew people with boats. After a few false starts, Jennifer came up with the name of an acquaintance who, for a staggering fee, was willing to let the Keelers use his boat, which he kept at the Norbury Yacht Club.

'It looks awfully big,' said Annie in sudden fear as she, Jennifer, and the boat-owner's wife stood on a wooden pier looking at the tethered craft. 'I hope Simon knows how to handle it.'

'If he can't handle this boat then he's no sailor,' declared the owner's wife. 'In the right conditions, my thirteen-year-old daughter can take her out single-handed.'

Annie felt a bit miffed. 'He's an excellent sailor,' she countered. 'I just don't know a lot about boats, that's all. This one seems more like a ship. But OK, we'll take it.'

Sunday morning dawned cloudy and humid; not the kind of weather she'd been hoping for, but at least it wasn't raining.

Over breakfast, Annie said casually, 'I promised Lydia we'd drive around and take a look at the autumn colours today.'

With a piece of toast halfway to her mouth, Lydia said, 'No, you didn't! I said could we go to the park with Patches, and you said—'

Annie gave Lydia a big, fake smile. '*Remember* what I said?' She winked meaningfully and jerked her head at Simon, who was lost behind newspaper and showed no signs of listening.

She and Lydia had discussed going out on the boat. Originally, she'd wanted the trip to be a surprise for Lydia too, but in the end she'd decided not to risk finding out, at the last moment, that Lydia had some sort of phobia about going on the water.

'Oh, I'm not scared of sailing,' Lydia had told her. 'It's just sort of boring. But I'll go.'

'Oh yes. Right,' Lydia said now, visibly remembering about the surprise.

'So, I thought we'd leave at about ten and maybe pick up some lunch along the way? It could be chilly so we'd better bring sweatshirts.'

'Hmmm?' Simon glanced around the paper at her, giving

a glimpse of weekend stubble and bed-head. She wanted to go over, sit on his lap, and run her fingers through his tousled hair – but Lydia wouldn't like it.

'We're going out,' she said loudly. 'A drive into the country.'

'OK,' he shrugged, looking faintly mystified. 'Fine by me.'

'I might as well drive,' she added. 'It's a bit of a tricky route.'

'A tricky route?' he asked. 'Where exactly are we going?'

'To look at the leaves. The famous New England autumn foliage. People drive all the way from New York city to see it – and I happen to know where the best trees are.'

'Good grief, do you always take your foliage so seriously?' he teased.

'Always,' she said, grinning back. Already, he was beginning to look less distracted – and more like the Simon of old.

'Hurry up and eat, Lydia!' Annie chivvied. 'We need to get going. Oh, and grab your trainers. Maybe a jacket too, in case it cools down. I've got the camera.'

About half an hour later, as they pulled into the unobtrusive driveway of the tucked-away club, Simon looked around in mild confusion. 'Aren't we going up north to see the leaves?' he asked. 'What's this place?' He obviously hadn't noticed the tiny Norbury Yacht Club sign, discreetly engraved in stone.

'Just wait, you'll see,' Annie told him, slowing down as

she approached a gate. 'Annie Keeler,' she told the man in the glass booth. He consulted a clipboard, made a laborious notation, and lifted the boom.

As they pulled into the car park, Lydia cried, 'Look at all the masts!'

Simon grabbed Annie's arm. 'What's going on?' he asked urgently.

She smiled a Mona Lisa smile. 'Come with me,' she said.

She walked confidently along the marina to the place where their vessel was berthed. The boat wallowed in the water, waiting for them, already stocked with borrowed life jackets and a cool box of picnic fare that she'd stowed on board on Friday: juice, champagne, cheese, smoked salmon, thin-sliced roast chicken, even a jar of peanut butter for Lydia. She'd made a loaf of bread overnight in the bread machine, and it was wrapped in a dish towel in the boot of the car, along with a bag full of towels, swimsuits, sunscreen and flip-flops – just in case the mercury rose. She'd packed the car that morning while Simon and Lydia were still asleep.

'This is our boat for the day,' Annie announced, waving her arms in a grand gesture.

For a moment, Simon said nothing at all.

Well, clearly he was speechless. That was all right – just as long as he was speechless with joy.

But when he turned to look at her, she knew right away that joy had nothing to do with whatever he was feeling.

'I can't believe you did this,' he said at last. She sensed by the tone of his voice that he was working hard to control some quite violent emotion. 'I'm sorry, Annie. I'm not going sailing on some rented boat on a morning so still you couldn't launch a bloody kite. You really know nothing at *all* about sailing, do you?'

Annie blinked hard. 'But the wind might pick up,' she said. 'And isn't there a motor on this thing?'

'You think I want to motor around on a glassy pond like some sort of ... Come on, Annie, let's just go home.'

Suddenly, Lydia raised her voice. 'Daddy, you're *mean*,' she said, her face clenched in reproach. 'You're hurting Annie's *feelings*. She was just trying to give you a nice surprise.'

Annie gulped and looked at Simon. His face had gone pale and still. For a couple of heartbeats, nobody moved. It seemed to Annie that none of them even breathed.

Then Simon put his hand on Lydia's shoulder. 'You're right,' he said. 'That was pretty uncivilised. I'm sorry.'

'Annie's the one you need to say sorry to,' Lydia told him, shrugging off his hand.

He pressed his lips together and turned to Annie. 'Sorry.' He sounded sheepish and sincere. 'I don't know what came over me. I can see you've gone to a lot of trouble. But if it's all the same to you, I'd really rather not go out on this thing. Can we just look at autumn leaves instead?'

Annie shrugged and managed a smile. 'OK,' she said. 'Mrs Van Hausen who owns the boat would be pretty miffed to hear you write it off that way.'

Simon cast a critical glance at the rejected vessel. 'It's built for stability, not for speed. I suppose they take the family out for little jaunts.' He spoke with such disdain for that sort of sailing that she cringed inwardly. She'd really misjudged his whole attitude to the sport; hadn't realised for a moment that pottering around with his family on board a nice safe boat would be absolutely abhorrent to him.

As Simon lugged the cool box off the boat, he suddenly said, 'I don't miss sailing, you know. It's all over and done with, for me. I'm quite happy to be a landlubber these days.'

Annie shrugged her scepticism. He took her by the shoulder and looked deep into her eyes. 'Annie, you need to believe this. I'm not hankering to go back out there.' He gestured at the smooth grey waters of the Sound. 'I'm happy the way we are. That was then, and this is now. I want to live in the now.'

And, suddenly, she believed him.

Against all odds, they ended up having a rather wonderful day; the sort of day that becomes a landmark in family history. They drove up north, where the leaves were indeed turning crimson, orange and yellow in a spectacular way. By accident, they stumbled on a pick-your-own apple farm and spent a happy half-hour watching Lydia fill bags with fruit.

'What on earth will we do with all these apples?' Annie asked, as Lydia put a fourth laden bag into the handcart Simon was pushing.

'God knows,' said Simon. 'But look at her face.'

And they stood together with their arms entwined, just watching Lydia's pleasure as if it were a spectator sport.

Hungry for something more substantial than apples, they drove on to a charming little waterfront town. They ate their picnic lunch barefoot on a rocky outcrop at the beach, gazing over the tranquil waters of Long Island Sound.

Stealing glances at Simon's thoughtful profile, Annie realised that he might never again look like the happy-go-lucky young man in the photos with Beth. And yet his face had more depth to it now.

He must have felt her eyes on him. He turned his head and looked directly at her, his pupils dilating slightly as if to take her in all the better.

'Happy?' he asked.

She nodded, speechless.

'Annie? Annie, guess what?' Heather's voice sang out over the phone one morning in triumph. 'I've just been over at the barn and – you won't believe it – but a space has opened up in Hailey's Wednesday class! The Moretons are leaving town, relocating to Dubai for a couple of years, all kind of sudden. So there's a slot for Lydia!'

Annie scratched her head, straining to bring her mind to bear on whatever it was Heather was babbling about so excitedly. 'I'm sorry, a what?'

'A slot! In the Wednesday class!'

'You mean a riding class?'

Heather groaned audibly. 'Yeah, that's it! A freaking riding class! But you have to move quickly, like *now*, because it's not going to last long. I told them you'd be calling, but they won't hold the space for more than a couple of hours. There must be ten families lined up to snatch it out from under you.'

'I— *what?*'

'Yeah, it could get ugly. There's a waiting list. I put Hailey on it right before kindergarten and she only got in halfway through first grade. These slots only come up once in a while. It's more competitive than country club membership, or getting a mooring for your boat at Norbury Harbor. You have to jump on it! Play your cards right and she could be riding this afternoon!'

Annie's heart began to pound with excitement. 'Oh God, Lydia would be thrilled, wouldn't she? Have you got the phone number?'

Heather rattled off a number, and then repeated it more slowly at Annie's request. 'Ask for Mrs Winter,' Heather instructed. 'She's a piece of work, but she owes me.' Annie wrote down the details and thanked Heather profusely. By now, it was beginning to seem to her that getting Lydia into the riding class had been her most fervent ambition ever since they'd arrived in Norbury.

As she hung up, she remembered that Simon wasn't actually that keen on Lydia riding at all.

But surely he'd think differently if she told him the circumstances? How the Moretons had left unexpectedly for Dubai, how ten other families were circling, how this was possibly their last chance to get Lyddie on a horse until she was a teenager? She was sure he'd be excited about the opportunity, but she'd better check in with him before signing Lydia up, just to be on the safe side.

Taking a deep breath, she punched out the number of his mobile phone.

The phone rang only once before Simon picked up.

'Simon? Oh, hi. I was just calling to—'

'Annie, is it an emergency?' Simon's voice was strangely hushed.

'No, but—'

'OK, because I'm in a meeting. Quite an important one. Can we talk later?'

'But it's about Lyddie—'

'I trust you absolutely to handle anything in that department.' He really didn't sound himself at all; very muted and brisk. Not particularly loving.

'Really? You trust me *absolutely*?'

'Of course! Look, I'm sorry but I really have to go now.' And he hung up on her.

Annie stared at the phone for a moment. She thought about calling him again and insisting on getting his opinion, but something in his tone gave her pause.

He was busy, clearly. Strategising about selling pies to the American market was a highly stressful job. Pies-as-fast-food was a foreign concept to American culture, and ChefPro was taking a huge leap of faith with this whole project. She knew that. She and Simon had talked about it often. Obviously, he was tense. Obviously, he hadn't cut her off on the phone just because he didn't feel like speaking to her. Of course he wanted to speak to her. He loved her, after all. He'd married her, hadn't he? He'd stood up in a register office and proclaimed his desire to be shackled in a monogamous bond to Annie Harleigh for the rest of his life. He'd done it of his own free will. The whole thing had been his idea in the first place! She couldn't have *been* more surprised when he'd popped the question. In fact, she'd been just about incredulous.

He'd proposed to her on a Wednesday afternoon during the lunch break. He'd taken her to a small restaurant on Islington Green, sat her down at a table, waved a waiter away, extracted an envelope from his briefcase and burst out, 'Have you ever given any thought to living in America?'

When she gaped wordlessly back at him, displaying a half-chewed mouthful of bread, he put the envelope down, raked his fingers through his hair, and muttered, 'God, Simon Keeler, try that again.'

Then he leaned across the table, disengaged her hand from her bread roll, took it in his own, and said urgently, 'I can't change my plans, Annie. Everything's in motion. The whole American pie push is my idea. It can't go forward without me. I've found renters for my house, told Maria to look for something else. But, the thing is, I can't let you go. I just can't. It's mad, I know, but would you consider, sort of, marrying me?'

Annie chewed and swallowed. A pulse was beating in her throat, and she put her hand over the place in case it was throbbing visibly. But she couldn't speak.

'Connecticut's a fantastic place,' he went on, impatiently declining a menu. 'They say the sky is blue most days, even in winter. And the town I'm thinking of is close to New York, so we'd be able to go in to the city for theatre and museums and shopping. The summers are really hot, and Norbury has its own beach. Plus the schools are brilliant, a really great environment for Lydia. I don't know how they do it, but they churn out kids with enough self-confidence to run for president by the time they're twelve. Look, I know it would be a sacrifice,' he added hastily. 'You'd have to give up your job, and I'm not sure we'd be able to wangle papers for you to work over there. So – well, I know I haven't got a hope in hell, but I'm asking you anyway.'

'What's in the envelope?' she rasped, ignoring the waiter at her elbow.

'Forms for my US work visa. Here, have a look.' He took some papers out and spread them on the table. 'I . . . I could put you down as my fiancée. That way they could get going on the paperwork. And we could get married before we go. Maybe in August? I mean, that's if you want to. I don't even know if you want to, but I feel as if maybe you do. Because I do. Very much. I can't imagine going off right now and never seeing you again. Or . . . or trying to have a long-distance relationship. Weekends here and there. Phone sex. I don't know if I could bear it.'

Phone sex? Golly, she didn't even know how to do that. Tears sprang to her eyes. 'Are you serious?'

'Deadly serious. Annie, I think I knew I loved you when I saw you that first time in Greece. I just sort of *recognised* you, in some weird way. I feel as if I've known you for ever.'

'I feel the same,' she whispered back, but he didn't hear her. He was delving in the envelope again, almost feverishly.

'Here, I have some photos of Norbury – you know, the town I'm going to live in. Look, this is the beach – it's right on Long Island Sound. And this is one of the elementary schools. And this is, let's see, I think it's a pond in the park. They skate on it in winter, apparently, and play ice hockey. Oh, and this is a typical house. They're all made of wood, with massive gardens—'

'Are these people taking the piss?' a low but carrying voice suddenly asked. Both of them became aware for the first time of a man in a white hat looming over their table. 'When are they going to order their effing food? We're trying to turn tables over here.'

Annie froze in horror.

'It's not *my* fault, mate,' another voice hissed back. 'I keep showing them the bloody menu but they won't look at it.'

'Oh God, I think we'd better order,' said Annie. 'I'll have the chicken. Any chicken. And yes, I'll marry you, Simon. Of course I will.'

Oblivious of the disgruntled chef and waiter, Simon stood up, pulled Annie to her feet, and kissed her across the table in a clatter of knives and forks.

Back then, Simon always had time for her if she called him at work. He never cut her off, never spoke to her curtly.

Annie found a tissue and blew her nose. Married life was different, obviously. Certain things were taken for granted, certain niceties could be dispensed with. It didn't mean that the way he felt about her had changed in any way.

Since it was up to her, she decided she would phone Mrs Winter at the barn. Lydia was bound to like riding lessons a lot more than she liked soccer. (So *there*, Simon.)

In about five minutes, she had secured the coveted spot.

Later that day, Annie stood on the pavement outside Bradley Elementary, holding a bag from Fairfield County Leisure, and grinning idiotically.

Waving at Lydia as she emerged from the building, she

pumped her arms up and down in a pantomime of running, but Lydia frowned, dropped her eyes, and came forward at her usual snail's pace.

'Lyddie! Hurry, hurry! Come and see what I have in this bag for you!'

Lydia's head shot up in surprise, and she did speed up ever so slightly.

'Here,' said Annie, thrusting the bag at her, 'take a peek.'

Lydia glanced around at the other children; some were watching curiously. She hesitated a moment, then reached into the bag and pulled out the contents.

'Oh, thanks,' she mumbled. 'A pair of trousers.'

'They're not trousers! They're jodhpurs.'

'Jodhpurs? What's a jodhpur?'

'Horse-riding trousers.'

Lydia stared at her in silence.

'That's right! You're starting riding lessons! Right now! Today! This very afternoon!'

Lydia's face went pale, then flushed painfully. 'Me? Riding lessons? Today?'

'Yes, now! Come on, we'll rush home and have a quick snack first. I hope the jodhpurs fit. I took a pair of your jeans into the shop and they said these should be the right size. We'll get riding boots as soon as we can, but for now you can wear your brown cowgirl boots.'

Lydia stood very still, not moving or speaking.

'Come on, come on, let's get going. It's going to be a bit of a mad dash to get there on time.'

Lydia remained frozen.

'Oh God!' Annie clapped her hand over her mouth. 'I'm such an idiot! You don't even *want* horse-riding lessons, do you? And I've gone and paid for four months upfront. Never mind. I totally understand. I wouldn't want to go either, to be honest. I can probably still cancel.'

Lydia tightened her hand around the jodhpurs. 'No,' she said, shaking her head. 'Don't cancel! I want to go.'

Annie stared at the child. Lydia wasn't smiling but when she glanced up at Annie her eyes burnt with secret elation.

'Oh, *you* ... You really had me going there.' Annie dived at Lydia, tickling her vigorously on the ribs and under her arms, overcome by the urge to blow the lid off her give-nothing-away composure. Startled, Lydia gave a hoot of laughter, then took off at a run, her backpack thumping up and down, the bag containing the jodhpurs ballooning up with air as she went. Annie followed, delighted. A small group of kids still waiting to be picked up stared after them in wonder.

What demon prompted Annie to take Patches to the barn that afternoon to watch the riding lesson, she couldn't really have said. Of course, she was a bit nervous about leaving him alone in the kitchen now that he'd chewed up several chair legs. She could only hazard the vaguest guess at the kind of damages they'd have to pay when they vacated the premises if Patches were left unattended too often. Because of his destructive streak, she'd taken to leaving him in the garage, where there wasn't much he could sink his teeth into. Lydia had even set up a little home for him out there – a folded blanket in a large cardboard box, a selection of chew toys, a bowl of water.

Annie was fully intending to leave him in this cosy holding pen, but when the minivan door slid open, Patches jumped into the back before she could grab his collar.

'Oh, can't he come?' Lydia begged. 'I've seen loads of people with dogs at the barn.'

Annie had seen them, too, these glamorous women and their dogs. They would pull up in their tank-sized SUVs, flicking the obligatory long, straight hair over their shoulders, and Annie would wonder how they got their highlights to match the exact shade of the golden retriever or yellow Labrador poking its head out of the passenger window.

The retrievers and labs wore bandannas, and sometimes plaid waistcoats. Their collars were in the style of the Fairfield County Leisure Store's famous hundred-dollar ribbon belts. Many were green, embroidered with pink flamingos.

Patches, of course, couldn't hope to hold a candle to these high-bred beauties. He was a mongrel through and through, with absolutely no pretensions to expensive pedigree, or any pedigree at all. But he was all dog, and she wasn't ashamed of him.

'OK, he can come,' Annie said, peering into the minivan at Patches cringing on the back seat with flattened ears, waiting to be evicted.

'Yippee!' Lydia yelled, jumping into the car and throwing both arms around the dog's neck. 'I can't wait to introduce him to Pompom.'

Annie's heart lifted at the exuberance in her voice.

As they nosed out of the driveway, Lydia suddenly asked, 'Annie, are you going to have a lesson too?'

'*Me*? Good grief, no.'

'But you're wearing jodhpurs.'

'Um ... yes. Well, you know. Just thought I'd show the right spirit.' She was beginning to wonder, now, if her outfit was a bit much. She'd noticed that jodhpurs were de rigueur among the women at the barn – but maybe that was only if you actually rode the horses. Maybe there was another dress code for non-riding mothers. She might just leave her new whip – no, 'crop' – in the car.

The riding instructor was holding the reins of a small, nondescript pony as they half-ran up to the arena, about five minutes late for the lesson. Heather had offered to drive Lydia to the barn, but Annie had declined the offer, thinking she'd better stay and watch, since it was Lydia's first time.

Hailey and another girl were already up on ponies, walking around the perimeter of the arena, looking very calm and collected. Several heads turned as Annie and Lydia approached, perhaps because of the strangled noise Patches was making as he strained against his collar. Every now and then he'd stand up on his hind legs and hop forward like a circus dog in his desperation to arrive more quickly at the scene of the action. Then again, the onlookers might have been admiring Annie's jodhpurs coupled with her knee-high patent leather platform boots. (Like Lydia, she didn't yet own actual riding boots.) The effect, if Annie said so herself, was pretty spectacular.

Lydia's new riding instructor, dressed in jeans, trainers and a fleece jacket, surged forward to greet them. 'You must be my new girl. Linda, right? Oh, *Lydia*? OK. I'm Christine, and your pony is Milkdud. Now, before we start this lesson we need to get one thing straight.' She lowered her eyebrows at Lydia. 'While you're up on the pony, what I say goes. If I ask you to sing the stars and stripes, you sing it. If I ask you to wriggle your fingers, you wriggle them. If I ask you to pat your belly and rub your head, you do that too.'

Lydia, who was usually mute when she met new people, looked up and whispered, 'I don't know the stars and stripes.'

'That's OK, I'm not actually going to ask you to sing.' Christine pushed her sleeves up to her elbows. 'But you get it, right? You do as you're told when you're up on the pony. Come on then, let's get this safety helmet on you. Oh, and Mom, could you take the dog behind the palings, if you're staying to watch?'

Mom? Wow, she *did* look the part, after all. Feeling highly satisfied with the whole turn of events, Annie gave Patches' leash a tug and retreated behind the fence Christine had indicated. The dog resisted with all his might, digging his paws into the ground, but she was able to drag him over by brute force. He was still making the strangled noises but at least he wasn't barking.

Beetle-browed Christine boosted Lydia up onto Milkdud's back, then spent some time showing Lydia how to hold the reins and where to put her feet. Annie was relieved to see that the pony stood stock still, looking bored out of its mind. At a click and a tug on the reins from Christine, Milkdud moved off at a lumbering walk, Lydia concentrating hard under her black hat. Christine shouted inscrutable orders to the other two – 'Change the rein across the diagonal, rising trot at K, sit deep and shorten the reins, get those ponies on the bit!' – turning aside every now and then to murmur something to Lydia. After a few minutes, she moved away from Lydia and into the centre of the arena. 'Prepare to walk . . . and *walk*,' she called to Hailey and the other girl, who slowed their horses down. 'Now, overtake Milkdud on the inside and let him follow you. I want all the ponies on a long rein, lengthening their stride please, girls. I want feet out of stirrups. You too, Lydia. Now, stretch your legs and point your toes down, down, down. Right. Feel that? That's absolutely the wrong way for your leg and foot to be. Now, toes up and push your *heels* down. Bend slightly at the knee, wrapping your legs around the pony but not squeezing. OK. Good. Now, let's move into a circle, bending the pony round your inside leg . . .'

As Annie watched, Patches began to act strangely. He started whimpering low in his throat then gave a high-pitched bark.

'Hush,' Annie scolded. 'You'll scare the horses.'

'That your girl on Milkdud?' drawled a vaguely familiar voice behind her. Annie turned to see Dan Morgan strolling up.

For some reason, an image of Dan and Sarah in a lip-lock in her loo popped immediately into Annie's mind, and she felt herself blush. At that same moment, Patches lost all self-control and gave a giant tug on his leash. Caught by surprise, Annie felt the leash slip through her slack fingers.

'Patches!' she yelled as the dog dived under the fence and began to charge the horses. 'Come back here! Come *back*! Come back at *once*!'

But it was no use. With helpless disbelief, Annie watched

as the dog streaked across the arena, barking fiercely, making straight for the pony Lydia was riding. Christine put her hands on her hips and bellowed, 'Get that freaking dog out of here!'

In slow motion, or so it seemed to Annie, Patches launched himself into the air and sprang at the mousy brown quarters of Lydia's pony. In mid-leap, he managed to grab a mouthful of the pony's shaggy tail. He locked his jaw, eyes bulging, and held onto the tuft for dear life. With a snort, the spooked pony began dancing and kicking. Lydia, her face rigid with shock, dropped the reins entirely and clung to the saddle. Patches, caught on the pony's tail like a burr, was shaken and tossed about – but not dislodged.

'Oh, stop that horse, stop it now,' Annie cried, her heart in her mouth, ducking under the fence and running at the animals with no idea of how to break up the fracas, but a vague notion of plucking Lydia off the pony's back.

'Get that dumb mutt outta here!' cried Christine. 'Get him outta here NOW!'

Suddenly Lydia's pony let loose with a giant two-legged kick that found its mark. Patches went sailing through the air, legs flailing. The pony skittered away, snorting with satisfaction, with Lydia still on board, though barely. Patches hit the ground running. He spotted Annie and went bolting back to her for protection, tail well between his legs.

The riding instructor stood and shouted at Lydia as she was jostled about like a bag of potatoes, 'Take up the reins and pull her in! Sit down, sit down, sit *down*, for God's sake. Whoa, whoa, *whoa*.'

It wasn't until Dan Morgan stepped casually into the

arena, strode into the path of the bolting pony and – somehow, miraculously – caught it by the reins, that Lydia lost her seat altogether, and slithered slowly off the pony's back to fall in a heap at Dan's feet.

'It's a miracle she didn't break every bone in her body,' Annie told Heather shakily as she dropped Hailey off home. 'Totally my fault. I've been banned from bringing Patches to the premises ever again. I think the woman was toying with banning me too, only I've already paid for the four months.'

'Are you all right, honey?' Heather asked, bending down to peer into Lydia's face. 'Any bruises?'

'I'm fine,' said Lydia with a shrug.

'You should've seen her!' Hailey piped up. 'Milkdud was going nuts, and she stayed up on him. It was so cool. She was like – like a circus rider. Was it scary, Lydia?'

'Really scary,' said Lydia, looking up with bright eyes, 'especially that big buck just before the pony kicked Patches. Poor Patches. I'm glad he's OK.'

'I saw your fanny come right up off the saddle then,' enthused Hailey. 'I don't know how you stayed on!'

Fanny? Good grief. Annie glanced at Heather but she seemed unperturbed by this sudden use of obscene language.

'Hey, I *wish* I could've seen that,' Lydia said wistfully. 'Do you think you could draw a picture of how it looked?'

Hailey raised her unibrow. 'Sure,' she said. 'Mom, can she stay and draw with me?'

Heather began to shake her head slightly, but before she

could say a thing, Annie cut in. 'Yes, yes, of course she can stay. Right, Mrs Gibson? It's late for a play date, but since it's been such a big day, we'll make an exception. Won't we?' She caught Heather's eye with a pleading look. Surely she wouldn't pull the plug on the first real overtures of friendship Annie had ever seen Lydia make?

'All right,' said Heather with a sigh. 'She might as well stay for dinner, too. It's only going to be scrambled eggs. Do you like scrambled eggs, Lydia?'

Lydia smiled, not the small, polite smile she sometimes forced onto her face when pressed by Annie, but a normal, genuine, child's smile. 'Yes, I like eggs,' she said. 'If they're not too dry.'

As the girls scampered into the house together, Annie found herself beaming too. 'I've never seen Lydia so happy. Thank God for those bloody horses.'

Heather nodded her head. 'Didn't I tell you to get involved with the riding?' she said. 'Horses are like dolphins, you know. They have a therapeutic effect on people.'

Annie laughed ruefully. 'Well, not on me and Patches,' she said. 'D'you know who came to the rescue, by the way? Your friend, Dan Morgan. He jumped in there like the Lone Ranger and caught the pony's reins. The stupid thing was still running around like a headless chicken even after it booted Patches. Poor dog, he was kicked a good twenty feet or more into the air. Flew off like a cannonball.'

Heather's grinned. 'Really? Must have been kind of funny. And Dan helped out? Wish I could've seen it.'

The story of the afternoon's adventures didn't go over half as well with Simon.

'I'm sorry, *what*? It sounded like you said Lydia fell off a horse.' He stood in the front hallway that evening, frozen in the act of taking off his coat. Perhaps she shouldn't have begun the tale the minute he set foot in the door. Maybe she should have primed him with a glass of wine first.

'Well – yes, that's what I said.' Annie could hear the tremble in her own voice. 'But don't worry, she's not hurt. Not even bruised.'

'Hang on, hang on. Backtrack a moment, here. How did she come to be riding a horse? Did she go over to the stables with the Gibsons?'

'No, Heather had nothing to do with it. Well, very little to do with it. The thing is, Lyddie was having her first riding lesson – mostly walking, you know, so very, very safe – when Patches—'

'*Riding* lesson?' Simon paused in the act of kicking his shoes off, his face incredulous.

Annie bit her lip. 'Um, yes. You see, Heather rang up this morning to say a slot had opened up in the group lesson Hailey goes to—'

But he was gone, thudding up the stairs in his socks, to see for himself that Lydia was really in one piece.

When he came back down again Annie was in the kitchen, stir-frying chicken and vegetables in a wok.

'You see?' She looked at him through the sizzle and steam. 'She's just fine. Not a mark on her.'

But Simon ran both hands through his hair and took a few quick, agitated steps around the kitchen. 'Annie,' he said with an audible effort to be calm, 'how do we know she doesn't have concussion? I thought I made it clear that I don't want her going up on a horse.'

Annie's stirring hand slowed right down. 'Well, um, the way I remember it, you said since she wasn't *asking* to ride, we should leave it at that . . .'

'OK, so maybe that's what I said. But I thought you understood. I thought you knew I didn't want her riding.'

'Well, yes, but—'

'Annie, my brother says that accident stats for horse riding are right up there with fractured skulls from trampolines and bunk beds.' Simon's brother was a senior executive in a major insurance company. 'He says he'd rather let his daughter ride a *motorbike* than get up on a bloody horse.'

'Come off it, Simon. I'm sure there are far more fatalities from road accidents than from falling off horses and bunk beds *combined*.' Annie was starting to feel indignant.

'Look,' Simon said firmly, 'I'm just not comfortable with this whole thing. She's already fallen off once. It's an unnecessary risk. A gratuitous bloody worry that we just don't *need* in our lives! You're going to have to cancel the lessons.'

'But . . . but I phoned to ask you. You left it all up to me. I mean, you *specifically* gave me the go-ahead to do whatever I thought was right.'

'Well, I made a mistake, in that case! I didn't know what the hell it was all about!'

'You mean you *don't* trust me absolutely to make any and all decisions for Lydia?'

'Annie, it's not a case of trust. I'm her *father*.'

'And I'm not her mother?'

'No,' he said. 'You're not.'

They stared at each other in silence for a moment.

Then Simon sank onto a bar stool. 'Bugger it,' he said. 'That didn't come out right.'

'No, I think it came out exactly right,' Annie said. 'Who am I to make decisions for Lydia? I mean, really? I've only known her a few months. I have no experience dealing with kids. She doesn't think of me as her mum. I have no more rights than ... than a nanny. Probably fewer. I mean, an experienced nanny would be a lot better at all this than I am.'

'Rubbish,' said Simon. 'You're doing a fantastic job with Lydia. I'm well aware of that. You *are* her mother, to all intents and purposes, and I love you for all that you do for her. It's just that a – a *biological* parent is a lot more likely to have irrational fears. That's all.'

Annie reached for the plates and began serving up their food with jerky little movements and lots of clattering.

'Annie,' he said, 'I'm sorry. I *do* trust you with Lydia. I trust you absolutely. But I just can't stop thinking about how big and solid horses are, and how small and breakable children are. So can you please just humour me on this?'

She turned towards him quickly, ready to forgive ... and knocked a glass of water off the counter with her elbow. It shattered on the tiles with an unnerving crash.

'Oh *bloody* hell,' Simon muttered, striding across the room and throwing open the pantry door. 'Is there such a thing as a dustpan and brush in this stonking great house, or are we too posh for that?'

She put her spoon down carefully on the glass stove top. 'So now you don't like the house?'

He was still throwing cupboard doors open. 'Of course I like it,' he growled, staring in frustration at a pyramid of plastic containers. 'We chose it together. How could I not like it? It's a bloody mansion! It just doesn't feel much like *home*, that's all.'

'The brush and pan are round the corner, in the cupboard next to the washer and dryer.' Annie worked hard to keep her voice even.

Shaking salad greens out of a bag onto their plates, she glanced at him, squatting on the floor brushing fragments of broken glass into the dustpan. He was still in his suit, his tie loose and crooked, his blond hair in disarray. She watched his broad, muscular hands wielding the brush, distracted by their brisk competence.

As she stared at him, his eyelids lifted and he looked straight up at her with his direct blue gaze. She was taken aback by the bleakness of his expression.

'Food's ready,' she said hastily. 'Let's just eat and deal with the mess later. I'll have to vacuum.'

He dumped the glass fragments in the bin, then sat down on a bar stool and accepted the plate she handed him. For a moment he sat staring at his food. Then he flicked his eyes at her from beneath raised brows. 'I just don't have the stomach for chances any more,' he said.

Suddenly, Annie's throat ached for him. She swallowed hard. 'No worries, the riding lessons are history,' she said. 'Um – and I know what you mean about the house. It's not that homely. I can't work out why, exactly. I suppose it's because we didn't pick the furniture.'

Simon held his loaded fork and looked around the kitchen,

his eyes resting on the toile 'window treatments'. 'I suppose so. But it's also, I don't know, so *tidy*. Beth always—' He caught himself immediately.

Annie took a quick gulp of water. 'Beth always what?'

He shrugged. 'I don't know. She had a lot of clutter, I suppose. And she always stuck bits of Lyddie's art up on the fridge.'

Lyddie's art? Lyddie didn't produce art. Annie hadn't seen a single stick figure to date. Oh God. That was probably a bad sign. She, Annie, must be crushing the child's creativity. Hang on! Hadn't Lyddie talked about drawing pictures with Hailey that very afternoon? She must ask Heather to check and see if she had actually put crayon to paper.

She cleared her throat and initiated a hasty change of subject. 'So what do you think of my Japanese stir-fry?'

Simon came back from some faraway place and glanced at his fork as if seeing it for the first time. 'Right. Looks great.' He took a mouthful and chewed with a thoughtful expression.

'So?'

His brow wrinkled. 'It's – quite nice. But it doesn't really taste Japanese, to be honest. What sort of seasoning did you use?'

Annie looked down at her own plate. The food looked good, if she said so herself: nicely browned chunks of chicken vied for attention with a colourful palette of vegetables: red peppers, tiny sprigs of broccoli, and adorable, bright yellow mini cobs of corn. 'You know, just the usual simple elements of Japanese cuisine: garlic, ginger, a base of soya sauce.' She glanced over at the stove top as she spoke, her eye falling on the bottle of soya sauce.

Only it wasn't soya. It was the Worcestershire sauce she'd been so happy to find the other day in the supermarket's mainly Mexican 'international' aisle.

Simon spotted the Worcestershire sauce at the same moment she did.

His mouth quivered and his eyes glinted with appreciation. 'Tuck in yourself,' he urged. 'It's a bit of a carnival on the tongue.'

'Oh God, I'm sorry. But in fairness, both bottles are black with yellow labels!'

He burst out laughing, and she couldn't help but laugh with him. All the tension and strain that was thickening the atmosphere in the room suddenly went swirling round at high speed and drained away abruptly, like murky water disappearing down the pipes when you pulled the plug on the kitchen sink.

Promising Simon that she'd cancel the riding lessons was one thing. Breaking the news to Lydia was something else entirely.

Simon offered to do it himself, since he'd been the one to throw the spanner in the works.

'No, Simon, don't do it,' Annie said. 'Don't go telling her you asked me to cancel the lessons.'

'Really? Why not? It won't be fair if she blames you.'

'No, don't you see? If you explain everything to her, it's going to look . . .'

He stared at her a moment. 'It's going to look as if you're not allowed to make decisions about what she does and doesn't do,' he said slowly. 'Oh God. I hadn't thought of that.'

She nodded briskly. 'She'll be angry with me,' she said, 'but I think that's OK. She'll get over it. I just – I want her to think that I know what I'm doing, that's all.'

At six thirty the next morning Annie lay awake in bed, watching Simon get ready for work. Normally she slept through his daybreak rituals, but today the alarm clock had found her wide awake, staring into the darkness. 'I'm sure she'll take it OK,' she suddenly murmured. 'I mean, she does like riding, but it doesn't seem to be an all-consuming passion or anything. She'll be fine.'

'God, I hope so.' Simon ran a comb through his damp hair and snapped his fingers at Patches, who rose from the laundry basket with a resigned groan and tottered over towards the door. Patches was a bit of a night owl and didn't relish being turned out of doors so early in the morning.

Simon leaned down to kiss Annie goodbye. Drowsy and affectionate, Annie surged up out of the sheets to put her arms around his neck. He smelled of soap and toothpaste. She smelled a little earthier, apparently. 'Phew,' he murmured, setting her gently aside. 'Quite a lot of garlic in the food last night.'

She felt herself deflating on the pillow like a balloon with a slow leak.

Then, one hand on the door, he turned to give her an indescribably raunchy wink, perking her back up instantly. With his muscular build and dark tan, he looked indecently raffish in his white shirt. 'See you later,' he murmured, and was gone.

Annie stared at the closed door.

How was it possible to be married to a man and still yearn for him as if you'd just had a one-night stand after meeting him in a pub and weren't quite sure whether you were ever going to lay eyes on him again?

'Do you have any aches and pains from your fall?' Annie asked Lydia as she put her porridge in the microwave to warm up. Lydia, trailing around the kitchen in pyjamas and bare feet, swept the long hair out of her eyes and gave a confused shrug. 'No, I told you, I didn't hurt myself.'

'I know, but sometimes muscles sort of stiffen up overnight.'

'Is my porridge ready?'

'Yes, here you go.' Annie watched as the little girl settled herself on a stool and began sprinkling sugar. 'So – you and Hailey had fun yesterday afternoon?'

Lydia shrugged again.

'Did you draw any pictures?'

'Loads.'

'You didn't bring any back to show me.'

'No, we threw them away.'

'Oh. Why?'

''Cos Mrs Gibson says it's about process not product.'

'I see. Next time you draw something, could you give it to me?'

'Why?'

'So I can stick it on the fridge to brighten up the kitchen.'

'OK.' Lydia stirred her porridge and sampled it experimentally. Apparently, it needed just a soupçon more sugar.

Watching her sprinkle, Annie took a deep breath, closed her eyes a second, then suddenly blurted, 'I'm sorry, sweetie, but I'm going to have to cancel the riding lessons.'

Lydia froze mid-sprinkle.

'What did you say?'

'Um ... the riding lessons. I'm going to have to cancel them. You see, your dad and I were talking and we realised that we don't want you riding, after all. We would rather have you do something less dangerous like – I don't know – chess.'

'But – but you *said*! You said I could do it. You said you'd already paid for it! I didn't even ask to do it! You bought me jodhpurs and *everything*! You said we'd buy riding boots today after soccer!' Her voice was rising ominously.

Annie pressed her fingers into her eyeballs and breathed in through her nose. 'I'm sorry, love. We've ... we've reconsidered and we don't want you riding.'

'Is this because I fell off?' Lydia cried. 'I didn't even hurt a hair on my head! Not even my little finger! Christine said I did a great job staying on. She said I was a natural!'

'My darling, I'm sorry. I'm so, so sorry. But we've decided. No more lessons.'

Lydia jumped up, dropping her spoon on the counter and scattering sugar all over the place. 'You know what you are?' she screamed. 'You're a big, fat *meanie*!' And she ran for the stairs, heaving with sobs.

Annie stood in the middle of the kitchen, arms folded to stop her hands from shaking visibly. 'So,' she said out loud to Patches, who was licking sugar off the tiles, 'that went surprisingly well, don't you think?'

Chapter Eight

'She's moping,' Annie told Simon a few days later, 'definitely moping.'

'I've noticed it too.' They were sitting on a bench at the beach on a Saturday morning, watching Lydia wander aimlessly over the sand. It wasn't really a beach day. The wind was blowing, whipping the normally flat water into little troughs.

'So I have a plan.'

He looked at her with interest. 'Yes?'

'Let's tell her we're keeping Patches.'

His brows snapped together.

'Don't you see?' she said quickly. 'It's a great plan. I mean, what are we going to do with him, anyway? Take him to the pound to be put to sleep? Nobody's going to claim him, that's pretty clear. We've advertised him up and down Fairfield county.'

'Annie, it wouldn't be responsible to keep him. You seem to forget, we're only here for a couple of years. We're not permanent enough to be dog owners!'

Annie jumped up and stood in front of him, radiating energy and determination. 'That shouldn't stop us. It's much easier to take dogs around the world nowadays. You just have this chip thingy inserted under their skin, and they don't even have to go into quarantine. Come on, Simon! He's a good dog.'

'He's a nightmare bloody dog.'

'But you like him. I know you do. And think how happy Lyddie would be!'

'Oh, for God's sake, Annie. Haven't we got enough on our plates?'

'I've got hardly anything on my plate, to be honest. Taking Patches for a walk every day has been a godsend! It gives me something to do, gets me out of the house, even helps me meet people.'

Simon looked at her with narrowed eyes. 'You're serious, aren't you?'

'Of course I'm serious.'

He sighed. 'Well, OK then. I guess we're stuck with the cringing cur.'

Annie was already running across the sand towards Lydia. 'Quick, quick!' she called. 'We have good news.'

Lydia glanced up from the shells she was poking at with a stick. Seeing Annie racing towards her, she frowned in a resigned sort of way, threw her stick down, and began trudging to meet her.

'Is it time to go?' she asked.

'Probably,' said Annie. 'I don't know about you, but my hands are freezing. But come back to Daddy. We have something to tell you.'

'You tell her,' Simon said when they reached him. 'It's your idea, after all.'

'OK. Lyddie, your dad and I have been talking and . . . well, since nobody has claimed Patches, we've decided to keep him.'

Lydia held very still.

'Do you understand? We're keeping Patches. You'll have a dog!' Annie was disappointed. The child didn't look in the least bit overjoyed. She hadn't even cracked a smile.

Lydia rubbed her sandy hands against her fleece jacket. 'You're just saying that,' she said. 'Tomorrow you'll tell me you made a mistake. Just like with the riding lessons.'

Annie threw Simon a horrified look. 'No, honestly. I promise you! I'm not just saying it! You can keep Patches.'

Lydia looked at her father. 'Is it true?'

He stood up and put his hands on her shoulders. 'Yes, it's true. We're not going to change our minds.'

Lydia jumped up into his arms, pressed her face into his coat and began to sob. 'It's OK,' he said, patting her back and raising his eyebrows at Annie. After a moment the sobs dried up, and she rubbed her face on his sleeve.

'Let's go back and tell him,' Lydia said. 'Let's go and tell him he gets to stay.'

This was more like it, Annie thought. Far more like it! 'Yes, and let's go to the pet shop and get him his own basket,' she suggested. 'And his own feeding bowl.'

'And maybe another toy to chew on,' Lyddie said.

'Or several dozen toys to chew on,' said Simon, who had lost a slipper and sundry belts to Patches' incorrigible oral fixation.

*

On Monday, Annie took Patches along to the vet to have his jabs done. After he knocked the vet's glasses off his face, then urinated on the stainless steel examining table with excitement, the man in the white coat recommended manners lessons. He also recommended crate training, which apparently meant putting the dog in a cage every time you left the house. This was after Patches vomited on the table, giving him an opportunity to see the contents of his stomach, which included fragments of wax crayon, sticks, pieces of brightly coloured plastic, a small spring, and a length of string. He told her Patches was about one year old, and strongly advised her to get him 'fixed' as soon as possible.

'I'm not sure the world is ready for this dog to start reproducing,' he noted in a far from jocular tone.

But what did Annie care if the vet didn't approve of their dog? Lydia was happy!

She was happier still when a little note arrived in the post from a girl called Emily Cooper, who used to be her best friend at St Thomas Church of England Primary School in Kensington.

Annie had passed on Lydia's address to the headmistress of St Thomas. She had almost given up hope of anything coming of it when the letter, in its blue airmail envelope, appeared in their mail box.

'Der Lidia, how are you? I am fine. It is raning here. LOL Emily.' This riveting piece of correspondence was illustrated with a stick-figure scene of people holding up umbrellas. It made Annie feel quite homesick.

Lydia wrote back: 'Dir Emly, how are you? I am fine. I

have a dog. Love Lydia.' Annie photocopied the letter and stuck it on the fridge. The drawing of Patches was quite masterful, in her humble opinion.

The next day, as Annie sat in her idling car, waiting to take Lydia and Hailey to soccer practice, she found herself hailed through the car window by Donna Knopf, one of her Maple Tree Ridge neighbours.

'Annie? Hey, how's it going?'

'Very well, thanks, how about you?'

'I'm good. Everything's good. Hey, I'm wondering if you could do me a favour?'

Annie felt quite flattered. She would never have thought she could do anything to help out Donna Knopf, who was one of those highly organised women whose main job in life seemed to be to make other women feel inadequate. Recently, when the mothers had been asked to bring in treats for the staff at Bradley Elementary for teacher appreciation day, Donna had brought in a cheese moulded into the shape of an owl, layered with sun-dried tomatoes, and artistically decorated with pine nuts for feathers. Annie had brought in a plastic box of violently coloured cookies.

Annie smiled through the car window. 'Of course, happy to help. What do you need?'

'We're looking for a fourth for our tennis clinic tomorrow. One of the gals has something else on. So – are you up for it?'

'Aaah,' Annie's voice was a squeak.

'I know you play,' Donna added. 'I've seen you walking around in tennis outfits.'

'Well, um—'

'Of course, if you're a tennis snob . . .? I mean, we're just giggle and hit.'

Giggle and hit? Annie wanted to lean out of the window and kiss Donna with relief. She could do giggle and hit any day of the week. After all it wasn't as if she'd never held a tennis racquet in her life. She'd had several lessons at school! 'A tennis snob? Me? Gosh no, I'm just trying to keep my eye on the ball, myself. I'd love to play! I'm really bad, though, I'm warning you.'

Donna smiled. 'Oh, you English. Always so modest! I'll email you the details. See you later.'

Gosh. Tennis. Simon was bound to be impressed if she started playing tennis. He was definitely in favour of competitive sports, as testified by his initial excitement about the soccer. Come to think of it, he didn't really know much about Annie's athletic abilities. He wouldn't know how downright astonishing it was that she was going to make up a foursome at Winterton Indoor Courts. For all he knew, she could have been a schoolgirl tennis star.

'Annie, open up!'

Lydia stood on the kerb, banging on the car door. Coming out of her reverie, Annie pressed the button to open the remote-controlled sliding door for the girls. They piled in, throwing backpacks onto the floor and then walking over them with a fine disregard for their contents. Annie thought she could hear pencils snapping and leftover sandwiches squishing.

'Come on, girls, get out the soccer gear and start changing,' Annie called over her shoulder, easing out into the minivan traffic.

'Sock puppet!' yelled Hailey, holding up a hand encased in a navy-blue soccer sock. 'I'm Wally Worm and I eat nothing but blueberries,' she announced in a high, distorted voice.

Annie glanced at Lydia in the rear-view mirror – then did a double-take, her mouth falling open. Her stepdaughter's eyes were glittering with excitement! *Glittering!* 'I'm Molly Worm,' Lydia cried, shoving her hand into her own sock. 'And I eat nothing but . . . chewing gum.'

Annie squeezed her eyes shut and opened them again, then glanced quickly over her shoulder. Sure enough, Lydia still had her hand in a sock, and was still talking in the squeaky tones of Molly Worm. This was a side of Lydia she'd never seen!

Alas, by the time Heather delivered Lydia back to the Keeler house later that afternoon, her playful side had disappeared. As Lydia yanked off her shin guards, Annie asked brightly, 'So, how was soccer?'

Lydia shrugged and threw her boots into the cubby-hole where her shoes were stored. 'Bad,' she said. 'Like always.'

'Would you like a snack? Some juice?'

'No.'

'We'd better take a look at your homework, then.'

'I can do it by myself.'

'Well, OK. But I'm right here if you need me.'

'I won't need you.'

In a flash of sheer genius, Annie grabbed one of Lydia's socks. She hesitated a moment then stuffed her hand into its slightly damp depths. 'I'm Molly Worm,' the sock said, 'and I just love helping out with homework!'

Lydia pulled a disgusted face. 'You're putting your hand in a sock,' she said. 'That's really gross!'

'I thought we'd have steak tonight,' Annie told Simon later as he poured himself a large tumbler of iced water. 'Something quick and simple.'

The fine lines around his blue eyes seemed more deeply etched than usual as he glanced at her over the rim of the glass. Closing his eyes, he drank deeply, without stopping to breathe, as if he hadn't had the chance to quench his thirst all day. Then he put the glass down, wiped his mouth with the back of his hand, and took a gulp of air. Not looking at her he said, 'I think I'll pass on dinner tonight. We were sampling pies at the office, and I'm stuffed.'

'Oh. Fair enough. I'll probably. . .I'll just make myself an omelette or something. We can have the steak tomorrow.'

'I should've called and let you know.' He looked genuinely contrite. 'You could have eaten with Lydia.'

'Nah. Plain pasta with grated cheese on the side isn't my favourite splurge. Never mind, I feel like something light anyway.'

He wandered off to watch TV while she made her solitary dinner. By the time a leathery omelette was on her plate, she seemed to have lost her appetite, but she took it through to the family room on a tray and sat down beside him.

He was watching a programme about a man who travelled the world eating unusual foods. 'Ah, goat's scrotum,' the man was saying, holding up a bowl of some indescribably foul-looking stew to the camera, 'a specialty here in

Uzbekistan. Mmm! Slightly ripe, and rubbery on the tongue, but meaty and delicious.'

She took a bite of her omelette, chewed, and swallowed with difficulty.

Instead of watching TV, she was watching Simon's profile in the light from the giant screen. She liked to look at him. He felt her gaze and turned to look at her with a quizzical expression. A faint stubble shadowed his strong jaw, and a tiny smile played on his lips. 'Is the omelette good?' he asked, tilting his head at the forkful of food that lay untouched on her plate.

'What do you think?' she asked. 'It's slightly ripe and rubbery on the tongue, to be honest.'

She met his eye and they both burst out laughing.

'By the way,' she told him when they'd stopped laughing, 'I forgot to mention to you – I've been invited to play tennis tomorrow.'

He raised his eyebrows. 'Really? That's great! I didn't even realise you played.'

'Oh, I haven't played in ages, but I used to pick up the racquet now and then at school,' she said nonchalantly.

He stared at her in silence for a moment. 'Well, have a good game,' he said at last. She was half convinced she saw his mouth twitching, as if he were suppressing a grin. 'I'm glad you're getting out and meeting people.'

It was only at the last minute the next morning that Annie realised she'd made a horrible mistake. She'd promised to play tennis, but she didn't have a tennis racquet. She had the outfit, all right – in fact, she had several. Tennis gear was simply so common around Norbury that no one ever batted an eyelid to see someone pushing a trolley around the supermarket in a cute little skort and top. It seemed to be the only form of skirt you could wear in town without raising eyebrows. Plus, if she decided to go jogging – which she was often on the brink of doing – then she'd have something to jog in. To complete the image, she'd even bought some blinding white tennis shoes. But no racquet.

It was as she was closing all the kitchen doors and settling Patches down in the garage with a bone in preparation for her departure for the courts that she realised she was missing this vital piece of equipment. Clearly, there was no time to run out and *buy* a racquet. In desperation, she phoned Heather.

'Yes, I think I have a racquet,' Heather said, sounding a bit surprised. 'I can probably dig one up.'

'Oh, thank God! I'll be round in five minutes to pick it up. You're a lifesaver.'

Heather had the racquet ready as Annie pulled into her driveway. 'It's quite a good one, I think,' she said as she handed it to Annie through the car window. 'An Agassi.'

'Oh, great,' said Annie, suddenly feeling horribly nervous. 'I'll look after it.'

'Have fun,' Heather called as Annie inched out onto the street, keeping her eyes open for toddlers on bikes. 'Break a leg!'

By the time she pulled into the car park of the Winterton Indoor Courts Annie was in a bit of a nervous froth. 'Calm down,' she told herself as she got out of the car. 'It's only tennis, for God's sake.'

Once inside, she went straight to the changing room and locked herself in a cubicle, rather wishing she could stay there until the hour was safely over. Coming out at last, she bumped into Nancy McKenzie, a Maple Tree Ridge resident, tying her hair back in a ponytail in front of the mirror.

'Great to have you playing with us today, Annie,' said Nancy with unnerving intensity. 'Listen, if we're partners, which is your stronger side, forehand or backhand?'

'Um . . . forehand, I suppose. But I'm about the same with the backhand. Sort of ambidextrous.'

Nancy frowned at her. 'You're a leftie?' she asked.

'Oh, no. Definitely a rightie.' Annie made a few swishing motions with her right hand. 'But sometimes my . . . my shoulder sort of . . . seizes up on me. If it does that then my shots are all over the place. I'll even miss a few. With any luck it won't happen today.'

Nancy's eyebrows rose. 'Yeah, let's hope.'

As Annie followed Nancy through a sumptuous waiting area equipped with coffee makers and easy chairs, she worked hard on breathing normally. Just keeping your breath slow and even could go a long way towards curtailing panic, she'd recently read in a magazine. Nancy opened a door and led Annie into a narrow passageway cloaked on one side by a huge, heavy curtain made of something like rubber. As they walked through this dim corridor, Annie heard the repeated slams of racquets hitting balls with unnerving ferocity. People were making load moans and groans as they smashed the ball around. Annie's mouth was as dry as dust now.

Giggle and hit, she told herself. It's nothing but giggle and hit. You'll be fine.

At last they emerged onto a blue court, beneath bright lights. Other courts were visible through immense curtains made of something like fishnet. Two women and – oddly enough – a young man in shorts were standing beside a bench on the side, fiddling with water bottles and shoe laces. 'Come on, I'll introduce you to the pro,' said Nancy.

The *pro*?

'Hey, Jacques, this is Annie. She's taking Kelly's spot for the day. Annie, this is Michelle. You know Donna, of course.'

The boy in shorts – presumably Jacques – held out his hand. Annie took it rather gingerly, aware that her palms were so wet they ought to be wrung out and hung up to dry.

'Right, ladies, let's get going,' said Jacques in an exaggerated French accent that made Annie giggle – until she realised it was real.

Everybody began to unzip their racquets. Annie did likewise. The boy wheeled a huge trolley-load of balls to the side of the court and positioned himself next to it. 'Donna and Michelle, come to the net on my side,' he called. 'Nancy and, um, Annie? Go back to the baseline. We'll warm up down the line. Nice and easy, just keep it in play.'

Baseline? Down the line? What on earth did he mean? Annie looked at Nancy who was walking towards the far end of the court. She followed.

'Why don't you take the forehand? I'm working on my backhand right now,' Nancy suggested.

'Sure,' said Annie, shuffling over to a spot Nancy seemed to be indicating with her racquet.

'Remember, down the line, two balls in play at the same time,' said Jacques, and suddenly a ball came shooting at Annie. She lunged forward and managed to get it with the handle of her racquet. It flew out of the court at a strange angle, not even making it to the net.

'OK, Annie, nice and easy,' said Jacques, shooting a ball at Nancy. Nancy hit it convincingly with the string part of the racquet, and it sailed calmly over to Kelly, who blocked it mid-air and sent it sailing back to her. They began to bat the ball between them. Darn, they made it look so easy. Annie didn't notice any giggling at all.

Donna stood at the net, obviously waiting for a shot from Annie.

'Are you ready, Annie?' called Jacques. This time the ball came more slowly, and seemed to jump up straight onto her racquet. To her delighted surprise, she managed to send it back to Donna. Donna smacked it hard, it flew back at Annie, she put out her racquet, the ball caught the wood and shot straight up into the air.

Jacques stepped up to the net, holding out a hand to stop play, and beckoned Annie.

'Do you always play with a child's racquet?' he asked in a low voice, jerking his head in the direction of Heather's Agassi.

Annie stiffened. 'No, of course not,' she said, glancing at it. 'Now you mention it, it does look a bit . . . you know, small. Good grief, I – I must have picked up my daughter's racquet in my rush.'

She shot a look at the other women. They seemed to be biting their cheeks and exchanging sly glances.

'OK,' said Jacques. 'Take mine, I'll go get another one. Meantime, just keep warming up with some mini tennis.'

Mini tennis?

The others had stepped up towards the line in the middle of the court. Annie followed suit. They began hitting a ball between the four of them. Mostly, Michelle and Donna hit it to Nancy, whose backhand didn't seem to need any improving at all. When they occasionally hit a shot in Annie's direction, she was surprised to find that she could almost always get Jacques' racquet on the ball. The results were a bit mixed, though. Sometimes the ball crashed into the rubber curtain at the back of the court. Sometimes it flew towards the ceiling. Every now and then it behaved in a more respectable way and hopped over the net towards Donna or Michelle.

Annie began to relax a little. She was clearly a lot more coordinated now than she'd been as a schoolgirl. She wasn't exactly shining, but at least she wasn't swishing at air.

Jacques arrived back with a substitute racquet, and soon had them in a new formation, Annie and Nancy up at the net, Donna and Michelle behind the baseline.

'Just block the ball, don't hit it,' he recited as he directed a shot at Annie's strings. She managed to get it back over the net quite handily without even moving a muscle. Honestly, she was beginning to enjoy herself. OK, so she'd noticed Nancy doing miniature shrugs at Michelle after some of her more deviant shots, but she was improving in such leaps and bounds that even Nancy was bound to be impressed.

And she could always put down her duff shots to the dicky shoulder she had quickly invented in the changing room.

Maybe tennis was her thing, after all. Maybe she'd get really good at it, and start playing in tournaments, and Simon would bring Lydia along to watch and learn.

'Ready, Annie?' called Jacques – and popped a ball at her.

Ready? Boy, was she ready. She swung at the ball with all her might, every muscle in her body bent on hitting it hard enough to make the thwacking sound that had eluded her so far. And to everyone's amazement her racquet caught the ball exactly right, her arm drove through the stroke exactly right, and the resulting thwack was enough to turn heads on other courts.

Delighted, she watched the ball fly low and bullet-like back over the net.

'Oooof!'

Jacques was suddenly bent double beside his trolley, clutching himself. A moment later, he dropped to his knees, and by the time Annie got over to him he was curled up in the foetal position, groaning in agony.

'Oh my God,' said Michelle. 'Bullseye.'

'So, how was the tennis?' Heather asked, catching up with her as she walked to school to pick up the girls.

Annie winced slightly. 'Um ... you know, all right. By the way, did you realise your racquet is kid-sized?'

'No way! I'm sorry – I guess I bought it for Hailey at some point. Did they crack up when they saw it?'

'A bit. But it was OK. The pro got me another racquet.'

'The pro, huh? Was he hot?'

Annie pulled a face. 'Actually, he looked like a schoolboy. But he was nice. I just hope he's not a bruiser and sweller, like you.'

'Oh, why?'

'Well, I sort of – hit him in the privates with a ball. Quite hard. They were still applying ice packs when I left.'

Heather's eyes bulged. 'You're kidding! *Ice* packs?'

'That's right. They keep them at the front desk.'

'Is this guy married?'

Annie shrugged. 'I don't know. Do you mind awfully if we don't talk about it any more?'

Heather pressed her lips together, suppressing laughter. 'Fine, no problem. So tell me, are you ready for Halloween?'

'Ready as I'll ever be.' Annie shot her a slightly puzzled look.

'God, you're ahead of me then. I still have to go buy candy.'

'Oh, right. Of course.'

'I only have about four fifty-count bags right now. You always need way more than that, don't you?'

'You do?' Fifty-count bags?

'In this town, you do. Especially on a cul-de-sac like ours. It's a perfect street for trick or treating.'

'Do you know, nobody did trick or treating much when I was growing up. It's going to be a first for me.' Annie's dad used to say that if any of the little bleeders had the cheek to ring the doorbell begging for sweets, he'd show them what for with his cricket bat. He was a mild man, her dad, but he didn't hold with yobbos going around threatening home-owners with vandalism if they didn't cough up. And that had pretty much been the attitude of all the parents in the village, as far as she could remember.

For all she knew, trick or treating might be the norm in London for little kids; she just didn't move in those circles. Henny, who lived out in the country, was her only friend with small children. Certainly, no child had ever rung the doorbell of her Islington flat on Halloween. She herself had been to the occasional nuns-and-prostitutes party in honour of the holiday, but that was about the sum of it.

'You do have a costume for Lydia, right?' Heather asked.

'Um ... not just yet. Maybe I could make her something? Cut out some holes in a sheet?'

'You don't see a whole lot of home-made costumes around here,' Heather cautioned. 'Tell you what, why don't you come round and look at Hailey's costumes? She was a purple witch last year. Lydia could be that.'

'Thanks,' said Annie humbly. 'I'd really be stuck without you.'

When Simon came home at ten o'clock that evening, he didn't even ask her about the tennis. She didn't know whether to be relieved or annoyed. Obviously, he'd totally forgotten she was scheduled to play. With little more than a distracted hello, he declined dinner (again) and closed himself up in the den, claiming he had to talk to a pie company in Australia.

Perhaps it was time she enrolled herself in some cooking lessons.

*

She wasn't going to make a habit of watching daytime TV, Annie promised herself the next day. She was just doing it this time because there was a bit of a lull in her morning, and she owed it to herself to get a broader sense of American culture.

Daytime TV was a bit of a window into the soul of a nation, she reckoned. For one thing, she'd had no idea that so much American justice was meted out over the air. Once you stumbled on Judge Judy or Judge Alex on the job (judges were obviously a casual lot over here: first names all round and not a white wig in sight) there was very little hope of being able to tear yourself away for at least half an hour. You found that you absolutely had to know whether Luella had completely vandalised Billy-Bob's Ford Escort including the custom seat covers in yellow leather – 'Ain't *nobody* got that, man,' as Billy-Bob attested – or whether, as Luella insisted, she'd confined herself to breaking the windshield. And then, of course, you had to weather out the advertising to hear what lessons Luella felt she'd learned from the exasperated knuckle-rapping that Judge Alex had given her.

Better even than the courtroom dramas were the cooking and decorating shows. She almost wished she had a tailgate party to cater for, or a clapped-out old house to refurbish, just so that she could use the foolproof recipe for five pounds of Buffalo-style chicken wings, or create a faux marble headboard using only poster-board and paint. She had no idea what happened at a tailgate party, or what poster-board was, but it all sounded like a lot more fun than sitting in an empty house.

Best of all, though, were the ads for prescription medicines; they were absolutely riveting. It almost brought tears to Annie's eyes to see the difference that medicine was making in the lives of people suffering from all kinds of diseases, from insomnia, indigestion and genital warts, to migraines, attention-deficit disorder and incontinence. One minute these people were down and out, sitting around alone in darkened rooms. Next minute they were running along beaches with their hair streaming out behind them, or drinking coffee with good-looking friends, or even fly-fishing in the sunset.

She just wished the narrator wouldn't always rattle off a list of side effects just when your eyes were misting up. Every drug under the sun, it seemed, carried a small risk of dizziness, headaches, nosebleeds, diarrhoea, blood clots, stroke, and cardiac arrest.

The most common illness in America was erectile dysfunction, judging by the volume of advertising. A bit unsettling, that. Presumably it wasn't infectious. Annie's personal favourite among the ED ads showed a very affectionate couple – identified as 'older' by a few grey strands in their hair, but otherwise well equipped with teeth, hair and the glow of youth – sitting in a romantic restaurant, holding hands over a linen tablecloth and staring into each other's eyes in the candlelight. Suddenly, rudely, a hand knocks at the plate glass window. The lovers glance out to see another youthful elderly couple peering in at them, waving madly. Chums of theirs, obviously. The romantic music fades abruptly, the friends barge into the restaurant, the lovey-dovey couple draw apart. But all is not lost, the voice-over assures viewers. Although the romantic lead has already popped a pill in expectation, apparently, of a quick consummation on the tabletop between courses, he finds himself well able to put off the action until a more convenient time. This was the special magic of the pill in question. Competing pills, Annie gathered, required the pill-taker to get on the job immediately or suffer who knew what debilitating consequences.

As the morning wore on, Annie began to feel very ignorant. She hadn't realised social anxiety was even an illness. The danger of living in a country where it was illegal to advertise prescription drugs, she could see, was that you simply had no idea of the range of new diseases out there.

Around noon Annie jumped up, turned off the TV and decided to take Patches for a walk. A vague headache and a vaguer sense of guilt told her that she'd probably had enough cultural immersion for one day.

She was clipping Patches' leash onto his collar when the phone rang.

'Annie? Annie, is that you?' Henny's voice sounded strangely shrill.

Before Annie could reply, Patches jumped up at her in his pre-walk frenzy and knocked the phone out of her hand. It crashed to the floor, the dog grabbed it gleefully, and Annie went down on hands and knees to wrestle it out of his mouth. It was a little wet when she put it back to her ear, but still in working order. Patches ran off, trailing the leash.

'Yes, it's me. Sorry about that. Bloody dog got the phone. Are you OK?'

'Yes, yes, I'm fine. But Annie ... your mum ... she's had a bit of a turn. She's in hospital.'

Time slowed down. Annie watched a speck of dust swirl about in a finger of sunlight, twinkling like a tiny star before it disappeared.

She told herself to breathe. 'A turn?' she managed to ask. 'What's a turn, for God's sake?'

'She fell down. In the kitchen, making dinner. Managed to crawl over to the phone when she came round. The ambulance people called me. Apparently my number's on her fridge door.'

'Yes, I stuck it there when I left,' said Annie. 'For emergencies. Oh God, is this an emergency?'

'To be honest, I don't really know. They're not giving me a lot of information. But I think you'd better come.'

'Of course I'll come. I'll get on a plane this afternoon if I can find a seat. Have you got a number for the hospital? Maybe they can tell me more.'

She wasn't able to get much out of the woman who picked up the phone at Guildford Hospital. 'Gladys Harleigh,' the disembodied voice said. 'Let's see now. Maternity ward, is it?'

'No, no! She's in her sixties. She fell down at home and they brought her in by ambulance. For God's sake, nobody of childbearing age is called *Gladys*!' She clapped her hand over her mouth, shocked by her own rudeness. 'Look, I'm terribly sorry! You see, Gladys Harleigh is my mum, and I'm stuck over here in America, and I don't know what on earth is going on.'

'All right, dear. You just take a deep breath. I'm looking

it up. Yes, she came in earlier today and they have her in Ward D, room 23. It says here she's stable. She had a fall, apparently.'

'Yes, yes, that's her. Does it say anything else? Like, why she fell?'

'Oh, these old folk, it could be anything, my dear. Stroke, heart attack, or maybe she slipped on a wet spot. You'd better come in and see for yourself.'

'Well *obviously* I'm going to, but did I happen to mention that I'm calling from America?'

'If I were you, I'd get on a plane, my dear.'

Annie couldn't get hold of Simon. He was either in a dead spot, or he'd turned off his phone. After the fifth attempt to get him in person, she caved in and left a message. 'Simon, bad news. My mum's in hospital. She had a fall and they don't know what the problem is. I'm trying to get on a flight to Heathrow this afternoon. I'm going to ask Heather to take Lydia. Maybe she can take Patches too, if I beg her. Anyway, please call me back as soon as you can.'

Annie managed to find a seat on an evening flight, and Heather offered to drive her to Kennedy airport. To make it to the flight in time they pulled the girls out of Miss Scofield's classroom early.

'You're going to England? Without me?' Lydia asked as they sped along Main Street towards the I-95; Annie watched as the joy of being busted out of school abruptly faded from her stepdaughter's face. 'Why can't I come too?'

'I've told you. My mum isn't well and I need to go over and look after her. It won't be for long, I'm sure.'

'Yes, but what if it is? I saw your suitcase. It's big.'

'Mrs Gibson will look after you. And so will Daddy, of course. You'll be fine, I promise.'

'But I want to go to England. Why can't I come too?'

'You can't miss school. Besides, hospitals are boring places for kids.'

'No, *school* is a boring place for kids,' Lydia countered. 'I want to come *with* you.'

'Let's not talk about this now,' Annie said, rolling her eyes at Heather. 'I've said you can't come, and I'm sorry but you'll just have to accept that.'

'I'm not dying,' her mother told her the next day from her hospital bed. 'What a terrible waste of money, rushing over here like that. On business class too, you say.'

Annie blinked hard. Her mother's face was papery white and she was festooned with drips. 'Business was all I could get at the last minute. You're not allowed to get excited, Mum. How was I supposed to know you weren't dying, anyway? Am I supposed to wait until you're safely in your coffin before I book my flight?'

Her mother chuckled. 'That would be a waste of money, too,' she said. 'Anyway, it's good to see you. What did they tell you?'

'The same as they told you, probably. They've ruled out heart attack and stroke. They can't find anything major, but they're worried about you blacking out again.'

'How long are they going to keep me flat on my back? It's enough to make anybody weak as a kitten, lying about all day.'

'Not as long as you'd think. They're going to monitor you for maybe another day, then send you home.'

'Good. I can't stand the food in these places.'

Annie slid the box of chocolates she'd bought at the airport towards her. 'Have one,' she said. 'Chocolate always cheers me up.'

'If you were going to spend the money anyway, I wish you'd bought me a book.' Her mum gave a disapproving sniff. 'The government ought to ban chocolate – it serves absolutely no practical purpose, and it costs a fortune.'

'Well, how about giving it to the nurses? It might sweeten them up.'

Her mum shrugged. 'I suppose so. Goodness, don't I sound like an old battleaxe? I'm sorry, Annie-bean. I've had a bit of a scare, to be honest. Now listen, you'll find the house keys in my bag. I want you to get back there as quick as you can to check up on things. For all I know, I've left the thermostat on full blast. Lord knows, I don't want to get back to a runaway fuel bill.'

Annie laughed out loud, giddy with relief. 'A runaway fuel bill! Right, that would be a real emergency, wouldn't it?'

But her relief was short-lived. As she was leaving the ward, a doctor pulled her aside and said, 'About your mother. She's OK for now, but her blood pressure is almost too low, and she's having problems with balance. She's going to need to be very careful in future. Another fall and she could easily break a hip. To be brutally honest, with her profile she could faint again at any time. Ideally, she should have someone around to keep an eye on her until we work out whether this was a one-off. If you can, please persuade her to stay with you for a while, just to keep tabs on her. In the long run, if the syncope recurs, it might even be time to think about some sort of assisted living.'

He hurried away before she had time to say hang on, I can't cope with any of this, I live in America.

When Annie pushed open her mother's kitchen door later that afternoon, she gasped in horror. The white floor and cabinets were dramatically daubed in blood. People in big boots had walked around in the blood and tracked it all over the linoleum. The room looked like the scene of some ghastly massacre.

She stood stock-still for a moment, stunned that nobody had seen fit to mention that her mother had experienced some kind of major haemorrhage during her so-called turn.

Shaking all over and fighting a queasy stomach, she closed the door behind her, slipped her shoes off by force of habit, and inched her way around the blood to the sink, where she found some yellow washing-up gloves and a dishcloth. No paper towels, of course, because her mother 'didn't believe in' disposable goods. Creeping towards the splatters, she took a deep breath, turned her head away, and began to mop up at arm's length.

The consistency was all wrong for blood. So was the smell.

Annie risked turning her head to look at the gruesome mess again.

She gave a sudden peal of laughter, shockingly loud in the still and deserted house.

Tomato soup! Her mother seemed to have thrown a bowl of tomato soup at the cabinet before she fainted. How on earth could she have thought it was blood, for even a moment? Good grief, she must be going mental.

Weak with relief, Annie threw down the dishcloth and went straight through the kitchen, skirting around the soup, to the phone. She hesitated a moment before picking it up.

Annie's mother saw the phone as a dangerous instrument that could lead to unnecessary and uncontrolled spending if not kept under strict quarantine. To that end, she kept it tethered to a small walnut table in the hallway in the direct path of an icy draught that blew up the back of your legs from under the front door while you talked. Furthermore, the phone was so centrally placed that anyone in the kitchen or living room could hear your every word with ease, unless you kept your voice down to a virtual whisper. When Annie was a teenager, her mother's attitude to the phone had been a terrible blight on her social life.

Calculating the time difference in her head, Annie realised that Simon might already be in bed, but she hadn't said a word to him since she got the news about her mum, and she didn't care if she woke him from the sleep of the dead. She needed to talk to him.

Minutes later, she sat on the floor, arms wrapped around her knees, staring sightlessly at her reflection in her mother's glass-fronted bookcase.

She'd let the phone ring through to her embarrassingly sing-song recorded greeting at least six times. That was enough to rouse an entire household six times over, surely. But nobody had answered the call.

Where on earth could the man *be*, this late at night?

Really, there was only one thing for it. With shaky fingers, she dialled Heather's home number.

Somebody at the Gibson house was obviously up and about, even though it must be close to midnight. After a single ring, Annie heard a click and a voice said, 'Yes?'

'Um . . . Heather?'

'No, it's Rob.'

Oh dear. Bit of a clanger. What man wanted to hear that he could be mistaken for his wife on the phone? 'Sorry,' she muttered, 'bad line. It's Annie calling from England. Um . . . is Heather asleep?'

'Not that I know of. I think she's making lunch.'

'Oh, it's *lunch* time? Thank God, thank God! I thought it was the middle of the night. I was wondering where on earth Simon could possibly be at this hour. I've got it all backwards! What an idiot. Look, can I speak to Heather?'

'Hang on, I'll give her the phone.'

Annie heard a shuffling sound as Rob walked to the kitchen with the cordless phone to find his wife. Then his muffled voice said, 'It's Annie Keeler. She sounds a little spacey.' Moments later, Heather was on the line. 'Annie! How is everything? Is your mom OK?'

'Yes, thank God. She seems fine. How's Lydia?'

'She and Hailey passed out at around ten last night. It was cute – their first sleepover.'

'Around *ten*? Um, where was Simon?'

'He called in from the office. He had some huge meeting or other. It went on late. We decided he'd just leave Lydia here rather than come in and drag her home at midnight.'

'So . . . how did he sound?'

'Tired. Worried about you. I can't believe he didn't call you today.'

Heather didn't sound too bright and bushy-tailed herself, Annie thought but didn't say.

'Well, maybe he did. My mobile doesn't work over here, and my mum doesn't have voicemail. I'll try him on his BlackBerry again, I suppose.'

'All right. He said he'd make an effort to get home early today so that Lydia could sleep in her own bed. I told him she's welcome to stay here.'

Again, Annie thought she heard strain in Heather's voice. 'Well, I hope it won't come to that,' she said. 'Thank you so, so much. For everything! I'll pay you back some day. I promise.'

After she'd hung up on Heather, Annie hesitated a moment and then dialled Simon's mobile number. Her mother would go through the roof when she saw the phone bill, but that couldn't be helped.

She'd tried him so many times since she left Norbury without managing to get through that she was momentarily speechless when he picked up after just one ring.

'Hello, Annie? Finally! What's going on? Are you OK? How's your mum?'

He sounded so normal that Annie couldn't help herself. She started making the 'ack-acking' noise that indicates to the person on the other end of a line that you're either choking on a chicken bone or trying not to sob.

'Hey, Annie? Are you still there? Oh God, how bad is it? Should I get on a plane?'

Annie managed to bring her vocal cords and tear ducts

under control. 'No, no. I'm sorry. Mum's fine, absolutely fine. They're discharging her tomorrow. I'm just a bit worried because the doctor said she ought to be watched very carefully for a while, and I'm not sure how ... I mean, I wonder if I should start advertising for someone to come in and look after her, or something? They're worried about her passing out again, I think. Something to do with her inner ear, plus she could break a hip if she has another fall. She's not fit to be alone. This is when I wish to God I wasn't an only child.'

'Annie, can she travel?'

'Travel?'

'Fly. Is she up to it? Because if she is, bring her here. We'll look after her here.'

'Really?'

'Of course! It's the only logical thing to do. Well – unless you don't want her to come?'

'Good grief! You're a genius! If I can force her onto that plane, she's coming! God, Simon, I can't believe I didn't even *think* of it.'

'Well, people don't think straight in an emergency. Ask the doctors when she can fly. She can sleep in the third spare room, downstairs. I knew we'd find a use for it one day.'

Annie was in her pyjamas, about to brush her teeth and turn in for the night after eating a desultory meal of toast and Marmite in front of the space heater in the living room, when the doorbell rang.

When she peered through her mother's little spy-glass, she saw the faces of Henny and Sarah, distorted so that their foreheads looked huge.

She threw open the door and both women rushed at her with open arms. A little scuffle ensued, during which Henny managed to air-kiss Annie's left cheek, but Sarah bested her by getting Annie in a bear hug and pounding her on the back.

'God, it's good to see you,' Sarah said over her shoulder. 'Both of us have been trying to reach you all day. In the end, I just got on the train from London. Henny picked me up and we came over to see for ourselves. When in God's name is Auntie Gladys going to get an answering machine? And why have you turned off your mobile phone? Wow, look at your hair!'

Annie drew back from the hug, grinning all over her face. 'This is so nice,' she said. 'I was feeling all lonely and sorry for myself. I've tried to get through to you lot, too, but you're never home, Henny. And Sarah, I didn't know your work number. As for my mobile, it seems to have died on me. No Service, it keeps telling me. I don't think it likes all this roaming around.'

'The hospital says your mum's doing really well,' Henny said. Dressed in baggy jeans and a long-sleeved T-shirt, her wavy blonde hair scraped back in a messy ponytail, Annie's oldest friend still managed to look glamorous despite the wear and tear of bringing up three unusually bouncy children. 'Thank God! I can't tell you how panicked I was when they rang me up. And they wouldn't let me see her yesterday, because I'm not family.'

Annie shook her head. 'What a nightmare for you, Hen. But thank God it wasn't serious. They're discharging her tomorrow, you know.' By now, they were in the chilly living room and Henny threw herself down on the sofa as if exhausted. Sarah took off her military-looking coat and draped it over the back of a chair, but within moments she was shrugging it back on again.

'It's like a morgue in here. Is the heating on the blink?' she asked.

Annie laughed. 'Mum asked me to turn the thermostat down. She was dead worried about the cost of heating the place with nobody in it. You know how she is about waste.'

'*You're* in it, mate,' Sarah said, nodding her red head emphatically. 'Here, I'll go and crank it up a bit. I mean, Auntie Gladys always kept the place cold, but this is ridiculous. I'll put the kettle on, too.'

'So,' said Henny. 'Look at you, all blonde.'

Annie patted at her hair. 'Yeah, I decided to go native,' she said. 'I'm letting it grow out, though – I think it was a mistake. Things are pretty good, otherwise.'

'Oh, don't grow it out. I like it! Tell me, have you figured out what to give Lydia for packed lunch?'

Annie grimaced. 'Still working on that one. She seems to live on air and lemonade.'

'But she's happy? And you're happy?'

Annie hesitated a moment. 'Oh yes,' she said. 'We're happy. Of course, it's not like Simon and I are still on honeymoon. It's not that kind of crazy happiness. We have a ton of, you know, daily things that come up. Little arguments and stuff. But that's so normal in a marriage, isn't it?'

Henny raised her eyebrows. 'What kind of arguments?'

'Oh, just ... stuff. Like I might decide to do something

with Lydia, and he might not think it's the right thing for her. That sort of thing.'

Henny was still frowning. 'Well, I suppose it's a little different if you start off with a kid already in the mix.'

Sarah came into the room with a tray and set it down heavily on the coffee table. 'I found oatcakes, water biscuits, and a tiny wedge of old Cheddar,' she said. 'It's going to be a feast!'

As they settled down to this spartan fare, Sarah suddenly looked over at Annie, winked salaciously, and asked, 'So, do you see much of the sexy cowboy bloke? He's a dead good kisser. You should try him some time.'

'Sarah!' Annie and Henny chorused in protest.

'Crikey, I forgot for a moment. You're married! Let's pretend I didn't say that.'

After Henny and Sarah had left that evening, Annie had a phone call from Simon. 'Annie, can I ask you a huge favour?' He sounded strangely tentative.

'Of course.'

'Can you ... can you possibly visit Lydia's grandparents?'

'Um, yes, sure, why not. I'd like to see your mum again. Would I go up by train? I wouldn't like to leave my mum for too long.'

'I don't mean Mum and Dad. I mean Beth's people. Wilma's been in touch. She knows you're over there and ... well, she says she'd like to meet you.'

Beth's parents had been invited to Annie and Simon's low-key wedding, but at the last minute they had decided not to come.

'Really? Gosh. I wonder why. OK, well, if you think I *should*.'

'I think you should,' he said.

With a sense of dread, Annie set off the next morning in her mother's Renault 5, listening to Classic FM and trying to navigate from an ancient map book that showed roads that didn't exist any more.

Wilma and Don Forsythe lived in a village about twelve miles south of Oxford – some sixty miles from Gladys's house as the crow flew, but quite a bit further by road. By the time Annie pulled up in front of their house – a substantial two-storey brick building with a green door – she was clammy with nerves. She thought she'd sit in the car a bit, just to give herself a break from the driving before rushing headlong into another stressful situation, but the green door opened almost the moment the engine died, and a woman stepped out onto the gravel.

At a glance, Annie could tell that this was Beth's mother. She bore a striking resemblance to the slender, blonde woman Annie had seen in Simon's photo albums. Wilma Forsythe was tall and slightly stooped, with sharp elbows and rather prominent teeth, but her eyes were just like Beth's – piercing blue and fringed with thick blonde lashes.

She was dressed with old-fashioned precision in a navy-blue woollen suit and flat shoes of the kind that Annie believed were called brogues.

As Annie straightened up out of the car, slightly flustered in her very casual jeans and woolly jumper, the woman held out her hand and gave her a firm handshake. 'Annie, we are so pleased you could come.' She had a slight foreign accent,

Annie noted. 'Come and meet my husband. He was having a little nap, but no doubt he is now awake.'

Annie followed her into the house, which was very dim owing to yards of heavy fabric at every window. In the living room they found Don Forsythe dozing in an armchair. He woke with a start and stared rather wild-eyed at the stranger in the room, while Wilma explained to him with great patience that this was the guest they'd been expecting.

'I have prepared a light lunch,' Wilma told Annie when Don had calmed down a bit. 'We have only to heat the soup and slice the baguette.'

'Very nice,' Annie replied with a placatory smile. This woman, with her unshakeable poise and steady decorum, made her feel wrong-footed, somehow. 'My mum is a big one for soup.'

The woman inclined her head graciously. 'Come, sit down,' she invited, gesturing at the kitchen table. 'You know, of course, that for some time I have looked forward to speaking with you.'

Annie gulped. 'Really?'

'But of course! I was disappointed when Don's health made it impossible to come to your wedding. It has been a matter of great interest to me, to converse with the woman who now has the care of my grandchild.'

'Oh. Right.'

'Lydia is prospering, I hope? Simon tells me he detects positive signs of spiritual healing since she went to America.'

'Um, oh yes. She's definitely prospering.'

Wilma ladled out soup, threw in some sprigs from a herb growing on her window sill, and crumbled goat's cheese into the bowls.

Then she gave Annie a smile. 'You have come a long way for a bowl of soup. I hope you will enjoy it.'

While they ate, they talked about the weather, the sad state of the global economy, and the kinds of plants that grew in Connecticut. After Wilma had cleared away their plates, she set a tray for Don and took it through to his chair. Then she came back, put the kettle on, sat down, and looked Annie in the eye.

'I will say only this, and then be done,' she said solemnly. 'Lydia has had much sadness to bear in her short life. She is not, how would you say, a charming child. Not these days. But she has need of a happy home.'

Annie felt her throat constrict. She put out a hand. 'Mrs Forsythe, I mean Wilma, I want you to know that I plan to do my very best for Lyddie. She's safe with me.'

Wilma nodded briskly. 'I think you will,' she said. 'I have looked in your eyes, and I think you will.'

Chapter Nine

'I can walk, thank you,' Gladys Harleigh told the uniformed woman who was unfolding a wheelchair at the ticketing booth.

'Shhh, Mum,' Annie whispered. 'I'm counting on jumping all the queues with this thing. There's even a special fast track through security.'

Gladys's face lit up. 'Oh, I see. Good thinking.' Annie's mum had never asked for help in her life, and she wasn't about to start, even if she had a sore back and was covered in bruises. But she was always game to beat the system.

When they were ushered onto the plane, first in line with other wheelchair-bound travellers and a huddle of unhappy-looking parents of small children, Gladys was indignant to find that they were travelling first class.

'Simon booked the tickets,' Annie said in self-defence. 'I had nothing to do with it.'

'But it's outrageous! These seats cost as much as some people's annual salary!' She turned to an attendant. 'Excuse me, young lady, is there any way you can downgrade us to the economy section? We'd like to get refunds on these seats, if it's not too much trouble.'

The air hostess, eyes wide, shook her head. 'I'm sorry, madam,' she said. 'The seats are purchased now. It's too late to make any changes.'

'Mum! Relax,' Annie hissed in her ear. 'I'm pretty sure Simon used air miles to upgrade us. He travels so much for work that he has a ton. He's always trying to think of ways to use them up before they expire.'

'Really?'

'Really.'

'Well, all right then. I must say, it helps my back if I can put my feet up.'

Annie held her mother's elbow as she lowered herself into the seat, pretending not to notice her grimace of pain.

Simon hadn't been able to use his air miles. She knew that for a fact. They were travelling during some sort of black-out period. Despite the exorbitant price of these seats, he'd insisted that someone fresh out of a hospital bed couldn't travel with her knees in close proximity to her chin.

She must just remember to warn him not to spill the beans.

Simon was waiting at the airport, a tall, straight figure in a black trenchcoat, standing head and shoulders above the limo drivers with their scrawled handheld signs. His blue eyes crinkled as he smiled straight at her from across the room. They kissed briefly, aware of Gladys in her wheelchair, her string bag – bulging with newspapers, an umbrella, a scarf, cough sweets, and various oddments off the airline meal tray – balanced precariously on her lap.

Simon bent down to kiss his mother-in-law's powdery

cheek. 'Gladys, good to see you,' he said. 'The one silver lining in this whole business is that it got you to come and visit us.'

Annie watched her mother glow with pleasure. 'Well, I'd have come before if I'd been invited,' she said with a fake offended sniff. 'But a couple of newly-weds like you? No surprise you weren't begging me to come over.'

'Come on, you know we've been holding a room for you,' Simon replied. 'The day we looked at the house, Annie stuck her head into the downstairs bedroom and said, "This is Mum's room." You've been putting us off ever since we got here – admit it.'

He was helping her out of the wheelchair now, since the attendant seemed eager to be off.

She batted his hands away flirtatiously. 'Oh, don't fuss,' she said. 'Honestly. You'd think I was a complete invalid. Three days ago I was up a ladder pruning my standard wisteria.'

But in the end she allowed him to support her out into the mild day, across the busy road to the car park, while Annie brought up the rear, pushing the trolley. Watching them from behind – the wide-shouldered, upright figure modifying his long gait to accommodate his small, stooped companion – Annie's heart swelled again with gratitude. This was what it meant to be part of a family. You didn't have to shoulder your burdens alone.

She was brought down to earth with a rude shock a little later when she went to pick Lydia up from school. By then, her helpmeet was long gone (back into the city on the two-ten train) and she was waiting with Heather, who had come over to the house in the early afternoon to see if everything was all right, like the tried and trusted friend she had become.

As Lydia came out of the school building, frail body buckling under her large backpack, Annie smiled and waved – but couldn't catch her eye.

'She's been a bit quiet the last couple of days,' Heather had warned as they walked to school together, Annie hanging onto Patches' leash for dear life.

'Quiet?'

'OK, I didn't want to worry you, so I never said anything ... but she, um, she stopped talking a day or so after you left.'

'Stopped – talking? At school, you mean? She's always been quiet at school.'

'No, not just at school. At our house too.'

'Oh, she probably felt shy with you. Just as long as she was talking to Hailey ...'

'Sorry, nope, she wasn't even talking to Hailey. The only time she'd say a word was when she was over at your place throwing a ball for the dog.'

'But she was speaking to *Simon*, right?'

While Annie was in England, Lydia had spent her afternoons with the Gibsons, but Simon had made a superhuman effort to come home from work at around six so that she could spend the evenings and nights in her own home. Since the weather had been good, Patches had been able to stay at home for the most part, out in the backyard, restrained from wandering off by the new underground electric fence they'd had installed in the nick of time.

Heather shrugged. 'I don't know. You'll have to ask him. I do know he tried to take her trick or treating on Halloween, but she wouldn't go. Oh, and your house was tee-peed because he couldn't find the candy.'

'Shit. There wasn't any candy. I forgot to get it. What's tee-peed, anyway?'

'Toilet-papered. But Rob came over with a ladder and helped Simon get it down from the trees.'

Annie noticed for the first time that the normally vivacious Heather looked strained and subdued.

'Oh God, this has been a real trial for you,' she said with a guilty grimace, 'and all you got out of it was a bottle of perfume and a silk scarf from Duty Free. But I'll make it up to you somehow. I promise.'

But Heather shook her head and gave Annie's hand a quick squeeze. 'Don't get me wrong, Lydia was no trouble at *all*,' she said. 'I hardly even knew she was in the house. I've never known a kid who makes less of a rumpus. Sure, Hailey was a little bent out of shape when Lydia wouldn't play, but she understood when I explained that Lydia was probably just sad and scared. She was OK with it.'

Sad and scared. Yes, that sounded about right. Annie blinked quickly. She'd had her own sad and scared moments since that phone call from Henny.

'Anyway, I owed you one – remember?' Heather added. 'You took care of Pompom for me when you barely even knew me.'

'That's right – I did, didn't I? But then you got me the riding lessons.'

'Yes, but that doesn't count.'

'Well – OK. We'll call it even.'

Touched to hear that Lydia had missed her, Annie half expected her stepdaughter to come running out of the school building at full tilt, hair streaming out behind her and eyes full of happy tears, bent on throwing her arms around her stepmother in joyful reunion. But Lydia came out slowly, dragging her feet, eyes downcast, body ominously slumped, hair hanging limply down her back.

'Lydia, over here!' Annie called, thinking maybe she hadn't seen her. 'Here! Here!' Lydia (and most of the other kids pouring out of the building) finally looked at her.

Annie recoiled.

The resentment in Lydia's eyes could have stripped paint off walls, withered grapes on the vine, curdled milk in cows' udders.

It was a relief when the child dropped her eyes and walked over to greet Patches, who was as ecstatic to see her after six short hours of separation as he'd been to see Annie after six whole days.

Annie was beginning to think that people could learn a thing or two from dogs. Joyfulness, for example. Loyalty. Gusto. The ability not to bear grudges.

The short walk home was mostly silent, Lydia ignoring everybody, Hailey running ahead, Annie and Heather raising eyebrows at each other and shrugging.

Gladys was stationed at the sink when Annie and Lydia came into the house through the kitchen door. The old woman turned around stiffly, stripping off the washing-up gloves and holding her arms out. 'So, *there* you are, Lydia, goodness you've ...'

Lydia didn't even stop. She shrugged out of her backpack and jacket simultaneously, dropped them on the floor, kicked her shoes off without breaking her stride, and ran out of the kitchen. Annie and her mother stared at each other as they heard the child's feet pounding up the stairs, and then the distant slam of her bedroom door.

Gladys's eyebrows met above her nose. 'Don't tell me you're letting that child pick up American manners?'

Now, Annie hadn't minded when Gladys gazed around their minivan and said, 'Look at this *enormous* car! So these days a family of three needs, let me see, one, two, three ... *seven* seats?' Her mother knew nothing about car-pooling, after all.

Admittedly, when Gladys stood in the driveway looking up at their house and said, 'Oh, for heaven's sake! Look at the *size* of this place,' she'd begun to feel a prickle of annoyance.

But her own vehemence took her by surprise when Gladys piped up about Lydia's lack of etiquette.

'For God's sake, Mum. Give her a break. She's seven years old!'

Looking at her mother's startled face, she felt immediately contrite. 'I'm sorry, Mum. Turns out I'm a bit overprotective. Anyway, you're supposed to be in bed, aren't you? So for heaven's sake, leave the stuff in the sink and go and lie down. Please?'

Gladys gave one of her mock-offended sniffs and said, 'Well, it seems I was able to drum some manners into *you*, at any rate.'

*

Annie knocked steadily on Lydia's door for about five minutes before a voice burst out, 'Go away. I don't want to talk to you.'

'Rubbish,' said Annie. 'Of course you want to talk to me. I have a present for you.'

'I don't want your stupid presents.'

'Fair enough. I'll give it to Hailey. She likes horses too.'

A silence followed. Annie waited. She was just about to turn away when she heard the sound of feet moving over the floorboards. A moment later, Lydia's door opened a crack.

'All right, what did you get me?'

'You can come to my room and look.'

Lydia paused a moment, weighing the pros and cons. Then she sighed and inched out of her room, arms crossed over her chest.

Annie turned and walked to the master bedroom, her ears on stalks. She was just able to make out the shuffling sound of Lydia's socks.

Her suitcase was on the bed, half unpacked.

Lydia came reluctantly into the room. She was obviously finding it hard to maintain her air of bitter hostility alongside her eagerness to see what horse-related treasure Annie might have brought her.

'Dig around under the clothes,' Annie suggested.

Lydia approached the suitcase slowly and stood staring into it, her nose slightly wrinkled as if she smelled something unpleasant. But she could only hold the pose for a second or two. Soon, she was up to her elbows among Annie's jeans and T-shirts, bringing stray objects up for Annie's inspection. 'No, not that, that's my make-up bag. Not that, not that ... Ah, yes! You've found it.'

Lydia was holding an object wrapped in newspaper.

'Be careful,' Annie said, 'it's breakable.'

Lydia put it down on the bed and began to unwrap it, throwing crumpled pieces of paper over her shoulder with abandon. Patches jumped up from his basket in the corner and began tearing the paper to shreds. Annie didn't try to stop him.

At last, the present was revealed.

It was a ceramic Thelwell pony, comically rounded and sway-backed, with a whimsical expression in its eyes, and a wild, curling mane.

Lydia held it tight.

'Do you like it?' Annie asked.

Lydia nodded.

'Good.'

Lydia ran her fingers over the pony's mane. 'You missed the last soccer game,' she said out of the blue. 'And you weren't here for Halloween.'

'No, I'm sorry. I wish I could've been here. Did you score a goal?'

'I'll never score a goal. Everybody knows that.'

Annie gulped. 'You might, if you stick with it. You're getting better every time you go out. Do you know, I've never been trick or treating before?'

'I hate Halloween.'

'You do?'

'Duh! Of *course* I do. Stupid, dumb holiday. Who cares

about dead people and ghosts and skeletons! And – and I hate you too! You're not my mother. You can keep your stupid, ugly *pony*.'

So saying, she threw the little china horse at the floor where it smashed into several pieces. She didn't wait to see the damage, but ran out of the room, slamming the door behind her – much to the dismay of Patches, who had jumped up to run after her, confident that this was the start of some energetic new game.

Annie stood still a moment. Then she bent down to pick up the pieces of the pony. Perhaps she'd be able to glue them together. Moving too quickly, she managed to jab her finger straight onto the sharp end of a shard.

Annie watched the blood bubble up, then put it into her mouth and sucked it. 'Stupid, dumb *idiot*,' she said to herself, and felt almost triumphant to have made herself cry.

When Simon came home that evening, everybody was in bed, even Annie. Yes, it was only eight p.m., but Annie and her mother had lived through a day five hours longer than any day had a right to be – six hours of which had been spent on an aeroplane. What was more, they'd set out from a place where it was now one o'clock in the morning.

Nevertheless, Annie managed to raise her head and rasp, 'Why didn't you tell me Lydia was acting up?'

Simon, bundling shirts and his suit into a dry-cleaning bag, glanced up in surprise. 'Hey! You're awake!'

'Yes, I'm awake.' Annie sat up, rubbing her eyes. 'So why didn't you tell me?'

Simon shrugged. 'There wasn't much point, was there?

Nothing you could've done. Besides, you had enough on your hands.'

'Well, yes, but next time I'd like to be kept in the picture. I know nobody wanted to worry me because of Mum, but it was a shock to come home and find Lydia so ... so *angry* with me.' She was trying to sound calm, but she couldn't prevent a little wobble from creeping into her voice.

Simon dropped the dry-cleaning bag and came over to the bed. 'What happened?' he demanded.

Annie shrugged. 'Oh, nothing really.' She suddenly found herself reluctant to tell him about Lydia smashing the Thelwell pony. Just as he'd said earlier, there wasn't much point. 'It's OK. I'm just tired. We'll all feel better tomorrow.'

He bent down and kissed her chastely on the temple. 'You're right,' he said. 'Get some sleep.'

Annie took perverse pleasure in the impeccable manners of her new American friends as they went over to her mother's chair in ones and twos to introduce themselves, ask after her health, and tell her what a darling accent she had. Annie didn't think the ladies of the Women's Institute in Leatherhead could have outdone them.

They were at the home of Donna Knopf, who hosted an annual pre-festive-season coffee morning in early November. 'I'm sorry, I can't come,' Annie had said when Donna phoned to invite her. 'I have my mum over from England.'

'Oh, that's so cool. Bring her along too,' Donna insisted. 'I know everybody would just *love* to meet her.'

And sure enough, the ladies of Maple Tree Ridge all

behaved as if they'd been waiting their entire lives to meet an old-age pensioner from Surrey with firm opinions about the recycling of yoghurt cartons, jam jars and tea bags.

'You see, during the war,' Gladys told a rapt circle of admirers, 'we didn't throw a single thing away. Not a single thing. We found a use for everything that came into the house, and what was more, we bought almost nothing.' She shook her head sorrowfully. 'I'm telling you, there was no wastage back then. Not like you lot with your pumpkins. People would queue up for hours just to get their hands on one measly orange; fruit was that rare.'

'Good times,' Heather said to Annie out of the side of her mouth.

Annie laughed. 'Mum wasn't born until *after* the war,' she whispered back. 'But she likes to think she lived through it. Mind you, I think the rationing afterwards was pretty bad, too. Scarred the nation for a couple of generations. There are still people with entire garden sheds full of yoghurt cartons and jam jars.'

They both giggled.

But when Heather stopped laughing her face fell into haggard lines, and Annie couldn't help thinking, as she had so often recently, that Heather seemed distracted and vague.

'Heather – are you OK?' she asked.

Heather frowned and shot a furtive look around the room. 'Sure, I'm OK. How about you? How are things with Lydia? Looks like she's talking again, at least.'

Lydia was talking, all right – to Hailey, to Simon, to Gladys, even once or twice to her teacher, or so Annie heard. Just not to Annie herself.

Annie shrugged. 'Oh, she's fine.' She didn't feel like discussing Lydia, not in the middle of Donna Knopf's pre-festive season coffee.

The truth was, Lydia was behaving as if she wished Annie would simply disappear out of her life. If Annie entered a room, she walked out. If she asked her a question, she shrugged. If Annie tried to hug her, she held herself still and stiff as if waiting for the ordeal to be over.

'Do you need help with that?' Annie asked later that same day as Lydia pulled her homework folder out of her backpack.

Lydia shook her head as she spread her papers out on the kitchen table.

'What have you got there?' Gladys asked. 'I can probably help, as long as it's not fractions. I can't remember those for the life of me.'

'What are fractions?' Lydia asked.

'Halves and quarters and things.'

'Oh no, we haven't done those yet. It's spelling and word problems.'

Gladys hobbled to the table and lowered herself into a chair. 'Spelling,' she said. 'Annie was always good at spelling. I'll test you on the words, shall I?'

Lydia hesitated a moment. Then, 'OK,' she said. 'This is the list. I never do the bonus words at the bottom.'

'What's a bonus word?'

'Oh, it's just an extra word. You can get more than twenty out of twenty if you know your bonus words. But who needs more than twenty out of twenty?'

'Young lady, if there's one thing in life you've got to do

it's the extra things. If I'm helping you, you'll do the bonus words.'

Annie steeled herself. But Lydia didn't snatch the list out of Gladys's hands, or get up and storm out of the room. She simply sat very still for a moment, then shrugged and said, '*OK*, but it still seems kinda dumb to me.'

'Dumb means unable to speak,' said Gladys.

'No, it doesn't. It means stupid.' Lydia looked a little unsure as she said this.

'Do you have such a thing as a dictionary?' Gladys asked. 'We'll look it up.'

'My pocket *Oxford* is upstairs in the den,' Annie said. 'I'll get it, if you like.'

Gladys nodded briskly. 'That's a good idea.'

When Annie came back into the room with the book, she stood at the door watching the two of them for a moment. Neither of them knew she was there. Gladys was calling out words in her clipped, imperious accent, and Lydia was bent over her piece of paper, brows together, tongue between her teeth. Gladys peered at Lydia's paper and reached out to pat her hand.

'Well done,' she said.

Lydia looked up at Gladys and giggled. 'It's easy when you say the words 'cos I can hear all the letters. Except the r's. You don't say your r's.'

Annie felt a terrible pang, like heartburn only worse. Her mother did this so well. It was beautiful to see – the grey head next to the blonde one, bent together over the books. Gladys was such a natural. By contrast, Annie was a pitiful excuse for a mother figure. Anybody could see that.

Annie put the dictionary on the counter and walked soundlessly away.

'Isn't that a bit of a skimpy outfit?' Gladys asked one morning when Annie came down to the kitchen dressed for the first of her beginner tennis clinics. Tennis, Annie had decided, was definitely a lesser evil than either bridge or riding. 'You're not a teenager any more, you know. And won't you be cold?'

'I'm playing indoors, Mum,' Annie said, filling a plastic water bottle up at the fridge. 'The place is heated. If I went in a tracksuit, I'd be sweltering in five minutes.'

'I can't get over this whole tennis lark, I must say.' Gladys was standing beside the stove, boiling up Annie's kitchen cloths. (No matter how Annie begged, she simply wouldn't sit still and do nothing.) Gladys's sense of hygiene had intrigued Annie for years. It was a creed of hers that kitchen cloths needed regular boiling, but she couldn't see the point of dirtying two separate boards to chop up salad greens and raw chicken.

'I wish you wouldn't do that, Mum,' said Annie.

Gladys swirled the cloths with a fork. 'You were never any good at tennis at school,' she mused.

'It's never too late to learn something new.'

'Oh yes, it jolly well is. I don't know how to swim, and I never will. You can't teach an old dog new tricks.'

Patches, in the corner, thumped his tail. He thought his other name was 'dog'.

'Mum, people here think nothing of learning a new sport in their thirties. They do it all the time! That's one of the things I like about America. People really believe it's possible to change and improve.'

'Oh yes, I know all about that,' said Gladys darkly. 'Dale Carnegie. Oprah what's-her-name. But the truth is, *nobody* can make a silk purse out of a sow's ear.'

Annie took a deep breath. 'So anyway, Mum, I thought you could come along to the courts with me. I mean, if you're not feeling too stiff and sore? Maybe bring a book to read. They have comfortable sofas and you can even make yourself a cup of tea. There's an urn and everything.'

Although Gladys liked to play the curmudgeon, she was quite willing to try new things and visit new places. When they stepped into the club's reception area, expensively decorated in shades of chocolate brown and pink, Gladys lowered herself into a squishy armchair and looked around her with real pleasure.

Nervous, Annie found herself missing every second ball the pro hit at her. 'Sorry,' she kept shouting across the net. Eventually the pro beckoned her to the net.

'Don't move your racquet when I hit a ball to you,' he murmured. 'Just hold still. My aim is good.'

After that, things went better. Now and then, she even managed to hit a ball with reverberating force. Every few minutes, she found herself glancing through the plate glass window to see if her mother was paying attention. 'This is pathetic,' she muttered to one of the other women in the clinic. 'I'm in a tennis lesson and my mum's out there watching, so I've gone all butterfingers. I feel about ten years old again.'

On the drive home, Gladys surprised her by saying, 'You

looked very good out there, Annie. Never knew you could thump the ball like that.'

Annie glowed with simple pride.

When they arrived back, Annie found a message on her phone from Miss Scofield, Lydia's teacher. Her heart pumping with alarm, she dialled the school's number, wondering whether Lydia had been taken ill or perhaps fallen off the giant plastic 'spider' in the playground. That spider had always looked lethal, to her.

To her relief, she got through to the teacher directly. 'Oh no,' trilled Miss Scofield. 'Nothing's wrong. I just wanted to share something with you. We're all so proud of Lydia. She did it!'

'Um, did what?'

'You know – her class presentation.'

'Right, of course. The class presentation.' What class presentation? She'd never heard of it until this minute.

'She did so well! She said she'd been practising with her grandma.'

'Um, yes, that's right. My mum's been helping her a bit with her homework.'

'Well, your mom should be proud! Lydia did a fan-*tabulous* job! We gave her a standing ovation. Most of her classmates have never even heard her voice before, and she blew them away with this amazing speech about how dolphins communicate! I had tears in my eyes.'

Annie was delighted. She really was. This was a huge breakthrough for Lydia. Huge. And she wasn't small-minded enough to wish that she'd been the one coaching Lydia for her big moment. Of *course*, she wasn't. She was very grateful to her mum, very grateful indeed.

But she did wonder why Gladys had never let slip a single nugget of information about the whole project, from start to finish. Her mum, perhaps noticing an odd look in Annie's eyes, was quick to explain. 'We wanted to surprise you,' she said. 'And I thought Lyddie would do better without the pressure, to be frank. Even her teacher didn't know she was going to do it – not until the last minute.'

When Simon heard the news, he said he'd come home early and take them all out to dinner to celebrate. They went to Lydia's favourite restaurant, a local hibachi grill. Annie's grin was just as big as anybody else's when they all raised their glasses for a toast. Perhaps it faltered just a little when Simon said, 'Here's to you, Gladys, fantastic job with Lydia! And Lydia, here's to dolphins – and speaking up in class!' But she didn't think anybody noticed, because nobody was paying any attention to her.

Monday started innocuously enough with a visit to Costco. Annie didn't really need to go to Costco, but she was always looking for an outing for Gladys, who was constitutionally incapable of lolling about and doing nothing. That very morning, Annie had been forced to manhandle her away from Lydia's dressing table, which she had taken it upon herself to reorganise – even though, by the look on her face, all that stooping was pretty painful.

Besides, some inner devil kept urging Annie to take her mother to the giant warehouse store, just to goad her.

Back in Surrey, Gladys seldom ventured out of her own

village to go shopping. She was quite happy to patronise the local butcher, baker and candlestick maker, even though they were ruinously expensive. Since she didn't do any comparison shopping, and had a deep mistrust of mass-produced foods, she wasn't aware of how very extravagant her boutique shopping habits were. The concept of buying in bulk was completely foreign to her. This wasn't surprising, really. Her fridge was slightly smaller than Annie's cool box. Besides, grocery shopping provided a framework for her daily life.

Annie herself had been appalled when Heather first took her to Costco. In her flat in London, she'd never had much in her fridge beyond a pint of milk, an apple and a carton of leftover curry. Looking around in disbelief at the giant vats of mayonnaise and dill pickles, she had vowed to Heather that she would never shop at such a place, not if she suddenly found herself catering for an army. But mere days later, she was back, seduced by Heather's claim that one trip to Costco kept her family in 'bath tissue' for three to six months, depending. (Depending on what, she didn't like to ask.)

So she paid her joining fee, was issued with a card, and began her monthly bulk-buying pilgrimages. After her very first trip, she was a convert. How could she not be, when she'd found a revolving wooden stand housing twenty – yes, twenty! – pairs of scissors, each of which cut paper in a different pattern?

She wasn't disappointed by her mother's reaction to the place. As they walked in, Gladys fell silent. She remained silent as they pushed their super-sized shopping trolley past rows of digital cameras and monstrous flat-screen TVs. The silence persisted as they wheeled past tables piled high with leather jackets, cashmere sweaters and waffle-weave spa robes. The food department, with its three-pound cartons of cherries, forty-eight-count boxes of brownies and six-pound trays of minced sirloin, didn't elicit a single remark. Gladys had nothing to say as they passed beneath a garden shed, suspended from the ceiling above flat-packed boxes that you could load into your trolley in case the hanging shed caught your eye and you thought, 'what the heck, let's have one of those'. She didn't even comment when Annie showed her a bag of sixty frozen waffles.

It was the chewing gum that finally undid her. She stood in front of the towering display in dumbstruck wonder, then burst out, 'Who in God's name buys fifteen packs of spearmint gum at one time? I mean, that must be more than two hundred pieces of gum!'

'I don't know,' said Annie, 'but I know who buys those giant bags of pigs' ears. I do – for Patches.'

Gladys shook her head. 'I wouldn't have the heart to get a single thing from this place,' she said. 'I mean, look at that bottle of shampoo. I don't think I'd be able to lift it. And even if I could, I'm not sure I'd live long enough to get halfway through it.'

'Well, Mum,' said Annie a little defensively; she had that very same bottle of shampoo in her bathroom, 'most people do wash their hair every day, nowadays.'

Gladys rolled her eyes. 'I don't know. This modern mania about daily showering and clothes washing. Sign of an overly affluent society. A bath every third day is more than adequate unless you're working out in a potato field, and only *underwear* needs to be washed after every wear.'

'Mu-um!' Annie glanced around hastily, wondering if anybody had overheard. She felt uncannily like a teenager saddled with an embarrassing parent.

'Well, at least they get one thing right at this place,' Gladys said a little later, as they trundled off towards the car. 'No plastic shopping bags. Plastic shopping bags are the scourge of the earth. They should be banned. If people would just learn to keep a handy string bag with them at all times . . .'

Annie was about to explain that Costco's no-bag policy was less about wastage and more about discouraging people from nicking things when she happened to glance into a parked car and spot a cloud of dark hair that reminded her of Heather.

She looked again, then rapped on the roof – because it was indeed Heather's cloud of hair.

Heather turned her head, and Annie gasped. Her friend's eyes were red and swollen, her nose was damp, and her lips were blotchy.

As Gladys loomed over Annie's shoulder, Heather made a desperate shooing gesture. Annie needed no second prompting. Taking her mother by the elbow, she steered her briskly towards their own car. Nobody wanted to draw a crowd when they were having a quiet cry in a car park.

'Wasn't that your friend, the one with the horse?' Gladys asked.

'Heather? It looked like her, didn't it? But it was somebody else.'

Gladys gave her a long look, and held her peace.

*

'I need to dash out for a bit,' Annie said after she'd unloaded the shopping from the boot of the car.

'Of course, you do,' said Gladys. 'Don't worry about me. I'm going to put my feet up after walking around that shop. I haven't had that much exercise since my car broke down and I had to walk a mile and a half to the garage in Croydon.'

Annie smiled. 'All right, Mum. Just keep the phone beside your bed. I'll be as quick as I can.'

'You tell her to keep her chin up,' Gladys said as Annie gathered her car keys and her bag.

After a quick reconnoitre of Heather's empty driveway and garage, Annie drove back to Costco. Sure enough, Heather's car was still there, and Heather was still inside it, not sobbing any more but staring into the middle distance.

Annie tapped on the window, and made a winding-down gesture. Heather seemed resigned but not surprised to see her back. She cracked the window open an inch or two and said, 'Sorry. This is dumb. I'll be OK in a moment. I don't need help. I'm OK.'

Annie didn't budge. 'Look, I'm not going anywhere, so you might as well let me in.'

Heather gave a shaky sigh and reluctantly pressed a button to unlock the car. Sliding into the passenger seat, Annie leaned over and squeezed Heather's shoulder.

'So what's it all about?'

Heather blew her nose and dabbed at her eyes. 'It's private,' she said.

Annie's stomach clenched painfully. 'Do you have breast cancer?' she blurted.

Heather's hand flew to her breast. 'God, I don't think so,' she said.

'Oh, thank goodness. You're not dying of something else, then?'

'No, of course I'm not freaking dying! I've had a miscarriage, that's all.'

'A . . . miscarriage?'

'Yes, you know, when you're freaking pregnant one day, and then you're bleeding like Niagara Falls the next day, and then you're not freaking pregnant any more?'

'Oh, God. I'm sorry. Um, when did it happen? Not – surely not while you were watching Lydia for me?'

'Yes, it was around then. But don't worry, it was OK. I mean, having Lydia in the house didn't make it any worse. It wasn't painful or anything. I didn't need a D&C. There was nothing to it, really. It's just . . . ten days ago I was having a baby. And now I'm not.' She blew her nose aggressively. 'I'm fine with it, I swear. I mean, I've always been pretty tough. I haven't cried at all, not until now. But . . . going into Costco today and seeing those economy boxes of diapers . . . I've been eyeing them out for the longest time. We've been trying for this baby ever since Hailey was three. Rob's sperm isn't at the top of its game, you see. Half of his little guys can't swim and the other half don't seem to know where to go. So I've been pricing those diapers for four freaking years. I nearly bought them outright the day I did the pregnancy test, but then I figured,' she blew her nose again, 'I figured I'd wait to get through the first trimester.'

'Oh, Heather! Do they know what went wrong?'

Heather shrugged. 'They couldn't pin it down. Advanced maternal age obviously doesn't help.'

Annie's mouth fell open. 'You're joking. Right?'

Heather shook her head. 'I'm thirty-eight, kiddo. If you're a minute over thirty-five when you conceive, they start reading you the riot act. The rule of thumb is, all risks go up fifty per cent once you pass the magic milestone. Down's syndrome. Cerebral palsy. Gestational diabetes. Miscarriage. You name it. It's all fifty per cent more likely.'

Annie was getting the picture. So. She herself had four more years, then. Oodles of time. She squeezed Heather's hand. 'I'm so sorry you had Lydia on your hands when you had all that going on.'

'You know, I was kind of glad she was there. It kept me civilised.' Heather looked out across the parking lot at the assorted shoppers pushing their groaning trolleys to their cars. 'Anyway, it's a bit of a relief. I wasn't looking forward to the sleepless nights.'

Out of respect, Annie averted her eyes from her friend's bleak face. 'I never even knew you wanted another baby,' she said. 'I thought Hailey was an only child by choice. So many people do that nowadays. It makes a lot of sense, in a way – only one lot of school fees, that sort of thing.'

Heather gave a hollow laugh. 'Not in this town. In this town, you're an under-achiever if you have just three. Four is the norm. Five shows ambition. Six is the height of chic, only attained by the chosen few.'

Annie had indeed noticed, when she glanced through the school directory, whole tribes of kids going by the same surname. 'That's weird,' she said. 'Sort of old-fashioned and traditional for a place like this; a place so close to New York.'

Heather shook her head. 'You still don't get the demographics, do you? Staying home with the kids these days is – well, it's unusual. It's a luxury. But you've probably noticed that most of the moms around here do it. That's because they can afford to. I'm telling you, half these women you meet on the PTO were captains of industry back in the day. They're all Type-A personalities, to a woman. And if they're going to do the mom thing, they're going to do it *right*. And they're going to do it *big*. They're going to do it with spreadsheets and clipboards and a full quota of kids. Oh, and a bunch of "help", of course.'

'But you don't care about all that! You don't give a damn about keeping up with the Joneses!'

'No, of course I don't. I just want another baby, that's all. Rob wants another baby too. To be honest,' she lowered her voice, 'we *need* this baby. We need more glue to hold us together.'

'Glue?'

Heather smoothed her eyebrows with her fingers. 'Rob likes to shake things up,' she said. 'He doesn't like more of the same every freaking day of his life. That's why we've moved so much. He likes new challenges, new people, big events. He doesn't like the day-to-day stuff so much.'

'Well, maybe, but—'

'He likes it when I'm pregnant. He's one of those weird men who gets turned on by the big belly.'

Annie coughed and shifted in her seat. She wasn't sure she wanted to hear all this.

'Believe me,' said Heather, 'we need the glue. But you know what? I'm not going to let a miscarriage slow me down. If I miscarried, it means I still have eggs.'

'Absolutely,' said Annie. 'Of course, you still have eggs.'

'And if Belinda Nielsen could squeeze out four nine-pound boys after her fortieth birthday, damn it, I can surely manage one measly baby while I'm still in my semi-fertile thirties!'

'Damn it, of course you can!' Annie agreed, punching the air.

It was hard to snatch a moment to talk to Simon, now that Gladys was in the house. But while they were getting ready for bed that night, Annie said, 'I was talking to Heather today. She wasn't going to tell us, but . . . well, she had a miscarriage while I was in England.'

'What?' said Simon, pausing in the midst of emptying all the coins out of his pockets. 'Are you serious? Come to think of it, she looked a bit down while you were gone. I felt pretty bad; thought that maybe taking care of Lydia was wearing her out.'

'No, she says Lydia was no trouble. Anyway. She's pretty shaken up about it. Reckons that after the age of thirty-five, the whole pregnancy thing gets a lot harder.'

His fingers stopped stacking coins.

'So, well, we haven't really talked about it, but at some point I suppose we need to decide about . . .' Somehow, she couldn't go on. Not without any encouragement. He must, after all, know what she meant. By now he should have chimed in with *something* – enthusiastic or otherwise.

He gave her a long look, then dropped his eyes. 'Yes, we'll have to talk about a lot of things,' he said. His expression was all wrong, somehow. 'But let's leave it until we know what's going on with your mum.'

Chapter Ten

At Simon's urging, Annie took her mum to a highly recommended consultant in Greenwich who listened to Gladys's tale of dizziness, and diagnosed her with something called benign paroxysmal positional vertigo.

'Um – and what's it caused by?' Annie asked, trying to memorise the terminology. It didn't sound at all benign, especially the paroxysmal bit.

'Age,' said the doctor, a plump woman in a voluminous jumper. 'Age or injury. Basically, your mother has what we call ear rocks floating around in her canals. Now, I'm going to do a manoeuvre to see if we can settle them back where they belong.'

Annie watched as the woman got her mother to lie down on the examining table, then tilted her head this way and that.

'Ouch,' Gladys muttered.

'Watch it! She's got a bad back.'

The doctor helped Gladys back into a sitting position. 'She might be a bit dizzy now,' she told Annie. 'Drive her home and keep an eye on her today. Treatment of this kind of vertigo is about eighty per cent effective, so she shouldn't experience much dizziness after today.'

'What? You mean you think you've *cured* her by twisting her head around like that?'

'I am *here* you know,' Gladys interrupted testily.

'The treatment is eighty per cent effective,' the doctor repeated patiently, still talking to Annie. Then she looked at her watch. 'Did you have any more questions?'

Naturally, they didn't.

On the way home, Gladys said, 'What a lot of hocus-pocus. The woman was nothing but a quack. And she treated me as if I wasn't there.'

But when they got back home, Annie did a little internet research. To her surprise, she found there really *was* such a thing as benign paroxysmal positional vertigo, and it really *could* be effectively treated by twisting the head about in a certain way.

She leaned back in her chair, hand over her mouth, speculating. Her mum never talked much about her dizzy spells, but by a process of intense questioning, Annie gathered they'd been fairly regular for some time.

What if they went away?

Would Gladys be able to live on her own again? Did she want to live on her own again?

Obviously, Gladys couldn't live here for ever. Obviously, Annie didn't want her to. And yet – she had the feeling that she'd been given a bit of a reprieve, now that Gladys had joined their household; from what exactly, she didn't know.

'Is she driving you crazy?' Annie's neighbour Jennifer Miller asked in a low voice over the top of her skinny latte, watching Annie's mum browse through paperbacks.

Annie had bumped into Jennifer at the bookshop by chance.

Annie gave a wry shrug. 'Oh, she has her moments. She's a bit full of herself today because a woman she met at Donna Knopf's pre-festive-season coffee morning phoned up and asked her to be the guest speaker at some "New Frugality" thing she's hosting in honour of the recession.'

Jennifer's eyes widened. 'Wow. So what's she going to talk about?'

'Let's see, now.' Annie began counting things off on her fingers. 'Reusing wrapping paper. That's one of her favourites. I don't think she's bought a new roll of wrapping paper since 1979. The funny thing is, the patterns have come back into fashion! Recycling gifts. The idea is, you just keep the things people give you in a cupboard, and then pass them on again when the time is right. There's a glass jar of bath salts that's been doing the rounds of the Guildford WI since the late eighties. Hmm. What else? She wanted to talk about reusing tea bags, but I told her people here don't drink tea in the first place. Oh, and she's got a recipe for making soup out of a chicken carcass.'

Jennifer pulled a face. 'She's a real high roller, huh. It's kind of funny. Everybody round here has been living large for so long, they'll probably have to go back to school to learn how stay inside a budget. How are things with Simon on the work front?'

Annie's eyebrows shot up. 'He's fine, thanks. Working hard, as usual.'

Jennifer nodded. 'Drew's OK too. For the moment. A

bunch of people lost their jobs around him, but so far so good. He's feeling a bit more optimistic.'

'That's a relief,' said Annie. 'Let's just hope the economy stops tanking soon.' But she was really just mouthing the things she heard people saying around her. She didn't feel any personal anxiety. ChefPro was as sound as ever; she kept tabs on their share price on the internet. It was worrying, of course, to see that journalists had started referring to ChefPro's most direct competitor by the tag, 'ailing British food giant, William Tell'. If William Tell was ailing, it was possible that there would be rocky times ahead for ChefPro, too. But for the moment, all was well.

Gladys was making her way back to their table. She sat down heavily, dumping a book of slow-cooker recipes on the table.

'Anybody got a pen?' she asked. 'There're a couple of recipes in here I'd like to copy out.'

Annie looked over her shoulder nervously. 'Mum, I don't think you're supposed to do that.'

'Well, I'm not slapping fifteen dollars down on the table for this book,' Gladys declared. 'That's what went wrong with the economy the world over, you know. Impulse buying. Getting into debt. Paying for things you don't need.'

Jennifer stood up quickly, her mouth curling behind her cardboard mug. 'Well, got to run,' she trilled. 'Nice seeing you, Mrs Harleigh.'

Heather invited Annie and her family to Thanksgiving dinner because, as she privately told Annie, she couldn't bear to face the sympathy of her own family after her miscarriage, any more than she could bear to face the blissful ignorance of Rob's family, who knew nothing about her loss and never would. As her parents had retired to Florida, and Rob's family hailed from Chicago, avoiding family was relatively easy.

'Can I bring the mashed potatoes?' Annie asked – she was reasonable at mashing potatoes – but Heather graciously declined. Annie hoped she wasn't remembering the disastrous dinner party.

'I'm having everything catered,' Heather declared. 'I don't want to spend days thawing a freaking turkey in my tub. And I can't be messing around with basters. My hair would frizz.'

Gladys was shocked to the core when Annie told her about the caterers. 'What? You don't mean the woman can't even roast a bird and boil up some green beans? What else would you have – sweet potatoes? Just throw them in with the juices in the pan. Maybe you could buy the pumpkin pie – pastry can be tricky. But everything else – good Lord, even you could cook it, Annie.'

'I don't blame Heather at all,' Annie snapped back. 'Why spend a whole day sweating over the details when someone else could do it all for you, and so much better?'

Gladys shook her head in horror. 'You Americans are so extravagant!' she declared.

Heather's house on the day of Thanksgiving wasn't likely to dispel this view. It was all set about with hay bales, turkeys in various media, and cornucopias overflowing with fruit and flowers.

Simon met Annie's eye over Gladys's head as the older

woman stood frowning at a wreath on the front door made entirely of miniature winter squashes in different shades of green and orange.

'The *sheer waste*!' Simon mouthed at Annie. She grinned and winked at him.

But her mother surprised them with a different tack. 'Wreaths are for funerals,' she pronounced. 'I don't know where people get this odd idea of hanging them on doors. Mind you, don't go buying a wreath for me when I pop off. I'd rather you spent the money on a good, sturdy headstone, something that will last.'

'You're not going to die,' Lydia said loudly. 'Not until you're really, really old. And you're not old yet.'

'Of course, she's not going to die.' Annie glared at her mother. 'Right, Mum? She's probably going to live till she's a hundred.'

'Some days it feels as if I already have,' Gladys muttered, massaging her back.

At that moment, Heather threw the door open.

'Hi Heather. Wow! You're looking very . . .' Annie trailed off, stumped for words. Heather was an astonishing sight in a deep purple wrap-around dress with a hem so high that Annie suspected it was really a blouse. A simple but stunning bead necklace slipped in and out of her generous cleavage and sparkled when she moved into the light. Her knees and thighs twinkled in luminescent tights above tall black boots.

'Thank you – I *think*,' Heather said with a wry smile. 'Come in, come in.' She graciously accepted the wine bottle Simon was proffering, and led the way to the living room.

Dan Morgan, wearing tassels, was standing over by the computer with Rob, downloading songs on iTunes.

Before anybody could speak, Hailey burst out from under the baby grand piano, brandishing a plastic horse. 'Come on, Lydia, let's go play upstairs,' she cried.

As the girls scampered off, the two men came forward to air-kiss Annie and shake Simon's hand.

'You must be Heather's husband?' Gladys was talking to Dan in her extra-high, socialising voice.

'No, that would be me.' Rob stepped up and treated an astonished Gladys to one of his scorching come-hither looks. Annie gave a nervous trill of laughter. Poor Heather, saddled with a husband who couldn't help giving the glad-eye to every female who came his way, including old-age pensioners. Well, just as long as he was all talk and no trousers.

'Good grief, I forgot the introductions,' said Heather. 'Gladys, this is my husband, Rob. And the guy in the cowboy boots is Dan.'

'And Dan is?' Gladys asked.

'He's a friend of the family,' said Heather. 'You've got to have a waif or stray over for Thanksgiving, and he's it, for us. He's from Texas, you see, so he doesn't have any family around here.'

Rob tore his gaze away from Gladys long enough to pour out several glasses of white wine, and began handing them around. When everybody had one, he raised his own glass. 'To waifs and strays!' he said – by which Annie understood that they, too, fell into this category. Then Rob turned to Gladys with a gallant air. 'And how are you liking Connecticut so far, Mrs— Gladys?'

Annie groaned inwardly.

'Come help me in the kitchen,' Heather muttered under her breath, and Annie needed no second bidding.

'Oh God, I bet Mum's telling Rob off about having the heating on too high,' Annie muttered. But Gladys, shaking Rob off with ease, had followed them into the kitchen.

'Right,' said Gladys, 'let's see what those catering people have fobbed us off with. I can always throw something together if it's too horrible. Do you have any Oxo?'

Annie caught Heather's eye and took a huge slug of wine.

'I like Thanksgiving,' Simon said later, when they were back in front of their own fireplace and Lydia and Gladys were in bed. 'Good to have a holiday about nothing in particular; just a taking stock kind of thing. Count your blessings, and all that. We should think about having a day like that back home.'

Annie screwed up her nose. 'What, two turkeys in two months? Englishwomen wouldn't stand for it.'

Simon laughed. 'Yeah, you're right. Funny sort of timing, really – just before Christmas.'

'Nowhere else to put it,' said Annie. She began to count off on her fingers. 'You've got Halloween in October, Christmas in December, New Year's Day in January, Valentine's Day in February, Easter in March or April, and then the weather starts warming up. You can't have a great big feast like that when it's sweltering. Plus you have to incorporate the whole harvest idea, don't you? No harvest in the spring.'

Simon sipped his coffee. 'That Dan chap was a bit cheeky, didn't you think?'

'In what sense?'

'Well, what kind of berk stands up and starts spouting about all the wonderful things going on in his life?'

Annie snorted with laughter. 'Darling, I think it's a tradition. I think that's what you're supposed to do at Thanksgiving: give thanks.'

'Well, nobody else did,' Simon pointed out.

'I don't think Heather and Rob are feeling very thankful at the moment,' Annie said quietly.

'Oh God, I was forgetting,' he said. 'It was good of them to have us over, considering.'

'What would *you* have said, if they'd put you on the spot?' Annie asked after a moment. 'You know, about what you're thankful for?'

He took a surprisingly long time to think about his answer. 'Well,' he began at last, but a loud cry from upstairs, followed by some bangs and crashes, stopped him in his tracks. Patches, blamelessly laid out at Annie's feet like a moth-eaten rug, leapt straight from a deep sleep into full-on, high-volume barking.

Annie and Simon jumped to their feet as one and stampeded for the stairs. Simon, in socks, skidded towards the rug in the hallway, tripped over a wrinkle in it and took a nosedive, breaking his fall with his elbows. Annie leapt over his body, barely breaking her stride, and raced up the stairs to Lydia's room.

She burst in and turned on the light. Lydia was lying on the floor, moaning, her hands over her head. Annie ran over and gathered her in her arms. 'Lydia, what happened? What's the matter?'

'The room is burning,' she said.

'The room . . .? You must've had a bad dream. Nothing's burning. There's no fire.'

'Go away. I don't want you. I want Daddy.'

'You're very hot, sweetie. I think I need to take your temperature.'

Lydia was sobbing quietly now, her hair clumped wetly around her face. 'Go away. I want *Daddy*.'

'I'm here, Muffet.' Simon knelt down beside Annie, and Lydia scrambled into his arms.

'I'll get the thermometer.' Annie rushed to the spare bathroom where she kept a first-aid box. She found the brand new digital thermometer and ripped it out of its packaging with her teeth as she ran back to Lydia's bedroom.

'Open your mouth,' she told Lydia. 'Pop it under your tongue.'

The child was shivering now, and as she accepted the thermometer, Annie caught a whiff of her breath. It was sour and fetid.

Sure enough, Lydia's temperature was 103.

'Do we phone 911?' Annie asked, staring at the number in awe.

'Good grief, no.' Simon had lifted Lydia back into bed and was stroking her brow gently. 'Kids are always getting cricket-score temperatures. Just find something like Calpol and get her some water. I'll open the windows.'

Annie rushed back to the bathroom and returned with some ibuprofen.

'Go away, go *away*,' Lydia cried as Annie came at her with the teaspoon, like a contestant in an egg and spoon race.

'OK, but you need to swallow this first.'

Lydia flailed at Annie with a hand, and sent the teaspoon flying. Red syrup splattered over her white duvet.

'Oh, for God's sake,' Annie said.

'It's OK, she's always like this when she's ill,' Simon told her. 'Just pour out some more and I'll get it down her.'

Annie watched from the sidelines as Lydia accepted the medicine from her father, putting her small hand over his large one to steady the spoon.

'I'm going to sit with her for a while,' Simon murmured. 'She'll be fine once the medicine kicks in. You might as well go off to bed. No point both of us losing sleep.'

Feeling distinctly superfluous, Annie went downstairs to switch off lights, lock doors, and let the dog out for a last walkabout. Slamming shut the door of the dishwasher, she straightened up and rubbed her eyes briskly. There. She'd go off to bed now, and make a doctor's appointment first thing in the morning. Lydia would just have to make do with her stepmother tomorrow, because Daddy would be at work.

'Annie?'

At the sound of her mother's voice, she froze with her hand on the light switch.

'Annie? What's all the ruckus about?'

With a sigh, Annie walked through to the downstairs room where Gladys slept. 'It's OK, Mum. Lydia has a temperature, that's all.'

Gladys was sitting up in bed, magnificent in a lacy nightgown. 'Come closer, my dear, I can't see you out there.'

Annie advanced a step or two into the room.

Gladys stared hard at her. 'You've been crying,' she said.

'Rubbish.' Annie sniffed vigorously. 'It's allergies, that's all.'

'Come over here,' Gladys commanded. She patted the bed. Annie hesitated a moment, then went over and sat down.

To her astonishment, her mother leaned over and put an arm around her shoulders. 'Everything's going to be all right,' Gladys said, patting her hair.

Annie reared back, breaking out of Gladys's clasp. 'For heaven's sake, Mum,' she said. 'Everything *is* all right, thank you very much. Now, I'm going upstairs to get some sleep. Do you need anything before I go? A glass of water, maybe?'

'You need to loosen up and communicate better,' Gladys told her. 'We Brits are too reserved. Dr Phil reckons lack of communication is the root of all evil. You need to get real with yourself about your life before you can achieve anything.'

Annie's draw dropped. 'Get *real* ...?'

'That's right. Think about it.'

Stunned, Annie made her way up to bed.

'It's like a pregnancy test,' said the doctor, holding up a little tube containing some gunk from the back of Lydia's throat. Annie suppressed a shudder. 'Two lines and it's positive. One line and we *think* it's negative, but we send it out to be cultured, just to make sure.' Carefully, the doctor squeezed several drops out of the tube onto a white plastic strip.

'Yup,' she said with satisfaction a little while later. 'It's positive, all right. I always like a positive strep test, because – guess what? – she's going to be all better in about twenty-four hours.'

Looking at Lydia slumped over on the examining table, pale, thin and listless, Annie certainly hoped so.

As they left the offices, Annie said in an enticing voice, 'Do you want to press the buttons for the lift, Lydia?'

Lydia gave her a look that could have scorched a rain-forest.

'I'm guessing that's a no,' Annie said with a sigh.

'It's called an elevator,' Lydia replied in a voice of deep contempt. Lately, she'd been absorbing American colloquialisms like a sponge.

'Not where you and I come from, mate,' said Annie.

Lydia's face screwed up in confusion. 'But we live *here* now,' she said. 'We should talk the way everyone else talks. Otherwise people will think we're weird.'

'No, they won't. They'll think we're foreign and exotic and interesting.'

'They'll think we're *weird*,' Lydia repeated. And that was when Annie noticed, with a tiny jolt, that she sounded completely American.

Back home, Annie left Lydia and Gladys in front of the TV watching the frenzied advertising of Black Friday sales, and sneaked up to the den to make a phone call.

'Sarah? What a relief, you're actually home. Look, Sarah, I need your advice. It's about Mum.'

'How's she doing?'

'Very well. She's a *lot* better, actually. She hasn't had a dizzy spell in two weeks. The aches and pains from the fall are gone, too.'

'Is she enjoying Norbury?'

'Oh yes. She's having a fine old time. She's got herself involved with this "frugality" group, and they've had her to speak at one of their meetings. She came home cross as anything because the hostess had gone out and bought twelve jars of jam, then chucked the jam away so she could use the jars as vases for centrepieces. Oh, and she's doing a lot of cleaning and cooking, not to mention laundry. When she does consent to put her feet up, she watches Dr Phil and Oprah – and they seem to be giving her odd ideas.'

'Odd ideas? She's never been short of those.'

'No, I mean she's talking about how we should *communicate* more. Share our feelings. That sort of thing.'

Sarah gave a low whistle. 'Is she driving Lydia crazy?'

Annie drew in a sharp breath. 'Um, no. Actually, Lydia thinks she's great. They do homework together. She's teaching her to darn socks. They're really bonding.'

'What about Simon? Is she getting on his nerves?'

'Oh no! Far from it. He's fascinated by her Dig for Victory tales. He's gone and put it into her head that she should bring out a recipe book full of wartime horrors like crow pie and carrolade and squirrel-tail soup.'

'Good grief.'

'Yip, everybody loves her. All the women on my street

think she's such a character. She's always helping out around the house. She couldn't be making herself more useful.'

'But?'

'How do you know there's a "but"?'

'Well, isn't there?'

Annie sighed. 'But Simon's barely laid a finger on me since she's been here. And he says there are things we need to discuss, but we can only talk when Mum goes home. And sometimes she makes me feel about ten years old.'

'Sounds like it's time she came home.'

'Well, she can't, can she? She's not well. She might have another fall at any moment. She's not fit to live alone.'

'Annie, we'll think of something. She can't stay with you for ever, anyway. She doesn't have the right paperwork. We'll have to get a companion for her – or something. I'll look into it.'

Annie blew her nose. 'Thank you, Sarah. The weird thing is, in some ways I *want* her to stay here for ever. That's the truly scary thing.'

By Monday, Lydia was all recovered and ready to go back to school. The antibiotics had worked with almost magical speed. 'Just wait till she has pneumonia or Lyme disease,' Heather said as they walked home together. 'You'll be *really* happy we're not living in the dark ages.'

Annie stepped into the kitchen with a firm tread, determined to turn over a new leaf today and not be all nit-picky about her poor old mum. After all, in the spirit of Thanksgiving, she knew she should be very thankful for the extra pair of hands in the house. Nowadays, the dishwasher seemed to unpack itself. (And there was even less for her to do than ever, a small voice pointed out. She quelled it imperiously.)

'I'm back, Mum,' she called into the house.

There was a silence, and then she heard her mum's footsteps on the stairs.

'Mum, I've told you not to go upstairs. What if you got dizzy on the staircase? What were you doing up there, anyway?'

'Oh, making beds. A bit of dusting. That cleaning team of yours doesn't always get to the window sills.'

Gladys came into view, wearing an apron and carrying a duster. 'By the way, my dear,' she lowered her voice and looked around quickly, as if casing the room for eavesdroppers, 'a word in your ear. With a child in the house, you need to be careful about leaving items of an, um, *intimate* nature lying around the place. I found *this* on your bedside table.'

In one latex-gloved hand, between thumb and forefinger, she held up a small, battery-operated gadget shaped a bit like a tumbleweed.

'Mu-um! For heaven's sake! That's a vibrating back massager.'

Gladys's eyebrows rose. 'I know it's a vibrating something,' she said. 'I suggest you stash it away somewhere. I'm surprised you leave it lying about.'

Annie yanked it out of her hand and stormed up to her room. She opened the bottom drawer of Simon's dresser and threw the back massager in among his socks.

'Annie!'

'*What?*'

'I've made you some tea.'

Annie caught sight of her own wild-eyed face in the mirror.

Right. That was it. She had to have a little word with Mum before she found herself pulling her hair out in chunks.

She marched downstairs, breathing deeply, and threw open the door to the kitchen.

'Mum,' she said, brushing aside the tea Gladys was proffering, 'we need to talk.'

'I know, my dear,' Gladys said, settling herself onto a stool at the counter. 'I've been meaning to have a word with you for a couple of days, now.'

Annie sank down into a stool, taken aback. 'You have? About *what*, exactly?'

'About going home.'

Annie's jaw dropped.

'That's right, love. I know it's time, as well as you do. So I've been writing some letters, making some arrangements. I've managed to persuade Flo Mitson to come and keep an eye on me.'

'Flo Mitson?'

'The nurse. You remember – my cousin Elvira's widowed daughter-in-law. Her varicose veins have been bothering her for years; all that walking around the wards. I told her she could put her feet up and watch TV most of the day at my place.'

'Mum! But . . . but do you even like this woman?'

'Oh yes, Flo's all right. Addicted to lottery tickets, but otherwise quite sound. We'll get along just fine.'

'But how will you set things up? I mean, if she's giving up work to come and live with you, presumably you'll have to pay her something. How will—?'

Gladys raised a liver-spotted hand. 'Annie, I'm old, not senile. I've been managing my affairs quite nicely, thank you, since before you were born.'

'Well, yes, of course, Mum, but—'

'I've sorted it out, Annie. Let's leave it at that.'

So Annie did.

Annie wasn't prepared for the sense of panic she felt as she watched an attendant wheel her mother away through security. (Gladys had suggested the wheelchair herself, this time.) 'Come back,' Annie wanted to call. 'I can't handle all this without you! Who's going to help Lydia finish her crocheted frog? Who's going to boil the dishcloths?' But she stood firm and kept waving, her face fixed in a smile.

Simon, standing beside her, squeezed her hand. 'She'll be OK on the plane, and Sarah's meeting her on the other side,' he said.

'I know.' She blinked rapidly. 'I'm not worried about her, really. She's well able to look after herself.'

'She's going to miss everything,' Lydia piped up. 'The soccer party. The Christmas recital. Everything. She said I should write her a letter.'

Annie glanced down at the little girl. She looked dejected and wistful, and distinctly unkempt. Nobody had reminded her to brush her hair all day; Annie and Gladys had been too busy rounding up stray items and forcing them into Gladys's suitcase. In the end, Gladys had taken an extra bag to accommodate the waffle-weave spa robe and giant jar of cashew nuts from Costco.

'Of course you should write her a letter,' Annie enthused, working her fingers absent-mindedly through Lydia's hair.

'Ow,' yelped Lydia, jerking her head away. 'You're so *mean*, Annie.'

Simon frowned at his daughter. 'Lydia, don't talk to Annie that way.'

'Well, she's pulling my hair out by the *roots*.'

Annie gave a rueful laugh, showing Simon a strand or two of golden hair caught up in her rings. 'Look at that; she's right. Sorry, Lydia. I didn't mean to hurt you. Anyway, why don't you write a letter this evening? I'll find an airmail stamp for you and help you do the address.'

'I could draw her a picture of Patches so she doesn't forget what he looks like.'

The corner of Simon's mouth twitched. 'Oh yes, she'd never want to forget the noble features of the dog who ate her reading glasses,' he said.

Without Gladys clattering dishes and talking back to the TV, the house was Annie's own domain again. On the first morning of her repossession, Annie took care of her kitchen chores with grim satisfaction. But she suffered a little setback when, after turning on the kettle, she found herself automatically putting out two cups. She shook her head, then muttered to Patches, who was looking at her in concern, 'How do you take your tea, then, dog? Milk and two sugars?'

Patches cocked his head.

'Oh God, I hope I'm not going to turn into one of those mad people who talk to their dogs all the time.'

Patches thumped his tail.

To hear another human voice in the place, Annie turned on the radio – but turned it off again almost immediately when she found herself humming along: 'Everything is dust in the wind.'

'I know!' she told Patches suddenly. 'I'll phone Henny!'

'Well, I'm glad everything's back to normal,' Henny told her. 'You and Simon are still such newly-weds.'

'Well, not *such* newly-weds. To be honest, we're thinking of, you know, moving to the next stage. He said – he said we'd talk about the whole baby thing once Mum went home . . .'

'The whole *baby* thing? Oh, Annie, you're not . . .?'

'No, no, I'm not pregnant. We're just, sort of, thinking about it. Well, I am, anyway.'

Henny was whooping with joy on the other side of the phone. 'Oh my God, Annie – this is fantastic! I'll be able to give you so much advice. Like, did you know you shouldn't eat swordfish when you're pregnant because of the mercury?'

'Um, Henny? Slow down a moment, would you? You see, I'm not entirely sure about Simon's position on timing. Frankly, I'm not even sure if he wants a baby at all.'

'Oh.'

'So don't go getting too excited. And for God's sake, don't say anything to Mum if you happen to talk to her on the phone. I don't want her to get her hopes up.'

'Of course not. My lips are sealed. So your mum got home safely and everything?'

'Yes, I spoke to her first thing this morning. She's fine. Sarah took some time off work and drove her home. I bet she'll call you soon. She's staying with Mum for a few days until Flo Mitson shows up to take over.'

'Flo Mitson?'

'Some sort of relative. A nurse, apparently. Didn't know we had any nurses in the family. She's going to—' Suddenly, she was drowned out by a barrage of barking from Patches. 'Hang on, Henny, I'll have to go. Someone's knocking.'

Chapter Eleven

The woman on the front porch was impeccably dressed in a black business suit and heels. What was more, she had a perfectly coiffed head of designer highlights. Patches, wagging his tail obsequiously, aimed a few squirts of wee at her shoes.

Luckily the woman, intent on rearranging a briefcase stuffed with papers, didn't notice this sycophantic gesture.

'Oh,' said Annie in surprise. 'Are you a Jehovah's witness?'

'A what?' Tinkling laugh. 'No, of course not. I'm Cindy Faig.'

'Cindy Faig?' The woman had said her name as if Annie was bound to recognise it. 'I'm sorry, I . . . Wait, are you the room mum for Miss Scofield's class?'

The woman laughed. '*God* no. I'm not a mum at all. I work with Si, of course.'

'Oh, right. Of course!' She'd last seen this woman the day she'd fallen asleep in Simon's office. This was a member of his famous pie team! 'Good to see you! Would you like to come in?'

'If you don't mind. Did Si mention I might pop by?' She was staring at Annie quite hard.

'No, actually, he didn't. It must have slipped his mind.' She ushered the woman through to the formal living room. 'Sit down, make yourself comfortable. I'll just put the kettle on. Would you like tea or coffee?'

'Thanks, I'll have tea.'

Annie hurried through to the kitchen to fill the kettle and set a tea tray. Why hadn't Simon mentioned that Cindy Faig would be popping in? she wondered.

Back in the living room, Annie asked, 'So you're still enjoying New York?'

Her guest gave a wide smile. 'Oh my God, I just love living in the city. It's fantastic. Don't you just adore Manhattan?'

'I do, actually,' Annie said a little wistfully. 'I wish I could get down there more often, but it's hard with school and everything. Simon never wants to go in over the weekends.'

'So how *is* Lydia? Si says she's doing well, settling in at school, playing soccer.'

'Um, yes, that's right. So . . . you know Lydia?'

The woman laughed. She wasn't pretty, exactly, but her face was superbly made-up, her slightly slanted eyes giving her a mysterious look. She didn't need to be pretty because her body was magnificent. Never had a business suit looked more like a Velcroed-on costume worn by an exotic dancer.

In her jeans, T-shirt and cardigan, Annie felt every inch the frumpy hausfrau.

'Oh, we go way back,' said Cindy. 'I've known Lydia since she was a baby. Gosh, I remember the day Beth first brought her into the London office. She was three weeks old.'

'Oh, wow. That is way back. We really should have you round for lunch or something!' Annie felt excited at the idea of an old friend, maybe a sort of aunt figure, for Lydia.

Cindy smiled. 'Sure, that would be great when things calm down. But as you know everybody's been under a lot of stress at the office. We've been working all hours God sends. Socialising hasn't really been on people's minds.'

'Well – quite. So, um, what brings you out here today?'

Cindy bent down to pick up her briefcase. 'I wanted to make sure he'd have this as soon as he gets in from Boston tonight,' she said, taking out a file. 'The Brewster focus group report. You know how desperate he's been to get his hands on these results. We didn't want to risk a messenger service, so I drove them up myself.'

'He's in *Boston* today?'

'You didn't know? He took the train – just a day trip. He's looking at the site.'

'The site?'

'You know, the site for the flagship restaurant. Head office finally agreed with us that Boston is the right place to start.'

'Of course.' She did have some vague memory now of Simon saying something about Boston, but she'd been too taken up with her mum to pay much attention. 'I'll make sure he gets that file. Hang on, I'll just go and pour the tea. Kettle should be boiling by now.'

As Annie entered the living room with the clinking tea tray, she found Cindy on her feet, peering at the titles of the books on the antique bookshelf. Good luck with that, Annie thought ironically. On the day they'd moved into this house, she'd discovered that the handsome, leather-bound library of classics was a façade. There were no actual books, just cardboard stage props.

'Oh God,' said Cindy, 'I hope you won't think I'm rude but I really mustn't stay for tea after all. I have a meeting in Stamford on my way back. You know how the traffic on the I-95 can be. Anyway, be sure to let him have those papers so he can read them before he comes in tomorrow.'

Annie set her tray down with a little thump. 'Of course,' she said, smiling with all her teeth but no conviction whatsoever. *To say you'd have a cup of tea, allow your hostess to make it, and then walk away from the steaming pot* – that would be letting slip the dogs of war, in her mother's book.

As she escorted Cindy Faig out, Annie couldn't help noticing that the woman stared into all the rooms with blatant curiosity as she went by.

She didn't have time to mention Cindy Faig's visit when Simon came home, because the moment he walked through the door they had to jump into the car and race off to an end-of-season soccer party at the coach's house. They arrived about fifteen minutes late.

The coach's wife directed them down to the family's 'media room' in the basement where they found the whole team plus parents sitting on the carpet, eating popcorn in the semi-darkness. The coach, a florid-faced man with curly dark hair, stood in front of the TV holding a handful of medals and a remote control. 'Ah, that's everybody now!' he said when Annie, Simon and Lydia slunk into the room. 'OK, as you know we've had another fabulous season, most of which was filmed by my lovely wife, Erin.'

There was a ragged round of applause. Annie exchanged an alarmed look with Simon.

'So, let's get this show rolling,' said the coach. 'First up, McKenna Trent.' He stepped to one side and pressed a button. The TV screen filled with an image of McKenna, easily the smallest girl on the team, stubbornly pursuing a ball, hampered by a T-shirt that hung down well below her knees. 'McKenna is one of our best defence players, and she did an excellent job keeping that ball away from the posts. McKenna, please come forward and get your medal.'

Huge applause broke out as the little girl stood up and picked her way through the audience to receive her medal.

And so it went, with the coach calling each girl by name, showing a piece of footage illustrating the high points of her game, and hanging a medal around her neck.

Annie felt an awful tension building in her stomach.

At last, there were only two girls left – Hailey and Lydia.

'And now,' said the coach, 'for our trophy of excellence. This goes to Hailey Gibson, for being our top goal scorer this season.' The screen jumped into life with an image of Hailey racing across a field, controlling the ball like a mini Beckham before smashing it into the undefended goal posts.

The media room rocked with cheers and clapping. Hailey, looking embarrassed and waggling her unibrow, went up for her trophy.

'Last of all,' said the coach, and Annie sucked her breath in sharply, 'I want to talk about a girl called Lydia Keeler. She came to us completely new to the sport of soccer, but we were happy to have her. I have to tell you, guys, I was excited. I mean, she had the right accent to play this game. Well, as most of us know, it took Lydia a little while to get warmed up.' On the screen, Lydia was shown squatting down to pick flowers as a ball whizzed by. 'But as the season progressed we saw her grow a little stronger every time she went out. And then, people, the very last game we played, we saw this.'

The TV screen flickered to life again, and Annie made out Lydia at the back of the picture, doing nothing much, as usual. But all of a sudden a girl on the opposing team kicked a long shot that went bouncing and bounding towards Lydia. Oh God, she probably scored another own goal, Annie thought.

But no, Lydia ran at the loose ball, stopped it with one foot, dribbled it up the field, dodged her own teammates as skilfully as she dodged the opposition, took the ball all the way to the other side of the field, then made a faultless pass to Hailey, who stood ready and waiting right in front of the goal posts. Hailey's quick, winning kick was a bit of an anticlimax compared to Lydia's long run.

'And that,' said the coach, 'is the beautiful game.'

People were clapping and cheering and standing on their feet. Lydia, as red as a tomato, was inching her way to the front of the room as people leaned in to pat her back and shake her hand.

'Without a doubt,' said the coach, holding up a trophy that matched Hailey's, 'this is our Most Improved Player of the season.'

'Why didn't you tell me?' Annie hissed at Simon, tears streaming down her cheeks.

'I missed it,' he said sheepishly. 'I had a conference call with a bloke in England, so Heather took them. She said Lydia played well, but I thought she was just being kind!'

Much later, when Lydia was asleep, her trophy perched on her bedside table, her medal slung over a post of her bed, Annie remembered the strange visit she'd had earlier that day.

'By the way,' she told Simon, handing him the file, 'Cindy Faig popped by today. She said to give you this.'

'Cindy Faig came here?' He looked amazed.

'Didn't you know? She said she had a meeting in Stamford, and that you'd need to look this paperwork over before tomorrow.'

He took the file from her, flicked through it, and stood up abruptly. 'I'll be up in the den,' he said, his whole body radiating tension.

For the next few days he was on edge and distracted, barely talking to her other than to thank her for the food she put in front of him.

'So, have you found a good pastry for the American market yet?' she asked brightly one evening as they were watching some programme about survival in the wilderness.

He didn't take his eyes off the screen, where a man was steeling himself to eat a handful of grubs. 'Please, Annie, when I come home I want to relax, not face a bloody inquisition.'

She didn't dare bring up the topic of babies.

Babies were not going to be in Patches' future, that was for sure. Annie was coming to agree with the vet that it was probably best for the environment if Patches was a one-off model.

Still she couldn't help feeling guilty as she loaded him in the car one morning to drive him to the 'animal hospital' to be neutered.

'But he's not broken,' Lydia had protested when Annie told her over the weekend that Patches had an appointment with the vet on Monday and would be there overnight, recuperating.

Ruffling Lydia's hair, Simon had explained, 'They call it fixing but it really means he'll be having an operation so that he can't have puppies.'

'Silly! He doesn't need to go. He's a *boy* dog. Boy dogs don't have puppies.'

Annie and Simon locked eyes. 'I'll just go and put the kettle on for tea,' Annie said with a devilish grin at Simon. 'Daddy can explain.'

She still hadn't asked him what he'd said to Lydia, but she'd noticed the child bending over with a creased brow to look at the dog's underbelly.

Patches was always happy to jump into the car, but he began to suspect foul play at the animal hospital when the receptionist took the leash out of Annie's hands and tugged him away towards a back room. Apparently he remembered the smell of the place, and he didn't like it one bit. Scrabbling fruitlessly at the slippery linoleum, he turned his head to give Annie a reproachful stare. As he was dragged off around the corner, she heard a high, despairing yowl, and then the thump of a door closing, and silence.

Feeling like a traitor, she turned to leave ... and walked

straight into somebody who seemed to have crept up soundlessly behind her.

'Godammit, will you look where you're— *hey,* Annie!'

With a jolt, Annie recognised the drawl and the cowboy boots.

'Dan? What are you doing here?'

'I'm picking up a vitamin supplement for my horse,' Dan Morgan said, grinning down at her with such obvious pleasure that she couldn't help feeling pleased. 'And you? Did you bring the mutt in? Is he OK?'

Annie nodded. 'Yes, he's fine. Just going in to be fixed, that's all.'

At that moment the receptionist returned from the back rooms. 'Hey, Dan,' she called out. 'Good to see you. Your lick came in this morning.'

'Great,' he said, extracting a credit card from his wallet and tossing it onto the desk. 'Put it on that, will you?'

'Well, nice to bump into you,' Annie told him with a small wave, beginning to back out of the room.

'No, hang on! Let me finish up here, and then why don't we go grab a coffee? You look kinda shaken up.'

'I – I don't drink coffee, to be honest.'

'Well, you could have tea then. Or hot chocolate.'

Aware of the receptionist looking at them curiously, Annie shrugged and said, 'The thing is, I don't have much time. Got to get back home and, you know, do stuff.'

Dan shrugged. 'OK,' he said. 'Maybe another time. Have a good day.'

But when she got behind the wheel of her silver minivan, the damn thing wouldn't start. It wouldn't even make a noise. No matter how often she turned the key, all she got was a hopeless click. To make matters worse, it was beginning to rain.

'Having trouble?'

Dan was standing at her window in a sheepskin overcoat, his collar turned up against the drizzle.

'Bloody thing won't start.' She demonstrated the clicking noise.

'Sounds like a flat battery. Tell you what, if you come out for a coffee, I'll jump it for you afterwards.'

'You think you can get it going?'

'No problem,' he said. 'I have jump leads in my truck. So how about it?'

'Oh – all right.' She glanced at her watch. It was after eleven and she was suddenly aware that she hadn't eaten breakfast. 'Do you mind if we grab a quick bite to eat, too?'

Dan raised his eyebrows. 'Lunch? We-ell, it's kinda early – but what the hell. I know a Tex-Mex place nearby.'

As Annie got out of her car, the rain began to come down heavily. The two of them took off running across the parking lot. By the time they reached a massive red pick-up truck, Annie was laughing and breathless.

'Climb in,' he invited, opening the door. She looked up at the distant leather seat, feeling like Alice in Wonderland after she'd eaten the side of the mushroom that made her shrink.

'All right, but why do you have such a monster vehicle?'

He grinned at her, drops of rain caught in his eyelashes. 'Are you kidding? Because size matters.'

Annie chuckled to herself as she scrambled up to her seat. He was really playing the cheesy Texan to the hilt. She liked a man with a sense of humour.

Towering over other cars, they cruised down the road, made a couple of quick turns, and pulled up outside the seediest-looking establishment Annie had ever seen in Norbury. A fly-speckled sign, wedged between the plate glass window and the closed blinds, announced that this was, 'Bobby's'.

As they walked in, shaking rain from their clothes and hair, Annie felt the world darkening around her. Inside this place – bar, restaurant, whatever it was – no natural light penetrated. The windows were shrouded, and the room was lit by fluorescent signs shaped like cacti and sombreros. Five or six stainless-steel tables stood around, completely empty. There wasn't a soul in the place.

Annie's heart began to beat rather hard. She gulped. She hadn't bargained on anything quite so off the beaten track. Why couldn't they have gone to Friendly's where it was bright and clean and busy? Could it be that Dan didn't want to bump into anybody they both knew? The thought made her uneasy. After all, surely a woman could have a perfectly innocent bite to eat with a male friend who was about to jump-start her car without having to hide away in some hole-in-the-wall dive?

'Don't worry,' said Dan, following her gaze around the room, 'I won't make you drink sangria. What can I get you?'

'Um . . . what are you having?'

'Scotch.'

'*Scotch?* What happened to the whole hot drink idea?' She glanced at her watch, feeling more nervous by the moment.

'Come on, have a shot to warm your bones.'

Annie pursed her lips. Well, she was here now. One drink wouldn't do her any harm. She was perfectly sure that when Simon went out to business lunches in the city he had a glass or two of wine. 'We-ell, all right, then. Just one drink. But I'm more of a vodka girl.'

'OK, one vodka coming up.'

He went over to the counter, which seemed to be completely unattended. By dint of banging and calling, he managed to flush somebody out of the back room. 'Hey, Juan, what's up?' he asked the thin, sad-looking individual who came in wiping his hands on an apron.

The man shrugged. 'Dan my man, how you doin'? What's it gonna be?' Then his eyes cut over to Annie and he gave a knowing smile.

'Give us a Scotch and a vodka.'

'On the rocks?'

'Sure. And how about you make us some chicken fajitas, medium spicy?'

Annie watched the drooping bartender extract a couple of bottles from a cupboard and dispense their drinks into two greasy-looking tumblers. Using his hands, he dumped in some ice cubes from the freezer. Then he disappeared again, no doubt to start grilling chicken.

Annie took the glass from Dan and sipped it gingerly. Her father, she found herself remembering, had always warned against allowing people to put ice in your glass in dodgy countries where the water could be bad. It was one of his cautionary tales, like not putting a plastic bag over your head, that seemed to have left an indelible impression on him, whereas he could never be persuaded that it wasn't safe to defrost meat by leaving it in the kitchen sink all day.

She felt the onset of sudden tears – thinking about her dad could still do that at odd moments – and hastily took another sip of her vodka.

'So,' said Dan Morgan, leaning back in his chair and squinting his eyes at her. 'That mutt doesn't know how lucky he is to have a woman like you going all teary-eyed over him getting his—'

'Right,' Annie said hastily. 'I'm not actually crying. I'm just having trouble with my contact lenses.'

'Oh, you can't kid me. It's funny, I didn't peg you for an animal lover the day we met at the barn.'

Annie grimaced, remembering Heather's mare going loopy over Dan's gelding. 'I don't *dislike* horses,' she said defensively. 'I'm just – well, a bit scared of them, to be honest. But I'm getting used to them. Sort of.'

'So you might just let that skinny kid of yours have one of her own some day?'

Annie took another sizeable sip of her vodka. 'She's not riding any more,' she said.

'You're kidding me. That little fall scared her off?'

'No, it wasn't the fall. It was ... well, it's my husband. He doesn't want her to ride. He thinks it's too risky.'

'You don't say! Kid must be sick about it.'

Annie gulped more vodka. 'She's been really good about

it, actually. She sulked at bit at first. Called me – called me a few names. But she's resigned to it now.'

'Whoa,' he said, eyeing her all-but-empty glass. 'Easy does it, now.'

For some reason, this spurred her on to pick up her drink and drain it to the dregs. 'I think I'll have another, if you don't mind.' A strange recklessness was coming over her. She slid the glass towards him. 'We're going Dutch, of course.'

He gave her a long look, then stood up and called for Juan. When he came back with the drink he said, 'You seem kinda rattled. It's not just the mutt, I'm guessing. Want to talk about it?'

Annie took a slug of vodka. 'Not particularly. Not at all, really. Hey look, here comes our food.' Juan clanked over with a large tray and began arranging dishes of chicken, flour tortillas, salsa, sour cream and grated cheese on the table. Annie helped herself to a tortilla and began piling strips of chicken onto it.

'You homesick?' Dan asked, serving himself in a more leisurely fashion.

Annie slathered on the sour cream and began to roll the tortilla. 'I do miss home,' she admitted. 'But maybe not as much as you'd think. The weather's so much nicer here. Blue skies every day. And people are friendly. I mean, maybe they're only pretending to be friendly, maybe it's all just superficial, but it's nicer than people pretending that you're not actually there.' She paused and took a large bite of her fajita. Ah. Delicious.

He frowned. 'What do you mean?'

'Well, back home people tend to ignore each other in public. You know, on the street, on the train. I think it's because London is just so packed. If you started smiling at everybody who walked by, your cheeks would ache. I don't think I ever spoke more than two words to my neighbours back in Islington; it would've been an invasion of their privacy. But here – well, here they give you a street directory when you move in; even the dogs' names are on it.' She smiled and wiped cream off her lip. 'I like that.'

'I like it here too.'

'You don't miss Texas?'

He grinned into his whisky. 'I'm allergic to fire ants.'

'Fire ants?'

'Vicious sons of bitches. The day they marched into my house through the crack under the door, I swore I'd leave and never go back. Plus my ex-wife lives out there and she's more vicious than a whole army of ants.'

Annie burst out laughing. She laughed until her eyes watered, then pushed her glass towards Dan. 'Is there any more vodka in that bottle?'

'Don't you think you've had enough?'

'Just one more, if you don't mind?'

About twenty minutes later, Annie walked out of Bobby's, heavily supported by Dan, breathing garlic and feeling exhilarated. 'That's a good game,' she told him happily. 'Quarters. I don't know why, but I didn't play a lot of drinking games at uni.'

'Misspent youth,' said Dan.

''Zackly. Didn't know what I was missing. Whoa!' she

said as he clicked open his car. 'Your number plate says "STALLION"?'

He grinned. 'You didn't notice before? Climb on up.'

'No, hang on. You're in no shit fate ... fit state to drive.'

He shook his head. 'As soon as you knocked back that second vodka, I knew I was the designated driver. I've been drinking iced tea ever since. That's right, I was playing quarters with iced tea.'

Annie shook her head so hard she stumbled and had to clutch Dan for support. 'I just don't *get* this iced tea business,' she told him. 'Tea is a hot drink! *Hot*, I tell you! It's filthy when it's cold.'

'Easy now, Annie,' Dan said, steadying her. 'Nobody's gonna make you drink iced tea if you don't want to.'

Annie snorted theatrically. 'Ha! That's what you think. But they keeping bringing me the bloody stuff in restaurants when I ask for tea. And if they do bring the real thing, they screw that up too! I mean, along they come with a polystyrene mug of lukewarm water and a box of fancy herbal *infusions* that have about as much to do with tea as ... as storks have to do with making babies.'

'Whoa there, Annie. Just get in the truck and I'll drive you home.'

'Drive me ...? But what about my car? We have to go and jump-start it. We can't just *abandon* it in the vet's car park.'

'Annie, there's no way I'm going to let you drive. We can pick it up later. When you've sobered up a bit.'

She stopped in her tracks. 'You mean I'm that drunk?'

'I mean you're that drunk. Come on, let's get going. We need to pour some coffee into you before your kid comes home from school.'

Annie gave him a sideways look. 'You know what? I think you're enjoying this.' But she allowed him to help her up into the high leather seat.

She didn't say much on the way home, mainly because she was suddenly very sleepy. Dan's truck was warm and luxurious, just the place to curl up and close your eyes, and maybe nod off for a moment or two.

'Here we are,' Dan said directly into her ear. He seemed to be shaking her. 'Let's get you inside.'

Annie opened her eyes to find herself in her own drive-way. 'Ah! Home sweet home. Come along in, Dan.'

Smiling blearily, she allowed Dan to help her out and support her up the steps to the kitchen door. She scrabbled for her keys in her bag for what seemed like ages, located them at last, then fumbled at the keyhole. 'If the bloody door would just stay still a moment,' she found herself saying. Dan took the keys from her gently and opened the door.

'Can I put some coffee on for you?' he asked, shrugging off his jacket as he toured the countertops. 'Where's your coffee maker?'

'I don't like coffee much, but I suppose I'd better have some. It's in the corner near the fridge. Thanks so much. This is very good of you.'

He laughed. 'You've gone all polite on me,' he said. 'I kinda liked it when you were cussing me out about hot tea.'

'Was I? Gosh, I'm sorry. That's right, coffee's down there. Um, have you got the time on you?'

'It's just after noon,' he told her, glancing at his watch.

'Good. Three hours until the school run. I can have a little nap, maybe.'

'Coffee first,' Dan said firmly, following her into the family room.

She promptly collapsed onto a sofa. 'Come, sit down,' she said, grinning up at him and patting the cushion next to her. 'The coffee will take a while.'

He hesitated a moment, then sank down next to her. As he turned his head to look her in the eyes, she realised that they were very close to each other. Very close indeed. She could see his eyelashes. His shoulder, just inches away from hers, looked strangely inviting in its faded denim shirt.

Almost without volition, she found herself leaning towards him and resting her head on that handy shoulder. 'A shoulder to cry on,' she said with a tipsy giggle that turned into a sob. 'So this is what "maudlin" means,' she muttered, digging around in her pockets for a tissue.

When she thought about it afterwards, she realised Dan Morgan hadn't had much option. What could he have done, other than put his arms around her? Anything less would have seemed boorish.

The feel of those arms, warm even through their combined layers of clothing, was very comforting. Annie gave a sniff and settled in for a snooze.

That was when Dan lowered his mouth onto hers like a suction cap onto bathroom tiles.

Even in her woozy state his sudden onslaught gave her a nasty jolt and she reared away from him, pulling herself up into a kneeling position. He gazed up at her in surprise, his eyebrows raised, his hair ruffled, his shirt rucked up on his chest. 'What the hell?' he demanded.

'I think I'm going to be sick,' she said, hand over her mouth.

That got him moving. Few men, no matter how aroused, would linger downstream of a woman threatening to throw up on them.

As he jumped to his feet, she said, 'You'd better go, Dan. You'd better go now.' She was shivering with fright. God! She'd nearly gone and mucked up *everything*. And all because of a few terse words from Simon, a broken-down car, and too many vodkas.

'You asked me in,' he pointed out, tucking his shirt into his jeans.

'I know, I'm sorry,' she said, fingering her lips, which felt bruised. He was a bit of a vacuum cleaner. Still shivering, she gave a nervous snort of laughter, then tried to turn it into a cough. His eyebrows lowered. He was beginning to look distinctly peeved.

'I've had a tough morning, and the vodka went to my head in the worst way,' she explained hastily. 'Plus you're very attractive. Almost irresistible.' There, that should soothe his ruffles. 'But I *am* married, you know. *Happily* married. I'm very, very sorry if I misled you. So if you could please just go home now?'

'Look what you've gone and done to me,' he said morosely, gesturing towards his jeans. She wasn't going to look in that particular direction. 'You're nothing but a lousy tease. What the hell am I supposed to do now?'

'I don't know,' she shrugged. 'People seem to recommend

cold showers. Look, I really am terribly sorry.' She was herding him towards the kitchen and the back door. Who knows how many neighbours had already seen and recognised his truck in her driveway, with its distinctive vanity plates. 'You were so kind to me today. I don't know what came over me. Can you please just ... go?'

They were in the kitchen now and he was pulling on his jacket. 'Of course I'll go. But sheesh, talk about leading a guy on. Hold it!' He lifted a hand as if he were stopping traffic. 'Your car. It's still stuck over there at the animal hospital. Want me to give you a ride back a bit later? When you're feeling better?' His tone said he'd really rather not.

She shook her head. 'No, I'll sort myself out. I'll call a garage. Honestly, I don't want to be any more bother. Goodbye then. And ... and thanks again for a ... a lovely time.'

'Yeah, yeah,' he said, stomping down the steps in his heeled boots. 'Whatever.' All the cowboy charm was gone. But then, he hadn't had the benefit of years of manners training with Annie's mother.

Annie followed him out into a world washed clean by rain. The sky was a thin, high blue and the puddles were gilded with sunshine. Annie felt dazzled, like someone emerging, all disorientated, from an afternoon movie. As Dan climbed up behind the wheel of his truck, she breathed a ragged sigh of relief. God, what a morning. She couldn't wait to get into bed and pull the covers up over her head.

She was turning back towards the house when a voice hailed her.

'Annie!'

She froze.

'What was that cowboy bloke doing here?'

Slowly, inch by inch, she turned around.

Chapter Twelve

Simon was standing in the driveway in his suit, his BlackBerry dangling at his side, gazing at Dan's enormous truck as it sped down the street. He must have walked up from the train station. Not surprisingly, Dan hadn't lingered to greet the master of the house.

'Simon! Good grief! Home at this hour? What's going on?' Time. She needed time to think.

He walked up and bent to plant a kiss, but she ducked down and fiddled with her shoe. She didn't want him getting a whiff of her breath.

'I had to come back for an overnight bag,' he told her, looking down at her with a puzzled frown. 'I have to go to Boston on the two o'clock train. I've been trying to reach you all morning. Did you forget to charge your phone or something?'

Annie's mobile phone was in the car, plugged into the cigarette lighter. In the vet's car park.

She looked up and gave a weak smile. 'Probably. Sorry.'

Since he was now walking briskly into the kitchen, she felt it was safe enough to straighten up and follow. You didn't kiss people hello after the hello moment had passed. At least, she hoped Simon wouldn't. Trying to breathe slowly, she pressed her icy hands to her face in the hope of cooling down her blazing cheeks.

Simon sniffed the air. 'Coffee? Since when do you drink coffee?' He walked over to the far corner of the kitchen and stared hard at the steaming coffee maker and the two mugs standing ready beside it.

Annie cleared her throat with a sudden, high squeak.

Simon's eyebrows snapped together. 'So. Looks like you were planning coffee for two. With Dan the Stallion, perhaps? But somehow you forgot to actually drink the coffee. Tell me, do you often entertain Mr Morgan in the mornings?' His voice was silky smooth, ominously polite.

Annie pressed her hands together to stop them from shaking. 'Um, no, never. He just dropped by. Out of the blue. He ... he was trying to sell me a horse. For Lydia, obviously. He's some kind of horse broker in his spare time, you know. I told him we didn't want a horse.'

He gave her a long, searching look. In the end, she dropped her eyes.

'Where's Patches?' he asked at last. 'I haven't had my daily dose of fawning.'

Annie perked up. Here was a nice segue away from the dangerous topic. 'He's at the vet's. Remember? Today's the day he's being neutered, poor bloke. They're keeping him overnight and he'll come home wearing a thing like a clown's collar around his neck.'

Simon was pouring coffee. 'Here, would you like some, since it's made?'

'All right, then.' She took the mug he proffered and drank

it quickly, almost scalding her throat. Coffee had a strong smell. Perhaps it would mask the vodka and the garlic.

'I can give you your daily dose of fawning, if you like,' somebody suddenly said in a smoky, sultry, suggestive voice.

Good God. She clapped her hand over her mouth. It was *her* smoky, sultry, suggestive voice!

What on earth was the matter with her? She couldn't let him get close enough to smell her breath, and yet she seemed to be offering him sex! What if he took her up on it? She'd have to develop a sudden migraine.

He shot her a sideways look. 'Are you feeling OK, Annie?'

'Absolutely. Couldn't be better. Why do you ask?'

'I don't know. You don't seem yourself.' He moved a bit closer, still staring. 'If I didn't know better, I'd say you'd been drinking.'

Ah. Shit. Now what?

She gave a guilty laugh. 'Well, you're absolutely right,' she said. 'I have had a little drink. Um – over at Heather's.'

'At Heather's?'

'Yup. She was serving champers and orange juice. Her birthday. I went round to her house for a little party. Just a few friends.' She was improvising wildly now. 'I'd just got back from Heather's when Dan Morgan showed up on the doorstep. That's why I put on the coffee. To sober me up.'

The web was growing more tangled by the moment.

Annie could see the tension drain out of Simon's body. He relaxed visibly, all the hard lines in his face suddenly softening into a grin. 'So this is what you women do in the mornings,' he teased.

'Champers, tennis, tea parties, it's a high old life,' she agreed.

'I'm glad you're having some fun,' he said, suddenly serious. 'It's such a lifestyle change for you, stuck out here in the suburbs, after London.'

She shrugged. 'It's OK. I'm adaptable.'

'I've noticed. So anyway, could you to drive me to the station in about half an hour? I don't fancy the walk with my luggage.' Simon didn't have a car. It was his gesture towards the Green movement. Since they lived so close to the train station, he was rarely inconvenienced by his sacrifice.

Annie spluttered and began to cough. 'Drive you? Um, the thing is, the problem is, I had to take the car to the garage this morning. So, um, I don't actually have it today.'

'To the garage? Really? I didn't know it was playing up.'

'It's not really playing up. I just – well, I reckoned it was time for a service. You know. You can't be too careful when you're driving kids around.'

He shook his head. 'Annie, you're not supposed to get it serviced randomly, whenever you feel like it. There's a log book in the glove compartment. You're supposed to do it every so many thousand miles.'

'Well, *sorry*. Take me out and shoot me for being over-conscientious.'

He pursed his lips and drummed his fingers on the counter. 'OK, well I suppose I'll take a taxi then.'

'Good idea.' Annie felt quite weak with relief. 'I'll call one while you're getting ready.'

*

Walking home from dropping the girls at school the next day, Heather shook her head at Annie in amazement. 'So you're saying that for the rest of my life I'm going to have to pretend to your husband that my birthday is in *December*?' she asked. 'What if I want to have a big party when I turn forty?'

'I don't know. Maybe don't invite us?' Annie felt weak and wan, probably because of the after-effects of the vodka.

'It wouldn't be a party if I didn't invite you!'

'Thanks.' Annie gave a pale smile. 'Maybe you could have a girls' thing. A brunch or something. I mean, it's years away.'

Heather pulled a face. 'Not *that* many years. But men never remember birthdays, do they?'

Looking hard at her cuticles, Annie said: 'Um, Heather? Another thing. Could you possibly drive me over to the vet's to pick up my car? And do you happen to have jump leads?'

She hadn't told Heather everything that had happened yesterday. For example, she hadn't mentioned her wrestling match with Dan Morgan on the sofa. She'd only told her that she'd agreed to go to lunch with Dan after her car conked out at the vet's, and then ended up too tiddly to drive.

Tactfully, Heather didn't ask why on earth she'd been drinking at lunch time. She wouldn't really have known what to say, except that she'd been feeling out of sorts because of Simon's recent testiness.

'We'll have to step on it,' Heather said as they attached jump leads to the car batteries. 'We're supposed to be at school at eleven for the Happy Holidays recital.'

'Oh God, I forgot all about that!' Annie gasped. 'I'm a feeble excuse for a mummy, aren't I?'

'A mummy's a shrivelled-up corpse from an Egyptian tomb,' Heather said. 'You'll never be one of those, but you've got the makings of a first-class mommy.'

'Really? What are the makings?'

Heather grinned at her. 'You *give* a damn,' she said.

Half an hour later, Annie pulled up at her house in her own car again, inching along slowly so that Patches wouldn't be jostled too much. The dog was a shadow of his usual self, too humiliated by his Elizabethan collar even to jump up and greet people. As soon as she got him into the house, Annie unfastened the oversized plastic contraption around his neck and threw it recklessly into the recycling bin.

'Now,' she told him, 'if you can just resist licking yourself, you won't have to wear that thing ever again.'

He snorted derisively, then slumped onto the floor, closed his eyes, and fell heavily asleep.

Annie ran upstairs, threw open her wardrobe, and considered what she ought to wear for a Happy Holidays recital. Fifteen minutes later she was clicking down the street in her long boots, a figure-hugging black wool dress that she hadn't worn since her working days in London, and her red coat. Surely a bit of glamour wouldn't go amiss at a concert?

But the other mums were still in jeans, albeit designer ones. They had changed into jeans at some point in early October, when their Capri pants became too chilly around the ankles, and hadn't looked back since. In honour of the occasion today, most of them wore cashmere jumpers.

Perhaps to make up for the boredom imposed by the jeans regime, they all carried fabulous handbags.

Heather, who had gone straight to school from the vet's parking lot to secure a seat near the front of the hall, beckoned wildly to Annie from across the room.

'I had to fight off five women including the freaking head of the PTO to keep this seat for you,' Heather told her as she slipped into the vacant chair. 'Wow, you look fabulous.'

Annie pulled a face. 'Does anybody but me ever wear a skirt around here?'

'Sure, to weddings and funerals. Oh look, here they come!'

The children filed in, wearing Santa hats. If Annie had secretly hoped that Lydia would have a starring role, she was disappointed – unless playing the triangle qualified. All the same, Annie filmed away like mad, like any other mum in the room, capturing every flicker of Lydia's eyelids, every move of her hands, so that Simon could watch and admire when he came home.

But he didn't get home until after midnight. Patches heard the front door click and gave a muffled bark, but he wasn't up to his usual mad dash down the stairs. Hearing him moving around downstairs, Annie turned over in bed and tried to fall back asleep. Simon usually made himself a snack and sometimes even watched a little TV when he came home late, so she wasn't surprised that he didn't make his way upstairs immediately.

But when she woke up again, hours later, she felt a pang of alarm to see his side of the bed smooth and flat. She squinted at the green digital display on the radio-clock. It seemed to be four in the morning. Where on earth *was* the man?

Heaving herself out of bed, she found a dressing gown and shrugged it on, aware of the dog's wheezing breath as he slept heavily on. Simon had probably fallen asleep in front of the TV, she told herself. She'd better go downstairs and rouse him or he'd wake up stiff and cold in the morning.

When she shuffled out onto the landing, she thought she heard the low buzz of the TV, but as she approached the stairs, she realised the noise was coming from the den. A strip of light under the den door confirmed that Simon was holed up inside.

Curiosity propelled her forward.

Standing in the dark outside the closed door, she hesitated a moment. Who could he be talking to in the wee hours of the morning?

Probably somebody in England. It would be – what? – about nine a.m. over there. Something to do with the pies, no doubt.

What compelled her to put her ear to the keyhole, she never really knew.

'No, I disagree, I think we're beyond that now,' she heard Simon say quite vehemently. '... Can't keep putting off speaking to Annie ... Yes, I'm doing it tomorrow ... We're in crisis mode. Right, completely out of her depth ... I know all that ... I know, I *do* feel responsible ... Yes, it's true, she gave up a lot, coming over here. I don't deny it ... Yeah, a gamble for her, too ... Look, I *know* she's been trying – to be honest she's been bloody trying! – but she's just not cut out for it.'

Annie stood frozen, her ears burning.

'Well, exactly, and I wouldn't care ...' Simon went on. 'But the fact is she's in bed with someone else ... OK, maybe not in bed, but at least at the heavy petting stage ... I don't see why I should stand by ... Look, it's time for action ... Tomorrow ... Yes, try to make a clean break. To be honest, I think she might even be relieved to go home.'

Very slowly and quietly, Annie backed away from the door and crept to the bedroom.

Shit.

Had she really just heard that?

No, no, she couldn't have. She must be asleep and having a nightmare. Simon couldn't possibly have said ... He couldn't think ... He *couldn't* believe she was sleeping with Dan Morgan. He *couldn't* be about to ask her to go home to England. And yet that was what she thought she'd heard him say on the phone.

She climbed back into bed, shivering, still in the dressing gown. She would go back to sleep, and in the morning everything would be OK again. Because this was obviously, quite obviously, nothing but a very bad dream.

But in the morning, when she jolted awake, she found herself still in the dressing gown, the other side of the bed still flat and smooth. It seemed Simon had never even lain down on the bed! Jumping up, she ran to the den, half expecting to see him still sitting at the desk with the phone in his hand.

He wasn't there, of course – he was always out of the house by this time – but a mug of half-finished cold tea testified to the fact that he really had been sitting at the desk in the night.

Oh God. So it wasn't a nightmare after all.

OK. It couldn't be as bad as she thought it was. Things were never as bad as you thought they were.

So, what she'd do was, she'd get Lyddie ready for school, and then sit down and try to remember exactly what he'd said, and then work out exactly what the words meant. And she wouldn't think about any of it now, because Lyddie needed her to be normal.

She woke Lydia in the usual way, by opening her blinds and calling her name. As usual, Lyddie muttered and groaned and told her to go away.

She made Lyddie's usual breakfast – porridge. She packed Lyddie's usual lunch – a butter sandwich, some cheese, a yoghurt, an apple, a box of juice.

'Are you mad at me?' Lydia asked as the two of them set out for school. They were unusually early.

'Mad at you? No. Why would I be? I'm just . . . just thinking.'

'Are you still going to talk to Miss Scofield today?'

'To talk to—? Yes, yes, of course I am.' With a lurch, Annie remembered it was parent–teacher conference day.

'I thought maybe you'd forgotten.'

'Why?'

'Because you're wearing Daddy's dressing gown.'

In horror, Annie looked down to see the red terry-cloth sticking out between her black wool coat and her sheepskin boots. She turned her gasp into a careless laugh. 'Oh, for goodness sake, I'm not planning to wear *this* to the conference.'

'Good. I don't want Miss Scofield to think we're crazy people.'

Annie hurried home, showered, styled her hair and changed into something she might wear to a job interview: well-cut skirt, silk blouse, flattering little jacket, elegant heels. There, she thought, posing in the full-length mirror; even Lydia wouldn't be able to find fault.

Miss Scofield welcomed her into the classroom warmly. 'So good to see you, Mrs Keeler. I've been looking forward to showing you some of Lydia's work. Of all the children I've ever taught, I don't think I've seen such an improvement in a child over such a short space of time.'

'Really?' Annie tried to smile, willing her mind to focus on the woman in front of her.

'Oh yes! When Lydia came into this room, I had real concerns about her, as you know. The main issue of course was her choice not to use her voice in the classroom.'

'Yes, she was very shy in the beginning, wasn't she? I have my own theory about that. I think she was waiting until she figured out how to talk with an American accent.'

'What do you mean?'

'Well, now and then I catch her practising to herself. To-mah-to, to-may-do, that kind of thing.'

'Good grief, do you think that could be it?'

Annie nodded. 'I think it could be part of it.'

Miss Scofield thought for a moment, her head on one side. She looked a lot like a plump, speckled bird looking sideways at a worm.

'You know, you could be right,' she said at last. 'She really doesn't have much of an accent any more. But her written work has also progressed impressively. Here, take a look at this. It's something she wrote in class recently.'

Annie took the piece of paper the teacher handed to her.

The writing prompt at the top read, 'If you could wish for anything, what would it be?'

Annie drew in a sharp breath.

'If I could wish for anything I wood wish for a new poney statew,' she read. 'My mom gave me a statew of a poney when she came home from a trip. She went to Englnd to look aftr my granny in the hosptl. But sumthing bad happend and I broak the poney. My mom was sad. So I wish I had a new statew to give my mom.'

'Mrs Keeler? Are you OK? Can I get you a glass of water?'

Annie shook her head. 'Um, you know what, I *don't* actually feel that well.' She sniffed hard. 'I think I'd better . . .' She stood up quickly. 'Thanks so much, but I think I'd better go home.'

Miss Scofield stood up too, the picture of concern. 'Yes, you look like you need to go lie down.' She held out a folder of papers. 'Here, take this with you. More of Lydia's work. You can look at it at your leisure.'

Sitting at her own kitchen table with a box of tissues at her elbow a few minutes later, Annie leafed through the small pile of Lydia's compositions. Her hands were shaking.

She blushed when she read, 'I ate porij for dinner last nite becos my mom didnt wont to cook bluddy mete again.'

And then she came to a page on which Lydia had written, in her cramped, slightly crooked hand:

'My mom is special because:

She is special becos she never had me in her tummy like ordnary moms. She is special becos there is no word for the color of her eyes. She is speciall becos she lisns to me. She is special becos she loves me. I love my mom becos she is specl.'

Patches jumped up against Annie's knee in concern. He had probably never seen a human howl before. After licking her face for a while, he wandered off and she could hear him lapping water from his bowl. The salt of her tears must have given him a thirst.

When Annie had recovered her composure, she went over to the sink and splashed cold water on her red eyes. Then she threw herself into the car and drove too fast over to Heather's house.

Without knocking or ringing, she crashed through the open door and went straight into the kitchen. Heather wasn't in it. 'Heather!' she yelled, walking into the family room.

A man with his jeans around his ankles was sprawled over Heather's sofa – and Heather was underneath him.

'God Almighty,' said Annie, and scurried to the safety of the kitchen, breathing in gulps, and struck by a terrible urge to laugh. She shoved her fist in her mouth, to be on the safe side.

She wished with all her might that she could simply leave the house altogether and go sprinting back up the street to the relative safety of her own kitchen, but she absolutely had to talk to Heather, even in these appalling circumstances.

Moments later, Heather appeared in the kitchen, still fiddling with buttons and zips. 'For God's sake, why didn't you *knock*?' she demanded.

'I don't know!' Annie tried to compose her twitching face. 'I'm sorry, Heather. Really, really sorry. I didn't mean to interrupt. I just – I have to tell you something.'

'It's not what you think,' Heather said, tossing her hair out of her face. 'I'm not cheating on Rob. Not really. You see, he's agreed we should try artificial insemination.'

'He— *what?*'

'That's right.'

'And that – that's how they do artificial insemination these days?' Again, an awful, inappropriate urge to guffaw was building up in Annie's mouth and nose area like an explosive sneeze that she had to quell, against all odds.

'No, of course not. But I don't like the idea of sperm from some complete stranger. I mean, what weirdo donates his sperm to a sperm bank, anyway? For indiscriminate use? You'd have to be some kind of megalomaniac trying to take over the whole freaking world with your gene pool, or something. And Dan just seemed like the best—'

Annie's hand flew to her mouth. 'That's *Dan* in there?'

'Oh shit. You didn't recognise him?'

'Well, I only saw his ... Heather, what the hell are you *doing*? You love Rob. I mean, don't you?'

Heather's eyes glittered. 'Yeah, I love him,' she said. 'That's why I'm freaking doing this. Oh God, Annie, you're making me second-guess myself now. I was so sure this was the way to go. I mean, Dan has the right body type and colouring and everything. He's smart too, under the cowboy act. And Rob's getting restless again. He's kind of like ... I don't know, like a half-tame wolf looking out into the woods at full moon. Sometimes I just get the feeling he wants to be released back into the wild real bad. You have *no idea* how much I need another baby.'

Annie shook her head. 'I think I'm beginning to have *some* idea. Look, don't listen to me, Heather. I mean, who am I to give advice about anybody's marriage?'

Heather narrowed her eyes. 'What do you mean? Nothing's up with your marriage ... *is* it?'

'I don't know! I mean, yes, everything's bloody falling apart, and I didn't even *know* it till last night. Simon's been tense, but I was such an idiot, I thought it was work related. See, at about four in the morning I heard him talking on the phone, and he – he was telling someone in England that he's planning to break things off with me. Probably his po-faced bloody brother. He seems to have this weird idea that I'm having an affair ...'

'What? With *who*, for Christ's sake?'

'Um, never mind. But the thing is, I've got to go into the city and talk to Simon.'

'Yeah, sounds like a good idea. Set the guy straight. Read him the riot act, Annie! What the hell does he think he's doing, talking about you to his freaking brother? Spreading vicious rumours?'

Annie felt her face puckering up. Heather strode over and folded her in a hug. 'Take it easy now,' she said, patting her shoulder.

'I'm fine, I'm fine,' Annie lied. 'I really just came over to ask if you could please pick Lydia up from school and have her over here this afternoon? I'm not sure how long I'll be.'

'Sure, no problem. She can come to the barn with us and watch Hailey ride.'

'Thanks a million. So sorry to burst in on you. I should've just called. I don't know why I didn't.'

'It's not the same over the phone,' Heather said.

'You're right,' said Annie. 'Anyway, bye, see you later. You'd better get back to . . . you know.' She jerked her head in the direction of the family room.

Heather grimaced. 'Are you kidding? I think the moment has passed.'

'I'm sort of glad to hear that,' Annie said. Then she squeezed Heather's shoulder and left.

Chapter Thirteen

By the time Annie arrived at ChefPro's offices, her eyes were no longer red. She had found some powder in her bag and used it to tone down the shine on her nose and forehead. But she knew she still looked a bit wild and frenzied, especially after a small boy pointed her out to his mother and said, 'Mom, is *that* what you call a fruit-loop?'

When she burst into the office on the twenty-fourth floor, the woman behind the reception desk looked up with wide eyes. 'Mrs Keeler?' she gasped. 'Is . . . is your husband expecting you today? It's quite a big day for everybody, and he didn't say anything to me.'

'No, he jolly well isn't, but—'

She was stopped, mid-sentence, by the sudden appearance of Cindy Faig who erupted into the lobby carrying a briefcase and a large pie carton. She powered past Annie and the receptionist without a glance, striding through the room and out of the glass doors, towards the lifts.

'One moment,' said the receptionist, and scuttled off after Cindy.

Without hesitation, Annie seized the moment to sneak through the doors into the inner sanctum of ChefPro's

New York headquarters. From memory, she made her way down the corridor to Simon's corner office. Propelled by adrenalin, she threw the door open without knocking. But the room was as empty as it had been the first time she'd seen it, the throne-like chair behind the big desk pushed out at a crazy angle as if Simon had left the room in a hurry.

Undeterred by this minor setback, Annie went back out into the corridor, as determined as ever to track Simon down and confront him. She was thankful to be in her parent–teacher conference clothes as she hurried down the carpeted hallways. Jeans and sheepskin boots would probably have made her a bit conspicuous.

She passed two men in suits walking along, deep in conversation, and asked, 'Where can I find Simon Keeler?'

Both of them looked at her with wide eyes. 'Conference room,' one of them said, pointing down a corridor. 'But he's already started.'

Started what? she wondered. Never mind, whatever it was, he'd just have to stop.

As she rushed past doors, she noticed that they had numbers on them, and sometimes a discreet sign, such as 'Kitchen', or 'Restroom'. This was helpful, as it meant she didn't have to keep throwing open doors and startling people. She'd done that once or twice, and was now vaguely afraid that someone would call security.

When she reached a door labelled 'Conference Room', she paused for breath. It would probably be better if she composed herself before she went in. It was possible he wasn't alone in there.

She took out her make-up compact again and powdered

her nose. Finding an eye pencil, she quickly drew a line along her upper lids. It was her signature look, after all. The line turned out a little shaky so she smudged the kohl as best she could with one hand. There! She always felt more confident when she was wearing her war paint. Now if she could just find some lipstick ... She didn't seem to have any, so she made do with chap stick instead.

She took a last deep breath and opened the door.

About a dozen faces turned to stare at her.

Simon was standing at the far side of a round table, close to a screen, with a pointer in one hand. On the screen was a large photograph of a golden-brown pie divided into slices, with various facts and figures superimposed on the image. Seated around the table were several men and two women, all dressed in dark suits, all gaping at Annie.

'Um, hello.' Annie gave a tiny wave with the tips of her fingers.

Simon put his pointer down and inserted a finger between his collar and his throat. '*Annie?*' he breathed.

'Yes, hi, I, ah, I just thought I'd come in. For the, um, the presentation.'

'Everybody, this is my wife, Annie,' Simon said. 'How she got wind of this, I'm not sure. But I'm happy to, ah, have her support.'

A few people smiled and one man clapped – although, looking at his face, Annie couldn't help thinking it was an ironic kind of clapping.

Annie slipped into a seat quickly. She would just wait here until the presentation was finished, and then she'd be able to speak her mind to Simon. She could bide her time.

She was on a slow burn. As she settled in, somebody pushed a sheaf of papers across to her, but she didn't look at it.

At first, she didn't even try to listen to Simon's speech. She was too taken up with rehearsing in her head what she was going to say to him afterwards. But after a while, the words began to penetrate.

'. . . the results of the latest focus group,' he was saying. 'I think you'll find this new information quite surprising. I'm aware that some of you have already made up your minds, but I'd like you, just for the sake of argument, to pretend for the moment that you haven't.'

People were shuffling through papers, and Annie heard a collective intake of breath.

'These numbers can't be right,' said a man with jowls.

Simon was smiling now. 'Ladies and gentlemen, these numbers are not bogus. These numbers are one hundred per cent authentic. These numbers are based on genuine consumer reaction to our new line of products. So, just to take you through it: Pie One garnered a ninety-five per cent approval rating across a sample group of approximately three hundred tasters; the largest sample group we have ever run. Pie Two performed almost as well with an approval rating of eighty-seven per cent. And Pie Three was still a huge hit with an approval rating of seventy per cent.'

Annie glanced through the stapled presentation pack in front of her. She soon found the page everyone was looking at. It was divided in half horizontally, with the top half depicting three pies, labelled respectively 'Steak and Kidney', 'Chicken and Mushroom', and 'Pepper Steak'. A large number 66 was printed over the steak and kidney pie;

62 was printed over the chicken and mushroom one, and 59 was printed over the pepper steak one. Above the three pies was the title, 'Approval Rating from Large-Scale UK Sample Group'.

The lower half of the page showed three more pies, mysteriously labelled Pie One, Pie Two and Pie Three. These bore the numbers, 95, 87, 70. This graphic was titled, 'Approval Rating from Large-Scale US Sample Group'.

'What the research is telling us,' said Simon with absolute self-assurance, 'is that our new range of products has the potential to outsell – yes, to *outsell* – our top-selling pies in England. Think, ladies and gentlemen, of what this could mean to ChefPro in these tough financial times. And we're talking the *US* market here. The biggest – yes, the *biggest* – fast-food market in the world. The fast-food market that makes our fast-food market in the UK look like nothing but a . . . a cottage industry.'

A hand shot up. 'That's all very well,' said a woman with fierce eyebrows, 'but what about the cultural issues? Last time you had some of us convinced that we could sell our pies on the "Olde World Made New" platform – the whole Robin Hood and Sherwood Forest concept. But that idea has been shot down in flames pretty convincingly. How do we know your new ideas have any more stamina?'

'Yes,' shouted somebody else in a heckling tone, 'how do you make our pies competitive in a market that research – *your* research, I might add – has shown to be predisposed to be resistant?'

At that precise moment a knock sounded on the door.

'Come in,' Simon called. The door opened, and in walked

a nervous-looking young man in a suit and an apron, carrying a large round tray of pies. 'Put them in the middle of the table, please,' Simon instructed.

The delicious smell wafting up from the pies made Annie feel quite light-headed. She hadn't eaten breakfast, of course.

'Ta da!' said Simon with a small, ironic bow. 'Ladies and gentlemen, I give you Pie One. But before you sample it, I'd like to fill you in on our process here. The thing is, we've all been well aware of the cultural barriers. Americans are about as likely to eat steak and kidney pie as they are to eat ... say, goat's scrotum.'

There was a burst of voices. Simon held up his hands.

'To the American market, pie is sweet. It doesn't involve meat. And pies are open, not closed. Plus, beef is generally consumed in the form of mince, or ground meat as it's known here. So how to address these issues? Well, I have to say, my wife was the one who gave me my first clue to a solution.'

'Me?' Annie mouthed, her face going red as people turned around to stare at her.

'We had a small dinner party at our house, and offered mini pies as hors d'ouevres,' Simon went on. 'Sadly, the pies went largely untouched. On the other hand, the shrimp cheese balls we were also offering went down a storm. That was when my wife made the incisive comment that we should have filled the pies with shrimp cheese balls.'

People were frowning and looking confused.

'Then it came to me,' said Simon with huge conviction. 'It's all about thinking outside the box. Why should we confine ourselves to traditional English fillings? So, before these pies on the table get cold, I'd like you to sample ...' he took a deep breath and flourished one arm in the air, 'the *hamburger* pie.'

A huge commotion broke out. 'Hamburger pie?' people were asking.

'It's a simple concept,' said Simon. 'Meat pie is unfamiliar to this market. Hamburger is tried and tested. So what do we do? Combine the two. It's a sort of entry-level meat pie for our American consumers. The idea is people then have enough faith in the product to try something less familiar. You can even make a cheeseburger pie – we've tried it. And guess, what? Our testers loved it. The only difference with this type of pie is its shape. The pastry is moulded around the burger, so you lose the traditional look – but that turns out to be a good thing. The traditional look seems to be associated with negative ideas about English cuisine. Gustav, would you please slice up the pies into bite-sized portions.'

The nervous young man brought a knife out of an apron pocket and sliced away.

Annie took a piece as soon as she could and popped it into her mouth. It was strangely delicious.

From the excited babble among the others at the table, Annie reckoned they thought so too – although some of the raised voices, she had to say, sounded faintly hostile.

'In the end we decided to stick with the original pastry recipe.' Simon was almost shouting to be heard, now. 'People don't seem to prioritise calorie counts when they buy fast food. Why should we be the chumps to force wholewheat on people?' Somebody cheered, but several people booed. Simon held up his hand. 'I'm not saying we won't have a healthy alternative line, but our main product will be the full monty. Gustav, you can bring in Pie Two and Pie Three.'

Gustav left the room and came back remarkably quickly with another tray.

'Pie Two and Pie Three are, respectively, pizza pie and All-American beef chilli pie.'

An even louder commotion broke out than before. Then a large man with a Scottish accent and quite a lot of crumbs around his mouth stood up, raised a hand for silence, and said, 'Simon Keeler, you're a bleeding genius.'

In spite of herself, Annie couldn't help swelling with pride. It was true – Simon was a genius! He'd presented the Americanised pie argument so persuasively that she was just about ready to cash out all her own savings and put them into the project herself. The only thing she didn't understand was why he'd had to make this presentation at all. Wasn't the American chain an established ChefPro venture already?

A thin woman raised her voice above the hubbub. 'This is all very well, but we can't make decisions on the spot,' she said coldly. 'We need to scrutinise all the facts and figures, look at all the research, go over all the backing documents before we say yay or nay to this.'

'You have those in front of you,' said Simon. 'Why don't I leave you to thrash it out? I'll be in my office when you need me. As I've already told you, I'm prepared to make considerable personal sacrifices to see this initiative go forward. My team is on the same page, too. Tough times call for tough measures.'

'Good plan,' said the Scot.

'Maybe, but will it be enough?' said the thin woman.

'Let's go, Annie.' Simon stood up and crossed to her side of the room, holding the door open for her to go out ahead of him.

Chapter Fourteen

They walked down the corridor in utter silence.

When they reached Simon's office, he shut the door and leaned against it, closing his eyes for a moment. Annie noticed then that his face was pale and strained. And so it should be, given that he'd been up all night plotting to make a 'clean break' with his wife.

Outrage boiled up in her all over again.

'How did you know?' he asked, opening his eyes. 'It was supposed to be a secret meeting. Who leaked it to you?'

'*What?*'

'Don't get me wrong, I appreciate the support – but I was gobsmacked when you walked in. We've been under strict orders to keep a lid on this. Don't want to risk panicking our shareholders. Was it Cindy Faig? Did *she* tell you?'

'I have no clue what you're on about.'

'You . . . hang on. You *didn't* come specifically to sit in on the meeting with the executive committee?'

'Is that who those people are? I noticed they were all Brits.'

'Annie, they've been flying in all week for this. They're meeting to decide the fate of the whole American fast-food push.' He began to pace the room. 'People have been panicking and wanting to pull out. There's a lot of money involved, a lot of risk. I'm trying my damnedest to save the project.' He stopped and stared at her. 'So . . . if you didn't come in for that, what on earth *are* you doing here? It's not another surprise lunch visit, is it?'

She threw her head back defiantly. 'I'm here to meet you halfway, mate,' she said. 'Were you planning to have it out with me this evening? On your own terms?'

He frowned. 'What the hell are you talking about now?'

'Oh, don't play innocent with me. I know you don't want a big scene with your precious executive committee sitting just a few doors down. But the point is, you've seriously underestimated me.'

'I've— *what*?'

'Yes, you bloody have. For one thing, I *am* Lydia's mother. Oh, maybe not biologically, maybe not genetically, maybe not even legally, but practically, emotionally, effectively – in all the bloody ways that really count – I *am* her mother. And I have documents to prove it.'

It was true. She felt like a lioness threatened with separation from her cub. Never again would she doubt she carried the maternal gene.

Fishing in her bag, she pulled out two pieces of paper and gave them to him. He took them, still looking puzzled, and read them swiftly.

'Lydia wrote this stuff?' he asked in wonder.

'Yes, she wrote it,' Annie said. 'So I'm here to tell you, mate, that I'm not budging. I'm here for the duration. I made a solemn promise to Wilma Forsythe that I would do my best for Lydia, and damn it, I will.'

'Wilma Forsythe?' Simon muttered. 'What on earth—'

'Don't interrupt. I've come all this way to have my say, and I'm going to have it. Whatever terms we have to work out, so be it. If you're fool enough to believe I'm cheating on you, then that's your problem, mate. But I'm not leaving that child. You saw what happened when I went away for just a few days. She pretty much went to pieces. If you reckon I'm ever going to walk away from her again, mate, you've got another think coming.'

Simon's eyebrows were close to his hairline now. 'Why in God's name do you keep calling me "mate" in that ... that *poisonous* way?'

She gave a bitter laugh. 'What's with all the backtracking? I heard you on the phone last night, mate. I *heard* you telling your brother that I was sleeping with Dan Morgan.'

'Sleeping with ...? Hey, hang on. This is just ... just crazy. I didn't even speak to my brother last night.'

'Well, maybe it wasn't him, but I heard you telling *somebody* that our marriage is in crisis and you were going to have to break the news to me today that you wanted me gone.'

Suddenly, Simon's face cleared and he sank down into a chair. 'Oh, God, I think I know what this is ...'

At that moment, there was a slight knock on the door and Gustav appeared, still wearing his apron.

'They want you,' he said to Simon. Then he noticed Annie, standing with her hands on her hips, chest heaving. 'Whoops! Didn't mean to interrupt.'

Simon stood up eagerly.

Annie felt pure fury flood through her body. He was about to walk out on her and go back to the executive meeting. His body language was unmistakable. If he walked out on her now, she didn't know what she would do – but it would be pretty spectacular, whatever it was.

'Does it look good?' Simon asked.

'Difficult to tell,' said Gustav. 'They're kind of quiet.'

'Quiet? Shit. That doesn't bode well.' Simon glanced at Annie, then back at Gustav. 'Can you go back and tell them they're going to have to wait a bit? I'll come as soon as I can. There's something really important I have to sort out first.'

Gustav's eyes widened. 'But Mr Abernathie says he has a plane to catch—'

'Tell them to *wait*.'

Gustav nodded mutely and left the room.

'Annie,' Simon said urgently, 'I had a conversation last night about sacking Cindy Faig. I think that's what you overheard.'

Annie shook her head. 'No, it definitely wasn't that. You mentioned my name. You said I was either in bed with someone else, or at the heavy petting stage. Why you would believe something like that on such minimal evidence is a mystery to me but if that's how little you think of me, well, it's your loss, mate. And don't try to fob me off with some bullshit story.'

Simon pressed a finger to the place between his eyebrows. 'Seriously, Annie. I know what I said. I said I thought *Cindy* was in bed with someone else. By that I meant I thought she was trying to sell our wholewheat crust recipe to our direct bloody competitor. Which is exactly what she was threatening to do.'

Annie frowned. Something about Simon's tone was beginning to give her pause. He didn't sound like a man trying to blow smoke in his wife's eyes.

She shook her head. 'I don't understand.'

'Look, it's quite simple, really. Ever since we arrived here, I've been aware that Cindy wasn't performing at the same level as the rest of the team. She was responsible for researching locations for the restaurants, but she messed up. Repeatedly. When she screwed things up in Boston, she knew her job was on the line. Do you remember the day she came out to the house to give you that file?'

Annie nodded. She was still smarting over the way Cindy had walked away from a hot pot of tea.

'Well, she tucked a little note in there, along with the Brewster focus group report, letting me know that she was in talks with William Tell.'

Annie's eyes widened. William Tell had always been the Goliath among British baked goods companies.

'She let me know that she had access to our most successful wholewheat crust recipe. She said she wouldn't hesitate to pass it on, *if necessary*.'

'You mean, if you fired her?'

'Exactly.'

Annie suddenly thought of Cindy storming through the reception area that morning, holding her briefcase and a cardboard box.

'But you fired her anyway?' she asked with a flash of insight.

'Of course I bloody did. I was talking to our top personnel guy last night, over in the London office. He wanted me to hold onto her, to contain the damage, as he put it. But I wanted her gone. I don't give a damn about the wholewheat crust recipe. She can publish it in the *Sunday Times*, for all I care. I just didn't want her spilling the beans about the hamburger pie before I could speak to the committee. That's why I didn't give her the boot until this morning.'

Annie put her hands up to her face. 'This all sounds ... sort of convincing,' she said slowly, 'but you *were* talking about me. I know you were. You even said my name. You said you felt responsible for bringing me here. You said we were "in crisis". You said you were going to break the news to me today.'

'Well, dammit, that's because I *do* have news to break to you today. I was going to wait until after the committee's verdict on the pie project – but what the hell, I'll do it now. Annie, I'm sorry but it's bad news. Even if the committee agrees to go ahead with the American venture, they're going to cut our budget down to the bones. They told me that when I went over to London.'

Annie had an abrupt memory of him in the shower after that trip, his face turned up to the water in an attitude of despair.

'It's not surprising,' he went on. 'After all, most companies have frozen their development initiatives altogether. So, well, the thing is, I've offered to take a massive salary cut. We'd lose the ex-pat benefits. ChefPro wouldn't pay our rent or our health insurance, or anything. We'd have to move into a much smaller house and cut out all our discretionary spending. No more housekeepers, no more landscape gardeners, no more tennis lessons. We'd have to trade in the minivan for something smaller.'

Annie gaped at him. 'That's the crisis?'

'There's more, I'm afraid. If they don't go with the project, they're going to cut my job. They're going to fire me.'

Annie continued to gape for a moment. Then her face creased in an enormous smile. 'Oh, this is fantastic!' she said. 'This is wonderful!'

Simon looked baffled. 'Annie, did you understand what I just said? I'm on the brink of losing my job. Even if I don't, we're going to be in a tough situation.'

'Yes, yes, of course I understand. You think I care if you lose your job? You think I give a damn about moving to a smaller house? As long as we're together, I'll live in a bloody *tree*house, if we have to. We'll get my mum to come and give us lessons in frugality.'

'You mean it?' Simon still looked strained and pale. 'You're not just saying it to make me feel better?'

'Oh Simon, you're an idiot but I love you.'

All of a sudden the strain and anxiety left his face, and it lit up with relief. 'I am an idiot,' he said, shaking his head. 'I should have told you what was going on ages ago, but I wanted to shield you from the worry.'

'I don't need to be shielded,' Annie said fiercely. 'Never keep secrets from me again, OK?'

'Are you sure you're not keeping any secrets from me?' Simon looked at her searchingly.

She blushed scarlet. 'Of course I'm not.'

'Then why the hell mention that clown, Dan Morgan?'

'Because he's the only single man I know in this entire country,' she said quickly. 'And because you were jealous when I offered him coffee.'

'Good enough,' said Simon, and pulled her into his arms.

As his mouth came down on hers, a thunderous knock at the door caused them to leap apart.

Gustav poked his head into the room without waiting for permission to enter.

'You have to come right now,' he told Simon, his eyes wild. 'They're getting restless.'

'All right.' Simon smoothed down his shirt and rolled his shoulders like a prize fighter about to enter the ring. 'You'd better stay here, love,' he whispered to Annie. 'This could get ugly.'

'You've got to be joking,' she hissed back at him. 'I'm coming with you.' She grabbed his hand, which was cold and clammy, and hung on tight.

He shrugged in a resigned way and followed Gustav out of the room. As they reached the closed door of the conference room, he gave her fingers a quick and rather painful squeeze.

'This is it,' he said. 'Take a deep breath. Here we go.'

As they entered the room, the buzz of talk died abruptly and everybody turned to look at them. Nobody smiled, not even the jolly Scotsman. Annie almost wished she hadn't insisted on coming.

'So,' said the thin woman, 'you've found the time to pop back in and see us, have you?'

'To be honest, I thought you'd be deliberating for longer.' Simon's voice was pleasant. 'Something came up on my side that really couldn't wait.'

'Evidently. I'm sure there are dozens of things more important in your life right now than this committee meeting.' A small titter went round the room in tribute to the thin woman's wit.

'No, only one,' Simon murmured.

Then the stout Scot spoke up: 'Simon, lad, you did a fair job presenting your case to us today. But we all know the American market is a tough nut to crack. We all know the odds are stacked against you.'

Annie felt her throat constricting. She glanced at Simon. His face was an unreadable mask.

A mild-looking man in tweeds spoke up: 'Oh, for God's sake. Put the chap out of his misery.'

The thin woman sniffed. 'Very well. Simon, it was by no means unanimous, but I'm afraid the committee has decided to let you go ahead with this ill-advised venture.'

Annie's hand flew to her mouth. She felt dizzy with relief. Nauseous, even.

Simon, meanwhile, was taking the news with calm self-possession, walking around the room shaking people's hands and accepting their congratulations. But Annie could tell he was chock-full of bottled emotion because the tips of his ears were very red.

'Well done, lad,' said Mr Abernathie (for that was the Scotsman's name), 'you proved to everybody in this room that you have a fire in your belly. I just hope that the miserable state of the global economy isn't enough to souse it.'

'I'm not going to let a recession get in the way of my game plan,' Simon told him firmly.

'Well, since I've probably missed my plane by now, what say we go out and drink to that?' Mr Abernathie suggested, looking mightily pleased with Simon's rejoinder.

'I'm sorry, sir,' Simon said, 'but I can't do it. I'm taking my wife out to lunch.'

'He's a cool bloody customer,' Annie heard somebody mutter, 'turning down the CEO for his wife.'

Annie's heart thumped with fresh alarm. 'What if he's really annoyed that you wouldn't do drinks, and changes his mind about the entire project?' she hissed as she and Simon stepped into the lift together.

'On no, Abernathie admires a show of spirit,' Simon told her, grinning from ear to ear.

And so it came to pass that Annie and Simon finally did go out for lunch together in Manhattan.

Sitting in a dim room holding hands across the table, they stared into each other's eyes like honeymooners.

'You were magnificent,' Annie said. 'You blew them away.'

'You were pretty fabulous yourself,' Simon said. 'It was a stroke of genius, coming in on the meeting like that. Much harder to sack a man in front of his wife.'

She laughed. 'God, on the contrary, I think that woman would have enjoyed the drama.'

'You mean Skinny Bitch? That's what the team calls her. Thank God, here's the champagne at last!'

As the waiter moved to pour champagne for Annie, she put her hand over her glass. 'I'd better not,' she said.

He raised an eyebrow. 'Oh, surely you can have a glass? Plenty of time for it to wear off before you get back to Norbury.'

But she kept her hand over her glass. 'How come you're not asking me about Lydia?' she said suddenly. 'School gets out in just over an hour. I'll never make it back in time.'

'Well, I trust you've taken care of it,' he said.

'You mean, you think I've learned my lesson, since last time?'

'Annie, I never thought you needed to "learn a lesson". Last time, if you remember, you fell asleep. This time you're conscious, so I know you've done whatever needs to be done about Lydia – because, as you pointed out earlier – you *are* her mother.'

'You really believe that?'

His face was deadly serious. 'I really believe it.'

'Good,' she said. 'Because, well, I *have* actually been keeping a bit of a secret from you. From everybody, really. I wanted to wait for the right moment to say anything. I mean, I know the timing is terrible with this recession and everything, and I certainly would have liked us to, you know, discuss things first, but sometimes you don't have as much control over life as you think you do—'

'Annie. What are you saying?'

'I'm saying I seem to be, sort of, pregnant.'

She looked at Simon anxiously. For a moment his face was completely still. Then he took her hands in his and held on pretty tight, but still he didn't speak. He didn't need to, though; his face blazed with joy.

Epilogue

It was May in Norbury, and the town was transformed by blossom. Drifts of crocuses and daffodils had appeared as if by magic under the beech and dogwood trees in Annie Keeler's tiny patch of garden.

Under one of these trees, Annie and Heather had set up a couple of folding tables and fifteen chairs. Heather was smoothing a tablecloth and Annie was tying balloons to the chairs when the school bus pulled up in front of the house and three girls came tumbling out into the street.

Patches, asleep under a folding table, woke instantly at the whoosh of the bus's brakes, and went hurtling across the lawn to jump all over the girls.

'Hi, girls. Go inside first and dump your backpacks!' Annie shouted across to them. 'Then you can play.'

But Lydia ran straight over to her and wrapped her arms around her waist. With a listening look, she pressed her ear against Annie's stomach. 'He's not moving,' she said after a moment, her brow buckling in worry. 'Is he OK?'

'Oh, he's sleeping,' Annie said. 'He sleeps all day and parties all night. You know that.'

'Come on, Lyddie,' Hailey called from the kitchen door. 'Let's get a snack.'

'Why don't we go in too; take a break,' Heather suggested. 'We're just about done out here. Plenty of time before the rest of them arrive, and you're supposed to be keeping your fluids up.'

'Yeah, I could do with a cup of tea,' Annie agreed.

In the tiny kitchen, Annie's mother, wearing a pink pin-striped apron, was cutting slices of bread and jam for Lydia, Hailey, and Courtney Phelps. 'Don't eat too much bread now, girls,' she was saying, 'you've got the birthday cake coming later.'

The children took their sandwiches and ran off outside to wolf them down in the treehouse, where there was a bit more space. Patches chased after them and positioned himself beneath the tree, watching for crusts.

As Annie put the kettle on, Heather squeezed herself along the wall to a seat at the kitchen table. 'What's this?' she asked, picking up a pile of papers.

'Oh, those are my notes for the frugality lecture at the library tomorrow,' said Gladys proudly.

'Wow.' Heather looked impressed. 'Listen to this, Annie! "Laundry: get over the idea that you have to wash every single item after just one wear. Instead, just give clothes in the hamper a good sniff. If something doesn't smell bad and hasn't got visible stains, fold it up and put it away for another outing." Eeew. That sounds gross.'

'I'm all for it,' said Annie, pouring out a cup of instant coffee for Heather. 'I've halved my laundry loads that way. Read out some more.'

'"Wash clothes in cold water unless they are badly soiled,"' Heather read. '"You will save on electricity and your clothes will last longer. String a washing line in your back garden and hang things out to dry. Again, you will save energy and your clothes will smell wonderful."'

'Oh God, that reminds me, I need to get the sheets off the line before the other kids arrive,' Annie said.

'Relax, it's taken care of.' Gladys nodded towards a basket of folded linens, visible through the kitchen door on the sofa in the living room.

'God, you're brave, hanging up your laundry in *this* town,' Heather said. 'I've never even laid eyes on a washing line around here.'

'On the contrary,' Annie told her, 'drive around a bit. It's catching on. You'll see.'

At that moment Courtney Phelps stuck her head through the door. 'Mrs Keeler, can we go on the trampoline now?'

'You can but you may not,' said Gladys.

'If you've finished chewing,' said Annie, shaking her head at her mum.

The trampoline was Lydia's birthday present, and it had been a huge hit ever since three men from the sports shop had set it up two days ago. Of course, it took up a good portion of the back garden, but Annie didn't mind the sacrifice. The grass would die in the shade beneath it, and there would be less lawn for Simon to mow.

'I still can't believe Simon got her a trampoline,' Heather said, shaking her head. 'I mean, weren't trampolines right up there with horses as waaaay too risky for Lydia?'

Annie smiled. 'Yeah, but Simon's making a huge effort

not to be paranoid about that sort of thing.'

'You mean he might let her ride?' Heather asked avidly.

Annie pulled a face. 'I didn't say that. For one thing, it costs an arm and a leg, doesn't it? But the pie places are doing pretty well. So you never know.'

Courtney Phelps poked her head in again. 'Mrs Keeler, can we take the bikes out?'

'Not now. There's no grown-up to watch you. Why don't you jump some more?'

'Short attention span, that one,' Heather muttered when Courtney had run off again. 'It's kind of surprising that she and Lyddie are so thick. Didn't they have a disastrous play date, ages ago?'

'Yeah, it was really bad,' Annie remembered, pulling a face. 'But Lyddie's sort of ... different, now. She likes Courtney's energy.'

'Darn right, she's different,' Heather said with a low whistle. 'Coach Matt tells me they're calling her The Assassin on the soccer field this season.'

'Why they can't play a nice game like netball, I don't know,' said Gladys, shaking her head. 'Whoever heard of little girls playing football?'

Heather met Annie's eye and gave a shadow of a wink. 'How long are you staying this time, Mrs Harleigh?' she asked.

'Oh, I don't know.' Gladys stopped wiping down surfaces and came over to sit with them at the table. It was a bit tight. 'This lecture tour Donna Knopf set up for me keeps getting extended. They want me to talk in libraries all over Connecticut, New York, Massachusetts and New

Jersey now. I might even be here when the baby comes. Flo will be getting a nice long break.'

'So it's working out with the companion?' Heather asked.

'Oh, she's all right but she's terribly hard on soap,' Gladys said. 'Goes through it like water.'

'Mum, should I tell her our plan?' Annie asked.

Gladys shrugged. 'I don't see why not.'

'Well, it's very hush-hush right now,' Annie told Heather, 'but I'm going to take Mum's frugality notes and make them into a book. *Bare-bones Living*. Something like that.'

'Hey! That's a *fantastic* idea! I mean, there's a huge market now for that sort of thing. Have you looked into finding a publisher, or is it too early for that?'

'Well, as a matter of fact, I've put out a few feelers,' Annie admitted. 'Just on the strength of my blog. Do you know, I have about five thousand followers now? So that gives me what they call a "platform". I already have a tentative—'

'MOM!' Lydia stood in the kitchen door, her eyes almost feverish with excitement. 'Mom! Come outside quick. People are coming! Samantha and McKenna are here! And Patches is knocking down chairs to get the balloons!'

So Annie and Heather and Gladys stood up and walked into the spring sunshine to throw a party.